CW01572452

Mark Stewart-Jones was born in London and brought up in south Wales. He is the author of four previous novels and two non-fiction titles, has edited two books of ghost stories for The Ghost Club and has also written for *The Independent*. Mark lives with his partner and his daughter Sophie and divides his time between Paris, Canterbury and New Orleans. He has played with a number of blues bands over the years and currently plays lead guitar with Boogaloo Jones.

By the same author

Martin Bonehouse (Book Guild, 1996)

An Ecstasy of Fumbling (Book Guild, 1998)

Sophie – Too Full of Heaven (Pascal Project, 2000)

Every Other Inch a Gentleman (Book Guild, 2007)

Daughter (Book Guild, 2009)

ROLL 'EM, MISTER BONES

Mark Stewart-Jones

Book Guild Publishing
Sussex, England

First published in Great Britain in 2014 by
The Book Guild Ltd
The Werks
45 Church Road
Hove, BN3 2BE

Copyright © Mark Stewart-Jones 2014

The right of Mark Stewart-Jones to be identified as the author
of this work has been asserted by him in accordance with the
Copyright, Designs and Patents Act 1988.

All rights reserved. No part of this publication may be reproduced,
transmitted, or stored in a retrieval system, in any form or by any
means, without permission in writing from the publisher, nor be
otherwise circulated in any form of binding or cover other than
that in which it is published and without a similar condition being
imposed on the subsequent purchaser.

All characters in this publication are fictitious and any resemblance
to real people, alive or dead, is purely coincidental.

Typesetting in Sabon by
Keyboard Services, Luton, Bedfordshire

Printed in Great Britain by
CPI Group (UK) Ltd, Croydon, CR0 4YY

A catalogue record for this book is available from
The British Library.

ISBN 978 1 909716 01 8

For Philip J. Blight
1960-2012

1

Recent Events

The odour of three-day-old human excreta is not one that hastily or easily departs the memory.

OK, OK, a powerful opening, he thinks, graphic and immediate, a statement of intent. It would certainly grab the reader's attention. Maybe if...

The stench of three-day-old human shit is not one that quickly abandons the memory.

He prefers this; he likes the use of the vernacular; it is somehow more passionate, more vibrant. Besides, in a bizarre way, it sounds to his ears more literary and less ... well ... you know.

The stink of three-day-old human shit is not one that is easily forgotten.

For six days and six nights now he has kept his promise.

He has tried not to think about any of it or allow the issue to cloud, as had become his custom in recent months, his every waking moment. He has forced from his mind any fleeting recollection, any memory of even the most trifling detail that might prompt reflection or consideration. By virtue of the kind of blinkered single-mindedness, in which there is usually no virtue whatsoever, he has concentrated upon only that which is sentient, immediate or tangible.

As an unavoidable and not altogether unpleasant consequence of this particular discipline, he has, during this same period, fully immersed himself in his entirely new role; that of foreigner and visitor. Indeed, for almost a week now he has been happy to simply regard himself as a tourist – no more and no less – one to whom the world is simply an entertainment passing in front of him and revealed only fleetingly in fragments and moments.

But now, finally, this morning, shortly after his breakfast, he has broken his vow.

It was not prompted by any particular incident as far as he is aware – the line had just popped into his head a minute before and when you had a line like that, promise or no promise, you just had to get it down. It was now sparking other ideas, ideas suppressed and unspoken for almost a week and now clamouring to be heard. At this stage, he thinks, it might simply be another letter to the editor of the *Gazette* in the hope that they might finally publish one or maybe a heartfelt confession for his own use. But maybe it needs a more personal introduction.

I am at this moment over four thousand miles away but the stench of three-day-old human shit is not something you forget in a hurry.

Maybe that is going too far the other way, he thinks – too self-consciously angry and basic. He restores the previous phrasing and continues.

I would, without a moment's hesitation, declare that I am innocent of all charges – but there have been no charges. I would naturally announce that there is no fabric to such ridiculous allegations – but there has been no direct allegation.

If I have learned anything these past months

These past *months*, he repeats the phrase silently to himself. He doesn't like this. He would have preferred an even less specific phrase – one that suggests a vague period of his life rather than a precise chronology; one which has dates and times. Markers and signifiers that he fears will follow him for years to come. In his mind, he alters the emphasis. A *few* months. But he draws little comfort from this. Indeed, for the

2

duration of the period in question, he has lacked, even for a moment, either the inclination or the capacity to trivialise the situation in any way. Not for a fleeting second has its absurdity been a source of mild amusement to him. Never once has he paused to delight in the possible irony of it all.

Never.

If I have learned anything from my experiences it is the following: implication is infinitely more toxic than direct allegation.

He turns away from the screen and makes a face.

Yet to deny an accusation is to give the accusation validity – the assumption being that it is something worthy of a denial.

No, no, no, that's just horrible. Worse if anything. If these were the attitudes and opinions he'd been so forcibly repressing in recent days then it probably qualified as an act of mercy rather than one of censorship.

Five yards away from a rat, they say, and never more than three sentences away from 'veritable smorgasbord' and you really never want to be any closer than that.

Select. Delete. Gone.

Actually, on balance, he'd rather take his chances with the rat. Martin Bonehouse now removes his reading glasses and rubs his eyes. He then stares blankly at the keyboard of his laptop. Rimbaud wrote somewhere that no one is serious when they're seventeen. Maybe the reverse is true and it's simply not possible to be frivolous when you're fifty.

'What a truly fucking depressing thought,' he says in a whisper as he finally succeeds in dislodging the piece of granola lodged between his front teeth with his tongue.

As has just been made so painfully obvious, another problem he has encountered these past months in his writing, while striving for some sort of dispassionate objectivity, is that he invariably lapses into this unnaturally elevated oratorical voice. Far from helping, this recent and unwelcome flair for flatulent overstatement has lent what he can only bring himself to term 'Recent Events' a grandeur and significance from which he could do little but cower and hide. Thus, he continues to cast himself as 'victim' and 'exile' whilst defending himself grandly and over-flamboyantly, in the manner of some terrible wartime courtroom drama.

No more now.

Just leave it.

Let's have the fantasy instead. What was that other line that came to mind over breakfast? He'd been absently spooning cereal into his mouth at the time when he suddenly caught himself staring intently at the reproductions of old photographs of Canal Street that lined the walls of the hotel's dining room. Usually such pictures are fairly bland and anonymous, he thought, but these were somehow different. Not great or noteworthy images in themselves, they did however convey a certain atmosphere.

He types quickly.

New Orleans is forever like Paris in the 1920s –

Should he try to justify this or just leave it hanging there?

Everyone here has a back story; it is a place for exiles and refugees.

He winces at his use of the word 'exile' but continues.

They say that every time someone sits down in New Orleans they glance over their shoulder.

Maybe they don't really say that but it's a good riff so who cares?

People come here running and the place just slows them raaaghhtttt daaahhhhnnnnn.

Awful and probably racist. Select. Delete.

The full effect of New Orleans is felt within a few moments of making its acquaintance or else it is not felt at all.

This is about as close to autobiography as he feels comfortable with at this moment. It was certainly true that upon first arriving six days ago he'd felt an immediate and instant affinity with the place. An experience that is, he has subsequently learned, a far from uncommon one.

Of course, it needs to touch on Katrina.

New Orleans itself now has its own perfect back story, one that is so brilliantly suited to its inhabitants. Look around you – it's rebuilding and rediscovering itself but mainly it's just trying to forget – it's just like the rest of us.

It is flowing easily now.

In tourist shops all over the city I have counted literally dozens of books written by a whole host of authors in which they try to understand the appeal of New Orleans; to try and distil the whole essence of the place in 40,000 words or less. It's a hopeless conceit and usually these books conclude with a confession that the author has failed in his task. But it is as though the place is a complicated mathematical equation, or some complex theorem that requires a detailed explanation. And perhaps it is.

You can't put this place into words; it's impossible. You can't put it into pictures either, maybe that's what the music was for; it's not from New Orleans it's about New Orleans.

He thinks about this for a few minutes.

OK, just consider the music – just imagine a great classic New Orleans band playing in your mind for a minute or two. Think of Jelly Roll Morton's Red Hot Peppers or Kid Ory's band or any of the great combos. Think of a grand old standard like 'High Society' being played on three frontline instruments – a cornet, a trombone and a clarinet – each wailing away at the same time but each playing a different melody; in short, three completely different tunes going on at the same time. Perhaps logic or common sense would tell us that this shouldn't work, that the end result would be a chaotic mess and not something a person would listen to for pleasure, but you don't end up with chaos you end up with something indescribably beautiful.

At this point, Martin glances to his left furtively and feels a knot forming somewhere in the pit of his stomach. Possibly the granola, he thinks, but he is not convinced. For this might be the time for Mr Bonehouse to admit that he has a problem. It's not a particularly new one either and for as long as he can remember he has had real issues with New Orleans jazz. Now, let's not rush to any conclusions here for Martin is an avid jazz fan and completely committed to the cause. In fact, apart from an occasional furtive dalliance with Delta Blues, he has for the past quarter of a century seldom listened to anything else. Sadly and perhaps inevitably, like so many others before him and despite his very best endeavours to the contrary, he knows and cares enough about the music nowadays to be both a snob and a bore on the subject. This has inevitably led to him to being selective (elitist) in his tastes (prejudices) and his great passion (obsession) remains jazz roughly of the period of the mid-forties to the mid-sixties. Or, in the language of his peers, 'Koko' by Charlie Parker at the one end and 'A Love Supreme' by The John Coltrane Quartet at the other. An indication of his level of dedication is that, on an intermittent rather than regular basis, he submits reviews of jazz reissues of this particular period to Amazon, a diversion for which he proudly affects the *nom de net* of BirdLives1960. Although he has never been fond of big bands, fusion, bossa-nova records or anything featuring strings (possible exception – Charlie Parker's 'Just Friends') or Stan Getz (no exceptions), it is traditional New Orleans jazz that remains his biggest problem.

He'd always promised himself that he would make a real effort one day and try to get to grips with it but he just never got around to it. He can (with a little persuasion) go back as far as Duke Ellington and obviously Louis's Hot Five and Hot Seven (and not just because in happier times they'd once sounded to him like a series of risqué books for adults written by Enid Blyton) but no further than that. It continues to defeat him in the same way ballet defeats him; he simply doesn't get it. It's all a bit too frantic perhaps, too jolly, too far removed from his idea of the music he loves so much. But every time he listens to one of King Oliver's records and those of the same era, he always thinks of cartoons. It's far too easy to imagine that every time Papa Joe stood up to take a solo his trousers would fall down revealing bright red polka-dot boxers.

Martin smiles for the first time that morning. He takes a deep breath and continues.

The three instruments play with and around each other and never against each other so you end up hearing the whole band as a single unified voice. The musicians negotiate their way around the song; they adapt, they communicate and they inspire. The needs or aims of the individual artist are secondary to the collective aims of the group. It is, in short, the ultimate democratic music and it could only have been born in New Orleans. For, in New Orleans at its best, one finds daily and constant evidence of its own particular brand of Social Polyphony.

That might be worth a paragraph or two.

New Orleans might be the world's most accommodating *city. It is a place of deceptions and duplicities – it is the ideal place to disappear and the ideal place to rewrite one's own history. It's a place where a man can lose whatever hellhounds he has on his trail . . .*

He inhales sharply. No. Better leave that out. Select and cut and gone.

New Orleans is a land within a land; it doesn't belong to Louisiana or to the USA. It is its own universe. You hear this in the regional idioms and their use of the definite article; Vieux Carré is simply the *Quarter, Storyville is* the *District and Hurricane Katrina is referred to as* the *Storm. This suggests that nowhere else in the world, nowhere beyond the shores of Lake Ponchatrain, has storms, quarters or districts. New Orleans has them. The strangest thing is that after a really short time in the place you begin to fully understand this.*

He likes this. Actually, he likes it a lot. This could really work; an outsider's impression of a city. Not what it is but what it means. Obviously this wasn't going to be just your normal bog-standard tourist guide; this was one man's take on a remarkable city and its metaphors. It was a completely different approach – possibly unlike anything ever attempted before. A book that did not seek to explain New Orleans, as so many had tried, but instead celebrated the fact that it could not be explained. It would be about the *idea* of New Orleans and why this idea was so important.

Yes, this could really work.

Sadly, his muse has never been a thing with wings; it's not clothed in the diaphanous garb of angels and saints – it is a simple clockwork wind-up muse with a big key in its back. It has no particular shape or design; it simply has a presence and now he hears for the first time the scraping and grumbling of those familiar rusty cogs as they begin to activate smaller cogs and then even smaller cogs. It is all the confirmation he needs at this stage.

Martin returns to the top of the document and writes:

Oh God! Not Another Book About New Orleans!

He looks at it for a few moments and then, not wishing to add blasphemy to his list of alleged current misdemeanours, he returns to the first line and amends it thus:

Oh No! Not Another Book About New Orleans!

He then adds cautiously underneath:

Notes From an Exile in The Crescent City

On rereading the line, he narrows his eyes and inhales sharply through his teeth; he immediately deletes the word 'exile'. He tries 'visitor', 'Englishman', 'tourist' and 'wanderer'. He even considers 'fugitive' before deleting the entire line. Instead, he writes:

Adventures in The Crescent City by Martin Boneh

At this point, he suddenly stops typing and deletes his name. He doesn't really feel comfortable about using it again like this so soon after 'Recent Events'. Even looking at his own name in hard 16pt. Goudy Old Style, on a page like this makes him feel uncomfortable. Like this was in some way related or he is about to embark on a sequel or some kind of... He shudders and takes a deep breath. He isn't prepared for this and so instantly seeks a viable distraction.

'OK, what then?' he enquires in hurried tones that betray his mounting anxiety. 'Let's keep the old initials then... Let's see... How about...?'

Montague Beresford

'Awful, sounds like a vintage car.'

Morton Buckley

'Actually worse. Probably a village in Hampshire.'

Milton Bewley

'Ditto.'

Morgan Beaumont

'Dodgy accountants.'

Mimsy Bagshot

'Oh, fuck off!'

Finally, after occupying himself in this fashion for at least ten minutes, he deletes all his previous attempts and smiling rather uncomfortably, he types:

Michael Barnes

He is very happy with this. It is a good solid name, a name you could depend on; the name of a man you could trust to write a fascinating and incisive new study of New Orleans. Michael Barnes was definitely the man for the job. Ah yes, the ever reliable Michael Barnes. Even the truncated Mick Barnes was good too. 'Please, call me Mick,' he could say to interviewers. That would sound good; it would break the ice and put everyone at their ease. It was an ambiguous name too insofar as he could be an English writer or an American. Then they could talk for a while about his accent.

He saves the document and for a moment a darkness passes across his features as he considers, just for a fleeting second, what might have been the possible implications of his inventing this Mr Barnes a year or so ago.

Now he starts to smell the shit again.

It is definitely time to get some fresh air.

On Gravier Street, New Orleans, west of the junction with Magazine Street, stands the Royal Crescent Hotel. It is a grand seven-storey structure and at this particular time on the third floor, in room 311 to be precise, we find the current residence of Martin Bonehouse. It has been his home now for almost a week and it is booked to remain so for another fortnight. Although he would be the first to congratulate himself on his astute choice of accommodation, its selection had been more the result of luck than judgement; evidently there was some annual dentists' convention in town for the week and availability of rooms had been an issue. But he has no complaints with the Royal Crescent, it is a fine establishment and Michael Barnes (the straight-up and fair-minded kind of guy that he is) would no doubt mention this fact in his book. Naturally, he would side step the obvious and avoid using words like 'charming' and 'delightful'. Instead, he would make allusions to the 'funky ambience' of the place. Although you had to be careful; such an adjective might still be regarded as less than complimentary in some quarters, particularly if your sense of the word leans towards the Buddy Bolden rather than the Horace Silver.

Martin's room faces the street but it's quiet and spacious and the tall sash windows let in a lot of light. It also has a rather large desk of which he has suddenly grown particularly fond. This is because for the past twenty-five minutes it has transformed itself into a writing desk and in his mind, it is now a piece of furniture as essential as a bed or a wardrobe.

Furthermore, at this precise point in his life, it will also function as a symbolic device with the greatest personal resonance. He rubs the palm of his hand along its edge affectionately and decides to quickly check his emails before closing his laptop down.

There is just one.

'Oh God,' Martin's sigh mutates quickly into a low desperate groan. 'Just tell me you're not serious, right?'

The email's subject is 'Great New Opportunities' and reading on from the unpromising opening, 'Dear Author,' Martin scans the communication from sales@authorland.net. It is something about an 'incentive offer' on marketing and Martin gets about halfway through before deleting it.

'You're having a laugh, aren't you?' he hisses quietly, all too aware that an unbiased observer would detect that there is now a suggestion of sadness in his voice. He quickly tells himself that this is simply an automatically generated email and not targeted at him specifically. Besides, this wasn't the first email of this nature that he'd received and there had been a few others from Authorland in recent weeks. It could be considered tactless perhaps, a little insensitive, but it would be difficult to ascribe any malice to the deed. No; leave it. Just forget it. Besides, Martin is currently in a reasonably buoyant mood and such moments have been rare of late. He is also fully aware that there are other more urgent matters that are currently requiring his attention. So, with a sense of renewed purpose that might have passed for a surge of enthusiasm, Martin now drags his suitcase out of the wardrobe and opens it on the bed. At the bottom of the case there is a large cardboard-backed brown envelope. He might be taking sensible precautions, he thinks, or he may simply be paranoid but he has hidden it quite well and there is no evidence that the case or its contents of socks and underwear has been disturbed.

'This your case, sir?' he whispers in a passable attempt at

guttural cockney as he removes the envelope. 'So, what've we got here then, sir? Drugs? Firearms?'

It's the same fairly humourless routine that Martin has performed these past couple of days with little or no variation. He opens the envelope and removes two identical copies of a paperback book and holds them up for inspection by his invisible inquisitor. The book is a shade over 200 pages long and entitled *An Unhealthy Interest*.

'It's worse than that, officer; it's books I'm afraid.'

'Oh dear, oh dear, sir, most dangerous thing in the world, books are!'

'Oh yes.' Martin nods and contorts his mouth into the smile of resignation which is in danger of becoming a permanent feature these days as he places the two books carefully in his inside jacket pockets. Then, after crossing out the number six, which is written on the envelope and adding a four, he returns the envelope to the bottom of the case and the case to the wardrobe.

He is ready.

He takes the elevator down to the lobby, sharing the trip with a friendly and very tanned middle-aged lady in a white baseball cap and a T-shirt emblazoned with the legend 'WHO DAT?' After exchanging the usual pleasantries, she fixes him with a knowing stare and asks him if he's a dentist. She is only about the fourth person in recent days to pose this precise question. He thinks about lying but in the end his nerve fails him and he informs her that he's simply on holiday.

'Have a good day, y'all,' she says as they part company in the lobby.

'Yeah, you too.'

Then, waving at the desk clerk who promptly waves back, Martin makes his way down the front steps and out of the hotel. He heads west on Gravier until he reaches the end of the block then he turns right on to Camp Street. The day is already warm and sultry and inhaling the morning air deeply into his lungs, Martin makes another mental note for Mr Barnes.

They never seem to mention the smell, do they?

It never seems to crop up in any of the books he's read. Maybe because it's so difficult to actually describe, but nobody ever alludes to the wonderful musky, dusty smell that permeates throughout the city. It's unique to New Orleans and it's everywhere; it seems to come out of the walls and up from the sidewalks. For reasons he has yet to fathom, the smell seems more pronounced in the mornings and today is no exception. It is an odd but far from unpleasant odour but it takes time for the olfactory mechanisms to fully assimilate and appreciate. The other day he felt he could discern an underlying scent of damp wood but then it vanished. Then, just for a second, it made him think of something vinegary ... but then it was gone again. But it adds something to the place; it makes the city seem alive and breathing.

Human maybe.

So, by extension, it is comforting and nurturing, maternal even. Martin stops walking and shakes his head. OK, maybe not the last bit but probably useable up until then.

He has now reached the junction with Canal Street, at the point where Camp Street leads you into the French Quarter, although it changes its name to Chartres Street in the process. As he crosses Canal, he momentarily loses the scent but he picks it up again on Chartres. This morning it is something very reassuring; it is certain and good and he smiles. After brief consideration, he concludes that there are only two other smells that he can recall having a similar effect on him, and both were childhood smells, nostalgic smells – wooden sheds and ironing. One reminded him of his grandfather or his uncles and the other was a smell he would always associate with his mother. All were gone now, long gone but something of them remained in the traces they left behind. Actually, never having paused to consider it previously, he now wonders why one smell was so definitely male and the other female. Maybe that was normal. Who knows?

Sheds, ironing and New Orleans; yes, he was more than happy with that and as he walks now there is a renewed slightly swaggering aspect to his gait.

A couple of blocks and a minute or so later, he is standing outside DuPont's Book Store. It is a small unprepossessing shop with a couple of old maps in the window but, according to his recent research, it boasts over 30,000 second-hand books in stock. This must be the place, he thinks, as he pushes open the heavy door and enters.

For as long as he can remember, Martin has loved second-hand book shops and without delving too deeply into the subject, he might go as far as to say that they conveyed to him a sense of sanctuary and reinforced the idea that there were still places in the world where books, just ordinary simple books, remain significant and important to people. He adores these shops: all the dust and the love and the license they have to be so untidy and disorganised, the shelves overflowing and books piled up on the floor. You would never see that in any other shop but somehow it was all part of their charm. Within seconds of entering, Martin concludes that DuPont's Book Store is a near perfect example of the type.

The interior is dark and cool, as one would wish, and opening the door activates a bell somewhere towards the rear. From behind a counter to his immediate right he is instantly greeted by a bearded white-haired man in a cravat and Panama hat.

'How you doing today, sir?' he asks, looking up from the morning's *Times-Picayune* and speaking in between mouthfuls of beignet.

'I'm very well,' says Martin. 'And yourself?'

'I'm good, good, thank you. Anything I can help you with today, sir?'

Martin ponders this question for a moment in a manner that is far from convincing and says simply, 'Fiction?'

'Certainly, sir. Back of the shop to your right,' the man says, gesturing with his beignet and covering his newspaper with sugar in the process.

'Thank you.'

'Y'all need anything I'll be right here. You just holler.'

'OK.' Martin smiles and quickly makes his way to the rear of the shop. As he does so, in order not to draw too much attention to himself as he is currently the only customer on the premises, he conducts a silent inventory – maps, atlases, a glass case with a few leather-bound volumes, loads of art books, large-format ones too, good-sized photography bit, biography, absolutely huge local interest section but you'd expect that, plays and poetry, a shelf or two, lots of music books, maybe come back later and have a look at that, and here we go now: paperback fiction, pretty reasonable size too and alphabetical by the look of it.

That always makes this next part a lot easier.

Glancing briefly now over his shoulder to ensure that he's still unobserved, he gingerly removes a copy of *An Unhealthy Interest* from his jacket pocket. For a fleeting moment he steals a glance at the now all-too-familiar cover, at the handwritten scrawl of the title and the image of the blank staring eyes. He'd never liked the cover; to him it looked like a teen horror novel, tacky, cheap and badly conceived. But if he's hoping that reflecting upon it again might prompt some sudden flash of insight or even emotion this morning he is destined to remain disappointed. He opens the book fractionally, just enough to read the words on the dedication page.

For Mr Price (1938–2009)

He smiles now, as he does every time he reads it.

Forcing himself to look away, he concentrates instead on the task at hand and in a movement made deft by recent experience, he squeezes the book onto one of the shelves next, in fact, to a title by J.G. Ballard. He quickly surveys the result and then repeats the entire procedure. On this occasion, *An Unhealthy Interest* is forced with some difficulty in between two books by William Boyd on the lowest shelf.

'Job done,' he says to himself and pausing one final time to inspect the results of his efforts, he turns on his heels and makes his way out of the shop.

'Y'all have a good day now,' says the proprietor as Martin exits the premises.

'Thanks. You too.'

The curious little scene that has just played out in DuPont's Book Store has previously occurred in three other book shops in the French Quarter over the past few days. Martin has found no need to improvise particularly or deviate from his original plan and he has so far found it a relatively simple task. As recently demonstrated, he would enter the shop in a friendly manner, ideally when it had just opened and was largely free of customers, greet the person behind the counter and then browse the fiction section. When he was confident he was not being observed, he would sneak a couple of copies of *An Unhealthy Interest* onto the shelves, after which he would smile, bid an effusive farewell and leave. The book being a paperback made its concealment in a jacket pocket a fairly easy procedure and now, after four attempts, his current 100% record of success probably flattered the guile of the perpetrator.

It was difficult to ascertain if he was actually committing a crime of any sort. If forced to, he could presumably defend his actions as simple gestures of philanthropy: small acts of generosity. However, that certainly wasn't the original intention and he would like to believe that his motives are a little more complex than that.

But he always likes to think like that.

This particular scheme had been hatched at roughly the same time as the trip to New Orleans was booked. Within moments of discovering that there are currently five second-hand book

16

shops in the Quarter, he had known exactly what the plan would involve. It was simple and if it made sense only to him then that was a good enough reason to proceed. Anyone who claimed to know him, or knew him reasonably well, would have perfectly understood him wanting to do something like this. Given the situation, it wasn't an act of folly or madness; it was the only action that made any sense to him.

Back on Chartres Street again, he adjusts his eyes to the bright morning sun and rummages in a pocket for his sunglasses. Already, one can sense that it's going to be another one of those beautiful sultry autumn days and satisfied that his tasks for the day are complete, he strolls towards Jackson Square with no particular purpose in mind.

'A good man doing nothing,' he says to himself and smiles at the possible irony.

As he draws near to the corner with St Peter's he finds that his path is currently blocked by two young men with a dog. From a distance of ten yards or so, they look vaguely Gothy, he thinks, or rather that particular Louisianan variant that is much in evidence on the streets of New Orleans nowadays. As he approaches the couple, he inhales sharply and then notices that they both now seem to be looking directly at him. This triggers an instant physical reaction and he feels short gasps of air being sucked into his lungs and immediately his heart begins to pound in his chest in perfect union with his footsteps – one, *two*, one, *two*, faster, *faster*, fight *flight*, too *close*, one *two*, too *close* to *turn* back… One, *two*, one *two*, whatdotheywant…?

'Hi there,' one of them says, stepping out of his way.

'Er, morning,' says Martin in the most bland tones he can muster under the circumstances.

The other one fixes him with a broad smile, which reveals two rows of perfectly even white teeth, and says, 'Those are some pretty cool shades, you know?'

And that is it. There is no altercation, no demands, no

threats, no insults, no harsh exchange of words or blows and absolutely no injury to person or property.

Martin mumbles a thank you, smiles and walks briskly away. Immediately, Michael Barnes reflects upon this incident and its implications in some detail. It is another aspect to New Orleans that is so obvious and is too often overlooked. This has always been a place where the outsiders, the marginalised, the unconventional, the oddballs and the loveable weirdoes all congregate. An adopted home for anyone who has ever felt different, ostracised or forced for whatever reason to very fringes of society, be it on account of ethnicity, disability or orientation. This is the city where all of us can join together and become one great united majority. Yes, we have taken over! A whole new sort of alternative democracy; an outsiderocracy, an exileocracy and isn't this the mirror image of all other cities? This is where being conventional or straight marks you down as different and thank God there is still a place in the world where you can be reviled for orthodoxy and complacency.

Stared at for wearing beige and grey.

That is why we all still come to New Orleans.

As though seeking confirmation, he turns around, hoping to catch sight of the two young men again. But they are nowhere to be seen.

2

Walking on Old Bones

Oh No! Not Another Book About New Orleans!
Introduction
Someone recently said
   'Well, actually, I just did.'
Someone recently said that travel writing is the new
pornography. Both trade on some facet of human longing,
both are engaging, diverting and ultimately succeed or fail
on the capacity to titillate. Therefore, in some ways, I feel
that I am as well placed as any to be writing this book, as
many years ago I scratched a pseudonymous living for myself
writing for a men's magazine. That magazine along with my
career as a budding pornographer is long defunct now. Its
dwindling sales and ultimate decline an early victim of the
Internet and
   Martin yawns, frowns and then exhales loudly through his
nose. Does he actually need to go into that much detail here?
The point is made well enough without going into specifics.
Otherwise, it starts to sound like a confession and that was
far from his intention. It wasn't that he was particularly
proud of the work he had produced – the stories he wrote
were usually little more than variations on a very few strict
traditional motifs – but he wasn't ashamed or embarrassed
by any of it either. There were worse jobs out there and it
had paid a few bills. He deletes the line and continues.
   To paraphrase the great Louis Armstrong when asked to

*define jazz; if you have to ask then you will never understand.
One could so easily apply that particular riposte to any
question regarding what makes New Orleans so special.
However, I will attempt in the following pages to record just
one man's thoughts*

Martin makes an animal noise. 'No, no, no... Make him
stop, somebody!' It is the morning following his visit to
DuPont's Book Store and Martin, naked apart from a ludicrously
oversized T-shirt recently purchased from the branch of Foot
Locker on Canal Street, is sitting at his desk again. It is still
early, the curtains are drawn and his room smells vaguely of
filter coffee and bed. On reflection, it might be better to leave
it until after breakfast, he thinks; wait until his head is a
little clearer. He'd awoken about twenty minutes ago with
the thought running through his mind about travel writing
and pornography. It seemed like too much of a good idea
to waste and so he'd forced himself to get out of bed and
record it before he forgot it.

He could elaborate later and provided that the rough idea
is saved, he is happy to leave it for the time being. He now
checks the time on his laptop, subtracts six hours and calculates
that they will start serving breakfast in just over an hour.
He thinks about running himself a bath but then decides to
check his emails.

There is one but it's not from Authorland this time. The
sender is Berni1104 and the message is as follows:

Hi Martin,
  *I don't know when you'll get this. I know you said
you were planning on going away for a week or two.
I've tried your landline a couple of times and as there's
no answer I'm now assuming you're away somewhere.*
  I hope you're having a nice time.
  *This is just basically to tell you that there have been
a few more problems with Wes at school. He's been*

suspended for another week for fighting. I think it's the same boy he was in trouble for fighting with last month. Anyway, I've been told to make an appointment to see the Head to discuss Wes's future at the school. Wes says that he's sick of it all and sick of being insulted and laughed at. He is very confused and he's still angry and very upset with you. He still says he doesn't want to see you and I know we said that we'd try and reschedule a visit for the end of the month but I don't think that would be fair on Wes.

I hope you can understand that I'm still really only thinking of Wes. And he is twelve now and so his feelings need to be taken into consideration. Let's give it another month or so and give him a chance to rebuild his confidence. Maybe meet him here after school one evening and take it from there.

I've kept the letter you sent him as he says he doesn't want to read it. Take care and enjoy your holiday.
B.
P.S. Thank you for the money towards his skiing holiday. He's very excited about it.

Martin now reads the email for a second time, slowly and carefully, as though hoping that he may have missed a vital word or two, misread the emphasis of a sentence, something that might change the entire tone and meaning of the text. Sadly, this doesn't happen and if anything, its general inference and manner strike him as even more condescending on rereading.

Angry and upset? Maybe he's not the only one.

The process by which common mortal sadness transforms itself into self-righteous bellowing indignation happens so quickly that it hardly seems like a process at all and within seconds Martin begins to compose a reply. To call his tone 'high-handed' would be a kindness and we will spare the author's feelings by not quoting him directly. Thankfully, within a few minutes he has abandoned the whole idea and deleted the document.

The only riposte he can actually summon at this moment is to say in a tone fractionally above a whisper, 'I do remember how old our son is.'

Martin had been divorced for a couple of years when he first met Bernice. That wasn't an obstacle to him remarrying and there were times when he thought he and Bernice would inevitably take that step. They lived together for just over fifteen years and would talk about marriage from time to time but somehow they never got around to it, not even after Wes was born, which both parties feel with hindsight to have been the most logical time. Indeed, the fact that it never happened has remained something of a mystery to both of them. But, as Mr Price used to say, it is always fate at the beginning and it's fate at the end and all you can do in the middle is make a bit of a bloody effort.

He was probably right too.

The recall of Mr Price's words has a calming effect on Martin and he starts to run his bath, reflecting on the fact that there seems to be a flexibility to the nature of time in all relationships. 'It feels like we just met,' 'Feels like I've always known her,' etc. etc. Temporal Elasticity, he decides to call it and it probably has something to do with the brain and pleasure sensors and serotonin. As evidence of this particular phenomenon, Martin would cite his own case history as an example.

M is twelve years older than B and while neither of them felt that this was an issue at the start of their relationship (M was thirty-two to B's twenty), as time passed, they both began to feel that the age difference became more significant. For some reason, which has yet to be established, thirty-two and twenty seemed less of a divide than fifty and thirty-eight, which were the respective ages of M and B when they separated a little over three months ago.

Even though 'Recent Events' had effectively ended their relationship, they've managed to remain on speaking terms; he doesn't hate her and she doesn't hate him. Although Martin looks back on their time together with the greater affection, tarnished not infrequently by something approaching longing: a fairly common deficiency of character he still awkwardly attributes to being Welsh.

Sadly, there is a strong possibility that this particular insight also functions as a creative inhibitor as this morning's breakfast is notable as it generates no further thoughts, ideas or riffs. But Martin knows that this is not the case and he is simply thinking about Wes again. He could not even claim to be the aggrieved party, that was the most depressing thing, and he could perfectly understand why the boy felt the way he did. Given an identical situation he would be acting in precisely the same way. If he could gain any comfort from this then he could at least claim to understand his son, so maybe there was hope.

For the second time in little over an hour, Martin now thinks about Mr Price, aware that he'd probably have known precisely what to do about Wes. That was the thing about the death of a close friend; you go through bereavement, mourning, that great sense of loss and isolation but there's an odd sort of anger too and all manner of agonies and confusions and then one day you are suddenly overwhelmed by the enormous fucking inconvenience of it all. This is more or less the stage he has recently reached with Mr Price. In fact, he had voiced more or less these very words on the first day of his visit when he had taken an early morning walk up South Rampart Street to Congo Square. He did feel as though he was keeping a promise of some kind, although no promise of this sort had ever been made. It was just a personal, very private thing between him and Mr Price. The square was all but deserted at the time and Martin had found a quiet bench and sat down. He'd obviously read a great deal about Congo Square over the years; way back in the eighteenth century it was the place where the slaves were permitted to gather once a week and where they used to make music and dance and keep the spirit of their African heritage alive. It is a site that is generally regarded as the ground zero of jazz. Nowadays, the place still exudes strange vibrations – it's like you're walking on old bones. Martin had sensed that immediately, together with the impression of something that was sacred and religious in a manner he would probably struggle to clarify. Nothing orthodox; it was just deep and old and profound.

Sunlight played on the leaves of the tall trees above him, while ancient branches rustled and ghosts observed. He'd remained there for about half an hour reflecting on his friend before the gentle morning breeze took the completely metaphoric ashes of the late Mr Price together with Martin's mumbled agnostic prayer.

There was no problem too great for Mr Price. There was no human agony or frailty unknown to him. He knew all weakness, all doubt and all fear, and nothing worried or alarmed him. He would do what he always did. He would sit you down on that big old sofa of his, offer you a couple of bottles of whatever brand of eccentrically named real ale he happened to be championing at the time and then put on some music. Usually, inevitably, at times of crisis, it was Bill Evans, either 'At The Village Vanguard' or 'Everybody Digs Bill Evans'. Then you would talk and he would listen. He never gave advice; he would simply offer a suggestion or two.

With very few exceptions, Martin usually acted on these suggestions. In fact, there was only one occasion when Martin completely ignored Mr Price's comments. Sadly, it was this occasion that was to have far-reaching and lasting implications.

* * *

'THHUUNNNCHHHHHHHCHK!' It is a sound that discourages elaboration. There is nothing open to debate here and nothing further to discuss. It is a simple and total finality, one that demands observance. An absolute. A given. A fact unto itself. There is no rejoinder, no epilogue. A single sharp percussive shock, after which the silence ranks only as conditional – post or après – entirely in relation to the prior event.

A door slamming, a shotgun blast, an exit – a sound that serves as its own conclusion. A denial, an obstruction – a sound that does not encourage enquiry and so no inquiry is made.

When the silence is eventually broken a very different question is posed.

'Did you read it, then?'

'Indeed I did. In fact I approached that very activity as something of a priority.'

Upside down, Martin now reads the familiar words on the cover of the 200 or so page manuscript that has just been dropped loudly and with a certain dramatic flair on the low coffee table in front of him. With some difficulty, he now reads the words backwards.

'tseretnI yhtlaehnU nA.'

It's a new alien language, he thinks, anxious to avoid asking the inevitable next question. Actually, the more he looks at it, the more it starts to resemble Welsh or what little he still remembers of it from school. A slight chill passes through him. He can delay it no more.

'So, what did you think then?'

It is a warm, muggy evening towards the end of June 2009 and Martin is sitting in the living room of Mr Price's airy flat in the centre of Canterbury. Part of a relatively recent development, adjacent to the old city wall, his flat boasts large sliding sash windows and these have recently been thrown open in the vain hope of generating some cooler air, but the room remains airless and humid. From the Bose speakers in the corners of the room, Hank Mobley blows some suitably sultry phrases from his 'Soul Station' album while the tireless flies trace their looping signatures around the lamps in the encroaching dusk.

'The manuscript,' says Martin, tapping the actual item with quite unnecessary emphasis. 'Your thoughts?'

'I will just hasten myself to the kitchen and take a merest moment to replenish our beers if I may. I'll be back momentarily.'

On first impression, this might appear to be a desperate attempt by the older man to avoid answering a difficult or awkward question but this would be to seriously underestimate the significance of Thurston's Old Crusty in Mr Price's life at this current time. Martin knows nothing about real ale but he does know his friend well enough not to take offence. He had first made the man's acquaintance in the early nineties and they had struck up a strong yet highly unlikely friendship, Mr Price being his senior by a little over twenty years. They have remained on very close terms all this time, their alliance being in some way sustained by their mutual love of jazz. But, in all this time, Martin has never referred to him as anything other than Mr Price. This is despite the man's fairly regular entreaties to be called Stanley. Martin never really knew why he did this. He'd always had a certain flair, if that's the right word, for rather stiff and mannered spoken English and this fact alone seemed to encourage a kind of awkward formality. So he remained Mr Price and any further speculation was discouraged.

Martin grew up without a father and is in no great hurry to make the obvious connection in regards to Mr Price. And neither is Mr Price. However, they have somehow drifted into their respective roles with comparative ease, although it seems to be generally understood that if they make any spoken allusion to this fact it will somehow tarnish or ruin their entire association.

Mr Price now returns holding two bottles, which he sets down with all the necessary reverence on the table beside the manuscript.

'Your very good health, Martin.'

'Cheers. Well?'

Mr Price manoeuvres himself into an armchair and takes a long sip of his ale. His face quickly contorts into the sort of expression that might easily be taken as a mild form of religious ecstasy. 'Well, if one might be candid, certain reservations aside, I have to say, Martin, I thought it was a most powerful work. I read it all the way through in one evening I was so gripped. It's most unusual, totally unencumbered by literary convention, I thought. But in a bold way, you understand. Challenging in many ways and I confess I found it most affecting.'

'Certain reservations?'

'Well, obviously the subject matter does inevitably, er...' Mr Price hastily imbibes once more as he considers what to say next. 'It inevitably takes you into some very dark areas, where I imagine it is the author's intention to make his reader feel uncomfortable or agitated even. It certainly provokes a reaction and I don't imagine it's possible to read the tome and remain unmoved. But surely that is the point, isn't it?'

'Maybe,' says Martin with a very deliberate shrug of his shoulders. 'But that's not the entire reason behind it.'

'But whatever one is attempting to say, given the choice of subject matter in this instance, it's always going to be problematical. You must realise that.'

The shrug this time is noticeably more feeble. 'I suppose so.'

'I can, with little difficulty, foresee a great deal of trouble if you fail to proceed with great caution; particularly in regard to publication. Talking of which, when are you going to start sending it off to publishers? Sadly, I fear it my duty to sound a note of caution at this juncture as I feel many of the major firms will be put off by the book's theme.'

Martin now takes his first less-than-delightful gulp of Old Crusty and winces. 'I think you're probably right. I don't know really what I'm going to do about that. I may just publish it myself. There's lots of these smaller companies opening up now on the Internet that do something called print-on-demand, which means they only print a copy when someone buys one – makes a lot of sense, I suppose. There's a company based in Croydon called Authorland that looks quite interesting.'

'Is it very expensive?'

'Not insanely. I'd have to save up or splurge on the credit card but it's an appealing alternative.'

'Sounds rather intriguing.'

'I just want to get something out there, just something with my name on it. I don't care if three people read it, I just want my novel somewhere out there in the world. Do you understand?'

'Perfectly.'

'If it exists then I know in some small way that I'm a writer. It's important to me.'

'But you are a writer.'

'I know, I know... But writing crappy little features, articles reviews and whatever else that pay a few bills is a completely different world. For as long as I can remember I've just wanted to write a novel. It's all I ever really wanted to do. I must have started dozens over the years but this is the only one I've even come close to finishing. It's just a shame it's going to be a difficult one to sell.'

'Please don't misunderstand me; it's a very fine piece of work and it certainly stands on its own literary merits.' Mr Price begins to chuckle to himself. 'It's just a shame that at the conclusion of every page one felt the overpowering urge to go and wash one's hands.'

Martin smiles at this. 'But surely you get to the end of the novel and your entire perception of what is going on is turned on its head.'

'Of course it is and I am in complete agreement with you; the twist in the tale shifts the whole meaning of the story and I fully understand now why you didn't want me to read it before you'd completed the first draft.'

'It changes everything hopefully and highlights our own knee-jerk prejudices. That's what I wanted it to do.'

'And you certainly achieve that but it's the content of the story before that point that troubles me. It's all a question of emphasis and interpretation.'

'But isn't it always a question of emphasis and interpretation?'

'Possibly, possibly. But I wonder if your average reader will get past the first hundred pages or so.'

Martin looks serious for a moment and leans back into the sofa. 'Oh come on. People aren't that stupid.'

'You think not?' Suddenly animated, Mr Price now lurches forward so he is sitting on the very edge of his chair. 'What about our man Mr Mobley there?' he asks, gesturing with his thumb over his shoulder towards his Bose speakers just as the late tenor saxophonist negotiates his horn around the introduction of 'Split Feelin's'. 'One should surely question the intelligence or the capacity for sound judgement of any species that fails to fully appreciate or indeed revere a man of such genius. That there are no statues of the man or great universities named in his honour is an inexcusable oversight.'

'OK, fair point.' This is not the first time Martin has heard Mr Price voicing similar sentiments but he is keen not to let the conversation drift away from the subject of his novel too much. 'I do think it attempts to make an important point. Well, that's what I was aiming at.'

'You'll hear no argument from me in that respect, Martin. Absolutely not. It makes that very point very well but I confess I worry that the common reader will not get past the sensationalist aspect, the shock value, if you will.'

'I think you might be underestimating the sort of person who might want to read a book like this.'

'Similarly, Martin, I have serious misgivings in that regard also. I fear that certain people with certain, shall we say, *inclinations* might be interested in the book for other more dubious reasons.'

Martin looks quite horrified at this suggestion and shakes his head. 'I doubt it. There's nothing graphic or salacious particularly and besides, a little controversy can be a good thing for a book. Think of *The Satanic Verses*.'

Mr Price looks across the room at Martin and smiles indulgently. He then lets Hank Mobley fill the space between them for a few moments before he continues. He speaks slowly now, deliberately, as though mindful of giving offence. 'If I might be allowed to make one small suggestion: one that amounts to just the tiniest of adjustments? There's no need to change anything that you've already written and this involves no alterations to any of the text.'

'Go on.'

Mr Price stands up and evidently agitated, he begins to walk around the room. 'Please, you can ignore me or just tell me to shut up but it is my feeling that the book would benefit in some way from a short foreword or an introduction.'

The author looks puzzled. 'A foreword?'

'Just a page, certainly no more.'

Martin raises his eyebrows. 'Why?'

His softly spoken question is elongated into a phrase of two syllables and is entirely free, Mr Price is delighted to learn, from any sudden surge of assertion or defensiveness. He returns to his armchair and leaning forward now and resting his elbows on his knees, he begins to speak. 'You see, my primary area of concern is the fact the book is written in first person. The book is in effect written by you, Martin Bonehouse, and whatever thoughts your character has these read like the thoughts of Martin Bonehouse.'

'But it's a novel; it's fiction.'

'Of course it's a novel. I perfectly understand that. My

worry is that it might be read by a person who doesn't fully grasp that: someone who might make all sorts of assumptions. Now, if you were to simply write a short foreword, perhaps even write in the character of an editor, just to put a sense of distance between the first-person character in the book and the author. You may very well need that sense of distance, Martin.'

This transpired to be a very sound idea and Martin would one day pay heavily for ignoring it. But on this particular day he says nothing. Instead, he looks down at the subject of their discussion and lifting the cover of the manuscript, he idly reads the first page.

AN UNHEALTHY INTEREST

Chapter One

They were always sending me for tests when I was a little kid. I admit my memory is probably a bit skewed on this but, as I recall it, it was like I was going for some test or another every week or so. I missed a lot of school back then. That probably didn't help either. But I wasn't interested in school much. Never was. I knew I was different – everyone kept telling me. I couldn't even be bothered to pay attention most the time, or at least that's how it seemed to my teachers. I don't blame them; I would have thought the same thing. I was in my own world most of the time. Completely detached from the lessons and the other kids, but I was always thinking about things. If I was given a book to look at it I would ignore all the writing and the pictures and instead I would become fascinated, obsessed even, by the book as an object. I was always doing stuff like that – my mind would just wander. I'd look at the spine of the book and the pages and think about the tree that provided the paper, the man who'd cut the tree down, the people who'd transported it and the

31

mill where it was turned into paper, the factory where they bound the pages into a book and all the people that worked there; this was a marvellous thing to me. I could imagine this amazing story that had delivered this book onto my desk; it was a far better and far more interesting story than what was in the actual book. So I would be concentrating on that all the time; it felt like I wanted to look through things and not at them. I knew I was different – everyone kept telling me. I'd sit silently during car journeys quite happily for hours and hours and stare at the handle of the door (which I wasn't allowed to touch) and wonder about the man who invented the mechanism and the man on a production line somewhere who had fitted it to our car. What did they have in common? Did those two people ever meet? Were their lives similar in any way? What was the person like who'd actually made the mechanism in my door? What about the metal in the mechanism? Where had that come from? Had it come from somewhere far away, somewhere very hot? Somewhere where there were strange languages and great brightly coloured beasts? I found such a sense of unending wonder in these deliberations I could entertain myself for hours. Everything I looked at or thought about became my connection to all things. I was a tiny link in a great chain that connected the whole universe. I had found the hidden meaning in all things! Yes and only I could solve all the world's mysteries! I knew I was different – everyone kept telling me. The strangest aspect I suppose, looking back, was that I was utterly incapable of applying this thought process to anything natural or living. A flower in my hand was just a flower; I didn't know or care why it was there. It was just there. Trees, birds, animals, the moon, the sea, a sunset – none of those things inspired me the way I might be diverted by looking at the corner of a carpet in my bedroom or a spoon in the kitchen. My mum was always talking about Jesus and taking me to church every Sunday but I never connected that to the way I saw things. She put

*three pictures of Jesus on my bedroom wall after my dad
died and I just wondered about the frames and how they'd
made the glass. In short, my distractions were exclusively and
entirely atheistic. My wonder was directed at all that was
manmade and all the people that had been involved in its
production. Emphatically construction and not creation. The
connection and the chain went no higher than that but that
was magical enough for me. But to an outsider I am certain
I just seemed isolated and detached from everything all the
time. So, I was sent for tests. Sometimes in these tests I had
to play with things, like arranging objects according to size,
or they had these cards with pictures on and I had to put
them in order so they told a story. On other occasions they
asked me to draw pictures. I remember once I had to draw
a picture of my family. I was about six or seven, still in
primary school definitely. I drew a picture of the whole family,
which was my mum, my dad and me, sitting on toilets in
our living room. Without being overly graphic, my recall is
that we were all involved in various bodily functions. But
the thing is, this wasn't out of any scatological impulse or
some deep-rooted urge to shock or anything like that. I did
it because I thought it would be funny. Seriously, I thought
it would make everybody laugh. I knew I was different –
everyone kept telling me. But I can tell you this much without
any fear of contradiction: educational psychologists have
absolutely no sense of humour! So I live with just my mum
now – it's been just the two of us since my dad died. I'm
glad he's dead, really I am. Sometimes I actually imagine that
I killed him and I relive the moment in my mind each time,
adding new details. Sometimes I push him off a cliff or under
a train. I don't remember the exact year he died. I didn't
want to go to the funeral but I was forced into it. I hated
it so much; I hated the way his life was being sanitised and
made decent, the way they pretended he was a good and
noble human being when I knew just what an abusive bastard*

he could be. Guess what? I made my protest by pissing my pants during the reading. After he died, my mum didn't like going out much and she used to rely on me to do the shopping. I don't think she could have actually been termed an agoraphobic because she loved the garden and spent a lot of time out there in the summer. She just got a bit nervous when she was around strangers.

3

Georgia Blues

For here they have always danced. They were dancing right at the beginning and they are still dancing now. Wherever there is music in this city there are people dancing. They dance out of exuberance not as part of some overture to foreplay or a ritual of narcissistic self-display or out of some didactic primitivism. Here, they dance from the sheer joy of the moment and a connection to the music. It is the order of things and part of their daily life.

This idea had come to him a few moments ago as he returned to his room after breakfast; it had probably been sparked off by recalling his trip to Congo Square again. It really was little beyond the very roughest sketch but he thought he should just get it down before he forgot it.

In New Orleans, they dance because that is what you do when you hear music.

Martin imagines that the point he is attempting to make might be best illustrated by having a couple of pictures inserted into the text, maybe a shot of some Mardi Gras revellers on Bourbon Street alongside a reproduction of that famous old engraving of people dancing in Congo Square. That would certainly make the connection an obvious one. He makes a note to this effect and continues.

Free from convention, restraint and self-consciousness, they dance in the streets or in the parks, mornings or evenings;

35

*they dance because they're alive and why stand still when
you could be dancing?*

But did he really want to include illustrations? That would
give the book an entirely different dimension and might
possibly lend it the appearance of just another travel guide.
Michael Barnes would doubtless have very strong views on
this subject and so the note is immediately deleted.

Martin gazes at the screen for a few moments and when
he next types something it bears no relation to any of the
above.

Dear Wes,
I'm really sorry to hear that you
This is quickly amended to:
I really am so sorry to hear that you
And then to:
SORRY SORRY SORRY SORRY!!!
At this point he decides to abandon the whole idea
and shuts down his laptop. He needs to think about all
this carefully and what would be the best approach; an
over apologetic, grovelling email was unlikely to move his
cause any further forward. Besides, there are another two
copies of *An Unhealthy Interest* in his jacket pockets and a
second-hand bookshop on Decatur Street is due to open very
shortly.

Possibly on account of an overnight rainstorm and a very
slight breeze, the smell is less in evidence this morning but
still detectable by those, like Martin, with a discerning, well-
tuned nose for such things.

Upon leaving the hotel, he heads westwards towards
Magazine Street whereupon he makes a left turn and once
again heads towards the Quarter. As he waits for the lights
to change on Canal Street, he glances inside his jacket, quite
unnecessarily, to ensure he still has the two books on his
person. For some reason, this prompts him to recall again
that evening with Mr Price and their first conversation about

the book. When discussing all the various possibilities for its future, Martin had insisted that his motivation was just to have something somewhere with his name on it, just to know that his novel existed in some quiet corner of the world. It remains a source of some regret that Mr Price had not lived long enough to witness the lengths to which Martin would go in pursuit of that precise goal.

The lights finally change and Martin makes his way onto Decatur Street. Now it would be out of sight, languishing on some dusty old bookshelf somewhere, largely forgotten but not entirely erased. Of course, in many instances a certain amount of controversy virtually ensures a level of success but this sadly had not been Martin's experience. In his case, the polemic had all but guaranteed that no one would ever wish to own, purchase, read or attach themselves to his book in any conceivable way, not even those with that permanent vague desire, common in so many, to gravitate towards the dark and forbidden or that which lurks beyond the mainstream.

Distributing his books in this manner is, he would concede, a small act of vanity rather than defiance. The alternative would be to admit that the past two years had been nothing but an exercise in wilful self-destruction. Bernice had made a point of saying to him at fairly regular intervals that he needed to move on, learn something from it all and maybe grow up a little. But Martin still has a bit of problem with all that. As he confessed to her on the day they finally separated, 'I don't know how to be old; I mean that I don't know how to be old in a manner I can recognise or even understand. I just can't even seem to grasp the basics. I just shuffle and stagger between events, issues and incidents.'

To this day, Bernice still believes this to be one of the truest things that he has ever said.

Beacham's Books in terms of floor space alone is by far the largest and most impressive shop of its kind in the Quarter.

An old, scruffy, two-storey building with high ceilings and more books than you and a thousand friends could read in a thousand lifetimes. Martin had briefly called in earlier in the week but the place had been too busy or too intimidating at the time for him to complete his intended task. But now, as he approaches, he is adept and confident and more than equal to the challenge. He strides with purpose towards the entrance and then promptly stops as he reads the small typed notice pinned to the door announcing that the shop will not be opening until eleven o'clock this morning.

'Oh fuck,' he says quietly, although not without a certain conviction. Looking at his watch, he calculates that he has about forty minutes to wait. Not enough time to go back to the hotel; not enough time to do anything much. Martin thinks for a moment but there really is only one reasonable course of action. About three doors down Decatur Street from Beacham's is the New Orleans Music Company, a smallish music shop specialising, according to the hand-painted sign over the door, in jazz, blues, Cajun, Zydeco and R&B and this would be the most obvious place to idle away half an hour or so. Actually, it was perfect. Martin had visited the shop a couple of times previously and browsed the second-hand section for possible bargains. The shop, which seemed keen to promote New Orleans's musical heritage and was therefore probably reliant on the tourist trade, had a kind of manufactured 'funkiness' about it that you had to instantly forgive because of its location.

Martin pushes open the door and greets the man behind the counter. 'Good morning.' A guitar fill.

'Hey there. How y'all doing this morning?' A drum roll.

'Yeah, I'm good thanks.' Another guitar fill, an organ riff behind it. The guitar was the giveaway. 'Grant Green, right?' he asks, gesturing at some indeterminate point above his head.

'Spot on, my man,' says the gentleman behind the counter, smiling broadly.

'Yeah, thought so. It's Grantstand, isn't it?'

'It sure is! My first customer of the day nails it in one! Give that man a balloon!'

Martin smiles and wonders if the gentleman is being polite or if he might actually be a fellow aficionado. If he fell into the latter category, was it feasible he'd logged on to Amazon in the past five years and looked up this particular CD? So might it also be within the realms of possibility that he'd read some of the customer reviews? If that was the case then he would have probably read BirdLives1960s' first ever CD review.

Martin had laboured over the review for hours and to this day, he can virtually recite it word for word.

Grant Green: Grantstand
* * * * One of Green's Finest
By BirdLives1960

Green's fifth album under his own name for Blue Note and a little celebrated hard bop classic. Teamed up with Yusef Lateef and Jack McDuff, Green's guitar skills stand out and it can only be a source of some regret amongst jazz fans that this line-up didn't record together again. Green seems to be continually edging towards that funkier style of playing that would later define his music. Unique amongst his peers of hard bop guitarists (Farlow, Kessell, Raney, etc.) with the notable exceptions of Kenny Burrell and early Wes Montgomery, Grant Green never lapses into what sounds, to contemporary ears, a little too close to easy-listening for comfort. His was always a very different groove. You need to check this guy out.

Martin slowly wanders over to the second-hand section and is happily and quietly browsing in a manner that he hopes is as inconspicuous as possible. But as the Grant Green track finishes there is silence for half a minute and it is obvious

39

that the man does not intend to play the whole album. This is awkward, he thinks, suddenly conscious of being the only customer in the shop. So it's a great relief when the silence is broken by more music. Anything would do but this is so far just a little piano vamp, now a guitar phrase, acoustic maybe, unfamiliar. Can't place it. Two people or possibly one person talking in two different voices.

'Hey there, wake up, man! We got to get together and sing us a real blues song!'

'Now why we want to go and do something like that?'

'Yes, sir, we gonna sing us a REAL blues song.'

'But ... but ... why? Ain't nobody wanna hear all that old stuff no more.'

'White folks do! Damn right! They jes' love all dem old blues songs, man. Yes, sir. They loves to hear all that wailing an a-moaning, man. They jes' love to hear the sound of us cryin'. Makes 'em all feel so damn pleased with the'selves, them righteous sons of...'

'But, but, but, but why's that then?'

'They love the sound of remorse, the sound of our pain, the sound of all that damn helplessness. Crying 'cause my pony done died or dem weevils ate the cotton, keeping us all lowdown and stuff.'

'Wait a mo'; let's get into it!'

Then, right on cue, the band kicks in. Martin doesn't recognise it. Sounds old but hard to place, maybe not that old, not Blind-Lemon-Jefferson old, more like Big-Bill-Broonzy old, late 1930s or 1940s maybe, but just played in an older style. But bluesy, definitely. Piano, guitar ... violin is that? Hard to tell; could be a clarinet? When the singing starts the words are easier to decipher; they follow the metre and phrasing of a thousand other songs. While the melody is instantly recognisable, the lyrics are quite different.

'Me try me a shotgun down in Texas. Me try poison down in Tennessee.'

For the second or third time in the past minute, he winces at what sounds like deliberately emphasised syntax and exaggerated, obviously mocking pronunciation. He now begins to feel uncomfortable, as though being in the same room as such a performance would forever associate him with its underlying philosophy. In his mind, it feels like singing along with a swastika.

After the first line there follows a little phrase played by the guitar and violin in unison. It reminds him of one of those priceless Leroy Carr and Scrapper Blackwell duos or the Harlem Hamfats but there was also a sort of swingy, country feel to it, almost like Bob Wills and his Texas Playboys, even though this is evidently a blues song in the traditional twelve-bar structure, confirmed when the second line repeats the first.

'Me try me a shotgun down in Texas. Me try poison down in Tennessee.'

A very slight variation on the unison riff is played and he likes this; it's catchy, it's buoyant and happy. Still hard to place, hard to know where it sits with things. It is still impossible to accurately guess the period. Then the singer concludes the verse.

'So now ah'm gwine down to Georgia – kiss de first white woman I see.'

As though anticipating the shock and bewilderment the line might engender, the singer is kind enough to repeat it.

'Yes, sir, ah'm gwine down to Georgia – kiss de first white woman I see.'

The line seems to run away from the music, detach itself and take on a life of its own; the song moves forward but the words remain fixed and permanent, forever now in their own space and time. The piano is still playing, the guitar and the violin restate that little unison riff but that line is still circling overhead; it blows though his hair and he feels it next to his ear, like a whispered private confidence. Utterly spellbound, Martin is terrified to move or even inhale for fear of destroying the moment. The second verse now quickly follows the first in which the singer claims:

'Me cut my throat in Jackson – me try candy up in Tallassee.'

The vocalist's diction is slightly less clear and for the first time, Martin is far from certain that he has made the words out correctly – was 'candy' a euphemism? But on hearing the phrase repeated, he realises his error.

'Me cut my throat in Jackson – me try canned heat up in Tallassee.'

This makes far more sense to Martin. According to the folklore and the classic song by bluesman Tommy Johnson, 'canned heat' was once a common term used to describe the alcohol derived from cooking fuel and shoe polish. It was notoriously dangerous as Johnson's own death would confirm. Once again, the verse concludes with the same final refrain.

'So now ah'm gwine down to Georgia – kiss de first white woman I see.'

Is he hearing this correctly? he wonders. Is there something really obvious he's overlooking? But even the most cursory reading of the song suggests that the character is a black man who has attempted suicide by various means before finally resorting to the desperate alternative of trying to get himself lynched for consorting with a white woman. Lyrically, this is unlike anything he has ever heard in his life; it is direct and powerful and doesn't seem to be born out of any particular tradition.

Still rooted to the spot, Martin listens intently as the band plays an instrumental verse. Not really a solo in the accepted sense of the word but the violin plays an approximation of the original vocal line. Then just as you are expecting the singer to come back in with a variation of the same refrain, the song suddenly changes its emphasis. The singer's voice is now joined by at least two others and they are all singing in a rough barrelhouse harmony:

'Roll 'em, Mr Bones, Mr Bones, Mr Bones,
I say Roll 'em, Mr Bones, Mr Bones, Mr Bones!'

At this precise instant, it happens and there is no virtue in ignoring or disguising the fact. Such things occur a few times in every lifetime and this is the latest in a sequence that had begun when Martin was eleven. One morning he had woken up as just a schoolboy but later that same day he went to bed as a schoolboy who had heard 'Jeepster' by T. Rex and nothing was ever the same afterwards. These are the rare, unplanned and absolutely unprecedented moments of complete and total connection we can experience with music. It also happens with paintings, literature and cinema but Martin has only ever felt it this intensely with music. You can't force these things; it simply doesn't work like that and if anybody claims to experience it when first hearing Wagner, John Cage or Archie Shepp they are very probably lying.

He feels his feet now standing squarely and firmly, taking root on a great strong timeline that rushes all the way back to that day in late 1971. A timeline which gives him reason to recall, amongst others, The Clash's 'White Riot' (only the original single version) in 1977, Howlin' Wolf's 'Moanin' at Midnight' in 1979 (mainly for the bit on the intro when the drums and guitar kick in) and Charlie Parker's 'Chi Chi' (take 6 – his last great masterpiece) in 1983. It's music that you understand without knowledge, without context, music that just makes you feel grateful you've lived long enough to hear it, music that hits you on some strange, deeper, unchartered level. Indeed, if the existence of the soul is ever proven, Martin is certain that it will only be done through music!

And now this! Suddenly there is this! Whatever *this* is...

The group is still singing what is obviously the repeated coda to the song.

'Roll 'em, Mr Bones, Mr Bones, Mr Bones,
I say Roll 'em, Mr Bones, Mr Bones, Mr Bones!'

There is absolutely no debate on the issue and he now decides that whatever crises, agonies or injustices life may heap upon him in future, he will simply affect a shrug and sardonic half-smile, whilst silently singing this exact chorus to himself.

Before the track has faded he has made his way to the counter at the front of the shop.

The gentleman behind the counter greets his return with a smile saying, 'C'mon, you're surely not going to tell me you know who this singer is!'

Martin shakes his head. 'Absolutely not. I haven't got the slightest idea but you *really* have to tell me,' he says, breaking into a mock manic grin. 'It's *so* important. Actually, it's essential that I have this information immediately.'

The man behind the counter laughs and reaches for an LP sleeve. 'So, y'all liked that one, then?' He is amiable and bearded and blessed with the sort of casual demeanour that puts others immediately at ease. Martin takes an instant liking to the man.

'It was – what can I say? – totally amazing. I don't think I've ever heard anything like it. I couldn't even guess what decade it came from.'

'Forties, I think,' the man says vaguely as he scan-reads the sleeve notes to the LP. 'Yeah, 1941, here it is. "Georgia Blues" by Tambo Bones and the Back O' Town Boys, originally released on the Hi-Tone record label. Um... All it says here is that Tambo Bones was a native Louisianan, born here in New Orleans... Recorded under a number of different names, blah blah blah, but this is the only known recording he made under the name Tambo Bones. Also it's the only record by the Back O' Town Boys, who were apparently just a studio group and never actually performed on stage together. Then it talks about catalogue numbers and the like. That's all it says.'

'What's the LP?'

The man obliges by holding up the sleeve for Martin to see. *Louisiana Folk Songs* announces itself in a typeface very typical of its genre and judging by the accompanying line drawing and general design of the sleeve, he would guess that in all likelihood the record dated from the folk boom of the early sixties.

'Is it particularly rare?'

'It's only twenty bucks if that's what you mean. I've had it for a while.'

'Is there a CD?'

The man chuckles to himself as though the very suggestion was absurd. 'No, my friend, I'm afraid not.'

Disappointed at this, Martin sighs and looks away; for a moment or two, he gazes vacantly at the walls, at the handbills, flyers and posters as if seeking some kind of inspiration. 'I don't own a record player anymore,' he confesses eventually. 'Is there any other information on this man ... this Tambo ...?'

'Tambo Bones.'

'Anything at all?'

The man considers the question. 'To be honest, he's pretty much forgotten nowadays. Very few books mention him, even books about New Orleans music ignore him and I've never seen that "Georgia Blues" on any other compilation. Yeah, that song is a true one-off, for real! There may be some other recordings under different names but it's not really my field to be honest. That's definitely the only recording by Tambo Bones.' The man thinks for a moment. 'Actually, there's a collector here in the Quarter who's very interested in all that stuff, lives somewhere over on Dumaine. I managed to get him one of the first issue 78s at an auction a while ago. I think he paid about three hundred bucks for that. Something like that.'

'It's an amazing record. Why is it not more widely known? I mean it's such a powerful song. It's almost twenty years ahead of its time, right? It's like one of the great civil rights rallying cries.'

Judging by the man's barely successful attempts to suppress a gale of laughter, this is evidently one of the most stupid things that anyone has ever said. He shakes his head and then proceeds to choose his words very carefully. 'No, that's not how it went down. No, that's not it at all.'

'What's so funny?'

'I do apologise; it just conjures up some amazingly surreal images in my mind.'

'Like what?' asks Martin, wondering if he should feel wounded by the man's outburst.

'Well,' the man says cautiously, 'Tambo Bones wasn't really a folk singer or a jazz musician, you understand? He belonged to a very different world. That's why you don't really hear about his stuff anymore.'

Martin says nothing but his expression would seem to indicate that he doesn't regard this as any sort of explanation.

Recognising this to be the case, the man now elaborates. 'Tambo Bones, you see, was kind of part of the old minstrel tradition; he worked with travelling theatre companies and the old medicine shows, which flourished down here in the South, believe it or not, until the late sixties. He was part of that world. It's not something we really want to associate ourselves with anymore. People find it offensive and to be honest, I would never usually play it in the shop. I just thought I'd play it to you this morning as it was the most obscure thing I could think of.'

'But it's still a great blues song; it's still part of that genre.'

'You know, that's pretty much what the man over on Dumaine thinks.'

'So does it actually matter?'

'Well, it does if you perform in blackface.'

The total and utter silence that follows this revelation is only broken when Martin is finally able to gasp, 'Fuck, no way,' far louder than he might have intended. 'You're joking, aren't you?'

'Sadly, I'm not. Ladies and gentlemen I give you … the lasting shame of the entertainment industry! Give it up for our very own Tambo Bones! Funny thing is, according to the fellow on Dumaine there, Tambo was actually a Creole by birth, which makes it all a bit weird if you think about it.'

Martin rubs his forehead with his fingertips as though trying to manually start the part of his brain that deals with ethical conflict. 'But surely,' he says after a few moments' consideration, 'isn't it the message and not the messenger? I mean the man in the song is drawing our attention to injustice and the terrible way black people were treated in places like Georgia and Alabama. And that bit at the start about white people liking blues makes the point pretty explicitly. Considering…'

At this moment, the door of the shop opens and a young couple with rucksacks stroll in.

'Hey there, how ya'll doing this morning?' asks the man and receiving no reply, he turns once more to Martin. 'Well?'

'Well what?'

'Do you want the record or not?'

Martin thinks for a moment. 'I don't know… I haven't got a record –'

'Yeah, tell you what, give me twenty-five and I'll burn you a CD of it as well. You can have them both. How does that sound?'

'Um … yeah,' says Martin vaguely. 'Great! Can you do that?'

'Takes a while but it's pretty easy if you've got the gear.'

'OK.'

'Y'all come back this time tomorrow and I'll have it for you.'

'Thanks,' says Martin, offering the man his hand. 'My name's Martin, by the way.'

'Very pleased to make your acquaintance, Martin. I'm Hugo.'

'Likewise, Hugo. This time tomorrow, then.' Martin wanders back out into the street and immediately the song begins to play in his head again. It stays with him all the way back up Decatur, across Canal, up Magazine and back to the Royal Crescent Hotel and it's only when he is crossing the lobby that he realises he still has two paperback books in his inside jacket pockets.

'A foreword?'
'Yip, that's what he said.'
'Really?'
'Yeah, his exact words,' says Martin airily. 'Actually, he seemed to feel quite strongly about it.'
'Well ... it's an idea, I suppose.'
Martin takes a grape from the bunch lying on the kitchen table. 'I don't know, I think he's worried that people will get the wrong idea or take things out of context. I'm not certain but I think his idea involved introducing a fictitious character to write a fictitious foreword to a work of fiction. I don't know, it just sounds a bit ... superfluous to me. A bit, I don't know, Victorian. Like when they have things that start' – and here Martin adopts a suitably elevated tone – 'these following accursed papers and journals came into my possession at the outset of my recent safari. You know the sort of thing?'
Bernice chuckles and nods her agreement. 'Yeah I do. So did he say anything else?'
'I think he liked it; he said a few positive things, but I don't know... I don't know if it was his sort of thing, to be honest. Anyway, is Wes still awake?'
She glances at the clock on the wall. 'Hmm... I doubt it. But you could pop up and have a look. I said you'd be in to say goodnight later.'
'OK, I'll go and check on him.'
Martin saunters out of the kitchen and then, as has become his habit, he runs briskly up the short straight staircase to his son's bedroom. He is rather proud of the fact he can still

run up the stairs; it's one of few things he actually enjoys about living in a cottage. If he is to be completely honest, he has never really fallen for the place in quite the way Bernie has and it is taking far longer than he might have expected to adjust to no longer living in London. After eight years, the fact that such an adjustment could still be regarded as *pending* is not a situation that particularly instils confidence or encourages optimism. Martin and Bernice had shared Martin's small flat in New Cross for a number of years; it was fairly cramped but they both adapted to the arrangement reasonably well. Then, when Wes was born, it was obvious that there needed to be a change in their living arrangements and so they agreed – Martin perhaps less readily – to sell the flat and buy somewhere a little larger out of town before Wes started school. Eventually they ended up buying a small two-bedroom Victorian cottage in the village of Wickham, a few miles east of Canterbury. They already knew the area reasonably well on account of their fairly frequent visits to Mr Price who, following his retirement as a publican, had been living in the area since the late 1990s.

It had thus once promised to be a fairly easy transition.

At the time Martin told himself that what was best for his son was best for him. He still repeats this to himself like a mantra at least two or three times every day. The truth is that the 60 miles that separated Wickham from London was misleading. Emotionally and psychologically the distance was incalculable and Martin could only envy the ease with which Bernice adapted to their new environment. She joined groups and committees and got involved and volunteered, she knew everyone's name and generally did all those things that are utterly alien to people in London; alien, in truth, to people just like Martin.

With a certain degree of encouragement on his part, his total lack of affinity with most aspects of village life allowed him periodically to feel rootless and nomadic – a fleeting but enormously satisfying sensation. In short, the cottage is Bernice and Wes's home – it is also where Martin keeps his 856 CDs.

He creeps stealthily into his son's room and, finding the boy deeply asleep, he simply kisses him gently on the head and then retreats downstairs. Returning to the kitchen again, where he finds Bernice sitting at the table with a glass of wine, the subject of his earlier chat with Mr Price is once again brought up.

'So you don't think he was shocked by it particularly?'

Martin repeats the anecdote about Mr Price feeling compelled to wash his hands at the end of each page. 'But,' he says by way of a conclusion, 'I really think he appreciated what I was trying to do. I don't think he found it salacious or that I was intending to shock in any way.'

'What about the ending?'

'What about it?'

'The twist and the way it changes the whole story.'

'Yeah, he thought...' But Martin is unable to complete his sentence as Bernice has suddenly begun waving her hands erratically in front of her.

'Wait, wait ... wait a minute.'

'What is it?'

'Hey, just had an idea,' she says emphatically as the hands settle once again. 'Now, listen very carefully...' One should not jump to conclusions here; Bernice's slightly condescending tone is not a legacy of her daily negotiations with a class of over-truculent eight-year-olds but rather her experience of dealing with Martin in similar situations in the past.

'Maybe that's what you need to do. You don't need a foreword but maybe you need to drop a few hints throughout the story so when it gets to the end people will kick them-selves for not working it out earlier. You know, like an old whodunit.'

Martin strokes his bottom lip with his forefinger and takes

a moment to enjoy what he hopes might be seen in his partner's eyes as a 'writer's moment'.

'Actually,' he says eventually in a tone of voice he keeps exclusively for these occasions, 'there are a few references dotted around the place. Right off the top of my head, there's one I remember in chapter three.'

'Well, maybe you need to make it really, I don't know ... explicit; just like really bloody obvious. Maybe that's the thing. What do you think?'

'I don't know,' says Martin, overplaying the dreamy nonchalance somewhat and sounding simply apathetic.

Bernice, however, is not one to be deterred. 'We're not talking subtle here, right? If there's a really strong, really in your face kind of hint or two earlier on, right, then maybe people won't read it as just a, you know...?'

Martin smiles. 'Yeah, I know.'

She reaches across the table and rests her hand on his. 'It wouldn't take much work, would it? Just put in a couple of really major ... not hints exactly, stronger than that, *clues* maybe – not enough to spoil the ending but something that gives your readers the idea that there's another aspect to the story: one that they're missing. Like I say, just two or three ... clues.'

Martin nods but says nothing and for a moment he loses himself in the space in between them. Then, uncomfortably, he reflects upon the difference in their ages being so perfectly demonstrated by seeing their hands in such proximity.

'Why don't you have a look at it now, just for ten minutes or so? I'm going up to bed anyway. I've got such an early start in the morning.'

'Um ... yeah, OK then. I'll have a look.'

For the second time in one evening Martin has been given a very sound piece of advice, advice that might have had a direct bearing on so many future events. For the second time, he completely ignores it.

AN UNHEALTHY INTEREST
Chapter Three

After my dad died and like I said I don't exactly remember when that happened, my mum sank into some sort of depression and she even stopped going to church for a while. Eventually, she stopped speaking. Well, that's not entirely true; she just stopped speaking in sentences. She'd say things to me like 'bed' or 'drink' and you had to figure out what she was going on about. Sometimes she'd give me a list and say 'shopping' and after a while I got used to it. I think that must have been around the same time I stopped bothering about school because I don't remember too much about it after that. We never answered the door and kept the curtains closed all the time and eventually people just left us alone. I think she stopped washing because there was always this, like, sweaty, dirty sort of smell around her. She'd just sit all day in her dressing gown with a blanket pulled around her and I remember she used to say 'cold' a lot. But it was so hot and airless in the house; it was totally stifling and before long it started to smell really bad. Sometimes, at night, when I knew she was asleep, I'd creep downstairs and open the back door just to let some fresh air in. But, day after day, she just sat in her armchair all the time and didn't do anything apart from write in this little notebook she kept with her all the time. She would sit and just scribble away for hours. I had no idea what she was writing; I was never allowed to see it and she used to get really agitated if I even mentioned anything about it. 'No,' she used to shout. 'No. Mine!' It was like how a child would talk. She used to keep it in her dressing gown pocket so she was never apart from it. I remember she had two pockets; the notebook was in one and she used to keep all her pens in the other. She probably forgot to put the lids on, maybe she just lost them, because they all leaked and the pocket ended up being stained blue and black for ages afterwards. Anyway, it went on like this for a while and I don't remember what happened exactly. I just remember coming downstairs one morning and seeing her dressed again and she'd washed her hair and put on some makeup, it looked like she'd made a bit of an effort. 'Doctors,' she said to me. 'Today.' And she sort of smiled at me and it was the first time I'd seen her smile in ages. I was so pleased, I volunteered to go with her but she shook her head and then she started crying. I don't know what happened at the doctors exactly. I don't know how she even managed to make herself understood; maybe she wrote everything down. But I think she was put on some sort of medication or another because right away she started to get better. She started washing again and keeping the place neat and tidy and after a while she started speaking again. She started going to church again and talking about Jesus. She also started attending Bible classes during the weekdays. She'd still have days when she cried a lot or got really angry with me for no reason. Then there were days when she would just keep hugging me all the time and saying she was sorry. I hated those days. They were the worst. Then she got really into cleaning, like really obsessively; everything had to be scrubbed every morning and I think that was about the time she started throwing stuff out, mainly stuff that reminded her of my dad. I don't know if she did this because she loved him or because she hated him; I didn't ask her and I suspect that she didn't actually know herself. It was just some other way of keeping herself occupied, I presume. She kept repeating the same quote: 'As long as it is day, we must do the work of Him who sent me.' It was another one of her Bible quotes, probably. But over a few weeks we filled bin bags full of this stuff; we even got loads of half-forgotten things out of the attic. That was quite sad, seeing all my old toys being thrown out, like all my Danger Mouse videos that I used to watch all the time. There were so many memories but then, like my mum kept saying, there are some things that are best left unremembered. Then one day she asked me to take a bin bag out to the dustbin for her but she hadn't tied it properly and I was just about to pick it up when I noticed that lying near the top, in amongst all the junk and debris, was that notebook of hers, the one she always used to be carrying around with her. I was really careful not to be seen but I took the notebook out and put it in my pocket. Then, later, I sneaked it into my bedroom and hid it under my mattress. Sometime in the evening, I think I said I had a headache and that I was going to bed early. But I just stayed up reading through her notebook. I don't know why I did this; I knew it was private but I just couldn't stop myself. I just read it all from start to finish. I don't really remember much about it. There were some poems that I didn't really understand; I don't know if she'd made them up herself or just remembered them from somewhere. There were loads of passages from the Bible and great long chunks about my dad; she seemed to blame him for everything that had gone wrong in her life. There were a lot of references to an abortion or maybe it was a miscarriage but I couldn't gather from the notebook if this had happened before or after I was born. There were whole sections about growing old and how much she feared it. The only bit I actually remember really clearly was about ageing and even now I can still recite it almost verbatim:

'I have absolutely no control over what happens to me. Sometimes, I feel like I'm a person being swept out to sea and every so often there's another wave that carries you further away from the shoreline. At first you are still able to see the people on the beach, you understand what they're doing and you even recognise someone you know but then wave after wave you are swept further and further away as it all grows more remote, ever more distant. Eventually they are just moving shapes – you can't relate to them in any way

and they can't even see you anymore. All I see nowadays are moving shapes.'

The strange thing is as soon as I read this I knew exactly what she was getting at, because all I have ever seen are the same moving shapes. They're not even separate or different anymore; to me they just blend into each other. They flash past you and are gone. Forgotten.

4

Well, Tambo, Let's Get Into It!

To anyone coming to New Orleans moderately well-versed in the story of jazz, so much of the modern-day city that confronts them is little more than a romantic and rather warped retelling of its own history. It is as though, for the first fifty years of the last century, people regarded jazz as some diverting yet unwelcome offshoot of the city's vice trade: white commentators having at that time what we might term a slightly cavalier or revisionist approach to African American culture. So many key locations are now long gone, ploughed down and redeveloped in the furtherance, one imagines, of decent, God-fearing

'No, I don't think I like that at all. What we might term...? Jesus! Come on! Wake up! Make a bit of an effort. Try Storyville.'

The legend of Storyville, the red-light district which flourished in the city from 1897 to 1917 and was by all accounts a rough and dangerous area, has been recast in the jazz consciousness as a key element in the birth of the music. At some point during this process, it has been conveniently overlooked that Storyville was segregated and catered exclusively to white patrons. But rather like the equally well-known legend of Robert Johnson's pact with the Devil at the crossroads, the birth of jazz has been for so long associated with Storyville that constant retelling and over familiarity has lent the story a kind of awkward credibility.

56

He deletes 'awkward' and replaces it with 'dubious'.

The truth is very different. While the piano 'professors' worked in the brothels along Basin Street, their repertoires would have been the hits of the day mixed with a few ragtime pieces. Very few bands actually played in Storyville and the leading established combos of the time, like Buddy Bolden's, were playing Uptown, at places around Perdido Street. Bolden, the first great trumpet king of New Orleans, as an example, played for dances, street parades, funerals and picnics, but according to his band members never for the clientele of a brothel.

But it is worth pausing to reflect upon this once-strong correlation between jazz and the notion of carnality. For it seems to be a rather durable association. Just ask yourself this: if you ever see a film and the director wishes to convey an atmosphere that is charged with erotic tension, what do you invariably hear on the soundtrack? It might be a solo piano or a sultry tenor saxophone but you can virtually guarantee it will have the phrasing and intonation we associate with jazz. Reduced to little more than a cinematic cliché, the music has been dogged for almost a century and perhaps it's time to call a halt.

Uncertain what precise point he is attempting to make, Martin now looks away from the screen in despair. The text seems to be gradually shifting towards a sort of jazz snob's manifesto and abandoning its original goals. Michael Barnes should be ashamed of himself! Isn't he supposed to be writing about New Orleans? But the simple truth is that the ideas just aren't coming anymore and for the first time since he hatched the concept of the book, there seems to be a lack of purpose and clarity to his thinking this morning. He saves the document without daring to reread it. He would go down to breakfast soon and assuage his frustrations with granola.

Glancing over his shoulder at the bedside clock, he realises he still has about ten minutes to spare and so he once again signs onto the hotel's Wi-Fi network. With a dismissive 'Yeah, yeah, whatever', he agrees to the $10.00 fee chargeable to his credit card and immediately returns to his search engine enquiry of the previous evening. This time he adds quote marks to '*Tambo Bones*'. Sadly there are no matches whatsoever aside from a dead link to a site called oldtimeymusic.com, which seems to have been offline since 2004, and a current link to an online record shop which has the track listing to the Louisiana Folk Songs LP. This is slightly disappointing but hardly surprising; the man is turning out to be just as obscure as Hugo claimed.

However, Martin had managed a little better the previous evening when he'd searched simply for *Tambo + Bones* and at least he'd been able to ascertain why the man had settled on that particular stage name. In the original minstrel shows of the nineteenth century, from which the later travelling medicine shows borrowed heavily, the entertainment followed a fairly fixed pattern. The opening of the show saw the minstrels sitting in a semi-circle at the front of the stage, performing comic dialogues and novelty songs. The instrumentation usually featured a banjo, an accordion or a fiddle, and the percussion was provided by the two musicians who sat at the opposite ends of the semi-circle. Known as the endmen, one played a tambourine and was called Tambo, while the other, who played castanets, was known as Bones. Tambo and Bones were traditionally the naïve and ignorant members of the troupe and much of the comedy was at their expense. They were poorly spoken and unworldly in their attitudes and usually ended up being conned or made fools of. As far as Martin could gather from an-hour-or-so's research, they seemed to be direct descendants of the original Jim Crow slave character. This had started Martin thinking. Perhaps involving himself in the same kind of irony that had been greatly in evidence on the record, had this Tambo Bones been simply paying his own sardonic, perhaps mocking, tribute to the old minstrel shows?

It was an interesting idea.

Martin now tries combinations of *Tambo, Minstrel, Endmen* and *Bones*, but sadly no new sites are forthcoming. He tries to summon up additional items to add to his search criteria but sadly, at this moment, his imagination struggles to conceive of any word other than 'granola'. However, as has become his habit recently, he decides to check his emails before shutting down his laptop.

'Oh fuck,' he says, opening his inbox and discovering another message from Berni1104. 'What is it now? More Alzheimer's by Proxy? Our son is called Wes? Your name is Martin? It is 2010? Go on, surprise me!'

Hi Martin,

Just to let you know that Sally has rung here a couple of times and left messages and yesterday I spoke to her. I told her you didn't live at this address anymore. She said she's been trying to contact you but doesn't have an up to date mobile number or your new email address. I told her you usually forgot to switch your mobile on!

'And thank you *so much* for that, my dear,' he says tartly.

So the best way of reaching you is by email. I told her you were away but were still picking up your messages. Hope that's OK. Her email address is the same as before she says – sallyb225@netmail.com
Regards
B.

'Well, that certainly was a surprise,' says Martin out of the corner of his mouth as he closes his laptop.

Sally is twenty-two and is Martin's daughter from a marriage that ended acrimoniously in the early nineties. Possibly as a direct consequence, he likes to think, communication between father and daughter has never been particularly good but in recent years it has dwindled to simply a Christmas card. Sally's mother had remarried about ten years ago and emigrated to Canada taking her daughter with her. Apart from a hurried lunch in Piccadilly in 2006, when Sally was over visiting her old friends, Martin had not actually seen his daughter since then. On that day, he'd really wanted her to meet Wes but there hadn't been enough time to arrange it and Bernice did wonder if it was really such a good idea. As far as he is aware she is currently attending a college in Montreal and doing a course in journalism or media or something. Or, of course, she might have finished by now.

To the fixtures and fittings of Room 311, Martin will now make his confession without protest. He had never been a good father to Sally. It wasn't personal; he just never quite understood what was required of him. Sally's mother would regularly berate and criticise him for being too lenient or too strict, often in relation to the same incident, and there was evidently a fine balance to such matters that was significantly beyond his abilities. The move to Canada was probably the best thing for Sally, he'd told himself at the time, and after ten years the sadness that he still sometimes feels usually passes, eventually.

Nevertheless, as Martin makes his way downstairs to the dining room a voice sings clearly in his head:

'*Roll 'em, Mr Bones, Mr Bones, Mr Bones. I say Roll 'em, Mr Bones!*'

Sadly, on this particular morning, Martin does not actually enjoy his granola very much. Maybe a person has to be in the right mood, he reasons, or maybe his mind is currently elsewhere. With an over-ambitious smile, he acknowledges the presence of the lady in the 'WHO DAT?' T-shirt as she manoeuvres herself behind an adjacent table, but this hardly qualifies as a diversion. What does Sally want after all this time? He swallows and makes a face. The most memorable thing about granola, he now concludes, is the fact that it is in no way memorable. You can't even describe it, which is why it's so hard to actively dislike... It's certainly strange that she's chosen this particular time or is it really so strange? It's easy to make some kind of a direct connection to 'Recent Events'. But nowadays his mind is permanently primed to think only along those strict lines and besides, she lives in Canada; how could she know? Another mouthful. Still nothing. Or is every mouthful a fresh, totally new experience because it's not possible to remember the previous one? Maybe this is a truly existential breakfast cereal and there you go, there's your new marketing angle right there. He fancies now that it's started to taste a little better... But could he realistically attribute this sudden contact to nothing more than coincidence? She might have been in England recently of course, visiting friends.

Maybe.

Maybe she just wants to have her say on the subject as well. Could anyone blame her?

Aware all too acutely that he is now approaching the point where habit tips over into ritual, he once again finds himself thinking about Mr Price. This seems now to be a fixed part of his day: an automatic response to any quandary, dilemma, crisis or simple inquiry. In the old days he was only a phone call away and nothing was ever too major or too trifling for him; he always found the time. A whole year now and he still can't think about real ale or listen to Bill Evans. He now abandons his granola and leaves his breakfast table. A sudden memory that he feels as a warmth in the corner of the eye and a tightening of the muscles around the mouth. Once again he finds himself recalling Mr Price's Bill Evans anecdote. How often it was imparted, how tedious he once found it and how much he now missed it. For many years, at the very slightest provocation, Mr Price would regularly and loudly announce that the great American pianist, due to his ancestry, could have played rugby for Wales. It might well have been true. However, what used to amuse Martin about this was the fact he imparted the information not as simply an interesting biographical detail, but because he seemed to be implying that there had been some terrible oversight on the part of the Welsh selectors by ignoring Evans.

What he would not give now, at this moment, just to hear that story one more time.

'*Roll 'em, Mr Bones, Mr Bones, Mr Bones. I say Roll 'em, Mr Bones!*'

At approximately five past ten that same morning, Hugo Blake unlocks the front entrance to The New Orleans Music Company and discovers that his first customer of the day is already loitering on the pavement just outside the shop. With limited success, this customer affects an air of practised nonchalance and saunters into the premises.

First thing in the morning the shop smells of weed and umbrellas.

'Hey... Martin, right?' asks Hugo, pointing to his solitary customer as though there might be some confusion over whom he is actually addressing.

'Yeah, Hugo, hi there.'

'How y'all doing today?'

'I'm good, thanks,' says Martin with a smile. 'And yourself?'

'No complaints.'

'I was just passing and er...' Martin is lying of course and if any proof were needed to attest to this fact he is currently performing a series of bewildering hand gestures as though attempting to imply that he has somehow been passing the shop from dozens of different directions. Some people avoid making direct eye contact when feeling embarrassed or being less than truthful; Martin simply gesticulates in this rather curious manner. It's a nervous, tell-tale reveal and one which he has had for many years. His ex-wife always took the credit for being the first person to spot it. She took unending delight in pointing out both his habitual dishonesty and the fact that his hand looked like Sooty at the gym.

Thankfully, Hugo picks up the drift without requiring his customer to elaborate further. 'Yeah, I know, you couldn't wait to get your hands on that little ol' record, right?'

'Absolutely. Did you manage to transfer it onto a CD?'

'I did indeed,' says Hugo, reaching behind the counter for a carrier bag. 'But I should warn you there's a bit of surface noise I couldn't filter out. But there are no major events as far as I can tell; nothing like clicks or jumps but there is a bit of a hiss on a couple of the tracks. But "Georgia Blues" sounded pretty clear to me.'

'That's great. Thank you.'

'It's my pleasure.'

They drift into silence for a moment or two as Hugo very carefully places the Louisiana Folk Songs record and the CD transfer into the bag and Martin hands over $25.00. No words are exchanged. It is as though their transaction has both the reverence of ceremony and the subterfuge of misdemeanour.

Martin looks inside the carrier bag and feels a tiny unmistakeable shudder of excitement.

'I looked him up, you know?' He now turns towards Hugo. 'Last night, spent ages at it. There's nothing about him anywhere. Not even a reference to him.'

Hugo shrugs and runs his fingertips over the stubble on his cheek. 'I'm not surprised. I did warn you.'

'But I thought that there'd be something, you know. A picture maybe. But there's nothing apart from the probable source for the name Tambo Bones.'

'Really,' says Hugo in tones that conspicuously fail to match the level of Martin's enthusiasm.

Perhaps not reading the situation as well as he might,

Martin now summarises for the shop owner all the information he has gleaned from the Internet regarding the pseudonym.

Hugo offers his customer an indulgent half-smile. 'That's ... interesting.'

'It's got me thinking, you know, about that particular choice of name.' Martin grasps the carrier bag to his chest and glances down at the floor in a furtive manner as though on the brink of some great confession. 'You said these sleeve notes stated that he recorded under a number of different names and he just used the name Tambo Bones for this one particular song, right? I think, given the nature of the song and all it implies, that choice of name was deliberately ironic and provocative and obviously intended to make a point; to make some sort of statement or political comment, maybe?'

'Yeah, it's possible, I suppose. Anyway, I hope you enjoy the record,' says Hugo, now with an evident urgency in his voice.

Meanwhile, impervious to any such nuance, Martin's tone becomes increasingly animated. 'Look, the irony is overlooked, the wit of the song is missed but in essence what we're talking about here is a classic protest song. I'm convinced that's what it is.'

'Well, give it another couple of listens, you may find another angle or two.' As a way of concluding their exchange, Hugo now offers Martin his hand. 'Anyway, good luck with it all, y'all!'

Their handshake is brief but cordial enough. 'Thanks,' says Martin. 'Just one more thing: you said there was a guy who collected this stuff.'

'Did I?'

'Yeah, he lives here in the Quarter, you said, you got him an original 78.'

'Oh yeah, that dude up there on Dumaine Street. Fella goes by the name of Clayton Palmer.'

'Is he still around?'

'Yeah, I see him all the time. He's quite a – what would you say? – a character. I think he's kept all his records but the last I heard he'd started collecting Tennessee Williams. So he hasn't asked me to do a search for him for a while.'

'What's he like?' asks Martin, in a tone that in an entirely different set of circumstances could have passed for coy. 'Do you think he'd speak to me?'

Hugo nods his head vigorously. 'Oh yeah, I'm sure he would, Martin.'

'I'd love to know what was on the other side of the original 78.' Hugo tears a piece of paper from the notebook on the counter and offers Martin a pen. 'Here you go, just write your cell number down on there and I'll make sure he gets it.'

Martin carefully writes down his name, his room number, the name of the hotel, together with his phone number. 'That would be great. Tell him I'm here for getting on for two weeks but I'd love the chance to speak to him.'

'Sure thing. I'll pass that on to him.'

'Thanks again, Hugo.'

'Now you have a good day now, y'all.'

'Yeah, you too.'

Within seconds of leaving the shop, Martin is hurrying back down Decatur towards Canal Street at a pace that takes him quite by surprise. The plans for the day have now changed. He's not going to be planting a couple of his books in Beacham's today – that can wait. All he can think about is getting back to the hotel and playing the CD on his laptop.

Suddenly, he finds himself recalling a very particular sensation, one he has not experienced for decades. It takes him completely by surprise but it is unmistakeable. It is precisely the same feeling he used to experience when returning home on the train from Cardiff on a Saturday afternoon. It was a happy-excited-nervous, pit-of-the-stomach thing. He was somewhere between fourteen and seventeen, still in school and a couple of times every month he would make the trip to Cardiff from the village where he lived, half an hour or so north of the Welsh capital. Sometimes he went with friends, sometimes alone but always with sole intention and objective to buy records. If he hadn't saved enough pocket money to buy new from Spillers, Sound Advice or Buffalo Records, he could usually cobble together enough cash to buy something from the second-hand LP stall in the indoor market. The day was usually unplanned and fairly spontaneous but the ritual commenced on the return journey. He would catch the train late afternoon and it would crawl its way through the northern suburbs and towards the valleys. But he would never notice; speed or journey time was never the issue. Neither was the scenery or even the people with whom he was sharing his carriage. Lost to time and the world, he would be thinking only about the record he'd bought. Then, when the moment was right, and it had to be just right and he'd always know the exact moment, he would take it out of its bag and just sit there gazing at the sleeve. There was no hurry, he knew that, he could just absorb every last tiny aspect. Then there was the moment of total connection after which he would read everything on the sleeve there was to read: all the details about the actual recording, from the timings of the individual tracks to the people who designed the cover; he wanted to know everything. If he was really lucky there might even be lyrics to read.

That was when you got that tingling feeling in your stomach.

You couldn't rush it. All you could think about was the moment when you would get home and that precise instant when you'd hear the hum of that old turntable and the crackle of a needle kissing the surface of the vinyl for the first time. But anticipation was an absolutely essential part of the whole experience. Sometimes the music failed these expectations but it didn't matter. Sometimes the expectations were the best part. Martin now crosses Canal Street, having concluded that between fourteen and seventeen, this particular Saturday custom was beyond simple ritual and was probably the nearest he ever came to foreplay.

To be fair, Martin is not usually prone to such outbursts of nostalgia. He is nowadays quite adamant on the subject and beyond a certain age (a reasonable and approximate estimate being thirty-five), memories are simply not to be trusted. He regards them not as some conscious, Proustian evocation of times past but rather as a synaptic bear pit into which he occasionally falls and from which he would subsequently resurface confused, disorientated and slightly annoyed with himself.

Back in Room 311, ritual and ceremony are quickly forgotten, ignored and denied as he rushes to power up his laptop. Pausing only to make sure that his *Do Not Disturb* sign is prominently displayed, he settles down to reacquaint himself with the song that has scarcely left his mind for a moment these past twenty-four hours. He selects the seventh track on the CD and holds his breath. The quality of his laptop speakers does little to enhance the sound of the music but that hardly matters as once again he hears–

'Hey there, wake up, man! We got to get together and sing us a real blues song!'

'Now why we want to go and do something like that?'

And, once again, within moments, he has lost himself in the song. On second, third, fourth … tenth, eleventh hearing, its power to enthral and amaze remains undiminished. God, it might actually be better than the version currently on permanent shuffle in his head. But now, after repeated listening, he is able to pick up all the subtle details that he missed during that first hearing in the shop. As an example, he can now hear clearly the final line of the spoken introduction not as

'Wait a mo'. Let's get into it!'

but as

'Well, Tambo, let's get into it!'

Also, there are actually drums on the record that he hadn't noticed before. Not particularly prominent, just keeping a sort of pulse in the background in what he could instantly recognise as the classic New Orleans style. From that alone, Martin would guess that the Back O' Town Boys, true to their name and like Tambo Bones himself, hailed from here in the Big Easy.

So, even if you manage to ignore the extraordinary lyrics, the song is still fairly remarkable from a purely musical angle as it seems to be coming from so many different traditions simultaneously. There's old-time New Orleans jazz, blues, folk, even a hint of something country in there too.

Despite a now growing familiarity, it remains defiantly unclassifiable and totally unique. But in common with all great music, every time he plays it he finds something new in it – something fresh, something startling, something slightly wonderful.

As he listens to the music again and again he opens the file entitled *Not Another Book About NO.Doc* and in one quick burst he writes the following:

Imagine something.

Imagine that somewhere, in the vast infinity of parallel universes, there is a world where rock 'n' roll is historically little more than a musical curiosity. It is simply an interesting fusion of the black blues tradition and white country and western. Regarded by critics as a worthy and perhaps fascinating marriage, it is grouped alongside other hybrid genres like western swing or Cuban bebop. It flourished briefly in the mid-fifties but it remains essentially a local musical form restricted to a few places in Tennessee and neighbouring states.

It is not a global phenomenon. It is not the universal medium. It has never touched the lives of millions of young people, placated, inspired, riled, comforted, soothed, enraged. It is not a shared experience. It is not the soundtrack to every moment of significance.

Imagine a little m

Martin now stops typing as he is suddenly reminded of another passage he wrote a couple of years ago.

AN UNHEALTHY INTEREST
Chapter Five

I thought I'd imagined it.

I really thought it was my mind playing a trick on me.

I used to spend a lot of time in the spare bedroom at the rear of the house. It has a great big window that overlooks the back garden. It faces west and so the room gets a lot of light in the afternoons, particularly in the summer. I used to spend hours in there working on my kits. Airfix were the best; Revell models were good too but they were always a bit harder to find. I always used to have a couple on the go at any given time. Bombers, I used to like, especially the big German ones and battleships, usually the Second World War period. If you'd asked me to pick my all-time favourite I'd say it was probably the battleship Scharnhorst. I always thought it was such a great-looking vessel; it looked low and sleek in the water like some great predatory, lurking beast. One of the great things about working on my kits was that no one used to bother me. My mum liked me to have a hobby and so she used to encourage me and she was always giving me money to buy the stuff I needed. I can clearly remember her urging me to branch out and maybe work on some bigger models. I had no ambition, she used to say; what if Jesus had just been satisfied with one disciple? But I kept telling her I was happy with my little planes and ships. But to be fair to the woman she would always leave me in peace all the time I was working in there. Even more than my bedroom, it became the place where I felt truly at home. Most of the time after Mum started speaking again she was always going on at me about something or other, but I was able to find something close to perfect tranquillity in that spare room. It didn't have any pictures of Jesus on the wall for one thing and it was good to be somewhere where I didn't feel that he was watching me all the time. The spare room just had two pictures on the wall: a landscape, an alpine scene or something, and a vase of yellow flowers. I've always loved that room and I was never happier than when I was alone in there with one of my kits. Then one day everything changed. It changed the moment I looked up from my model, actually I recall clearly that it was Heinkel HE 177, a kit I had been working on for a couple of days. You never forget stuff like that, do you? It could only have been for a split second, certainly no more than that. I just glanced quickly out of the window – a simple enough innocent gesture – but in doing so I was certain I had glimpsed something out of the corner of my eye. Like I say, I thought it was my imagination or something like eye strain which I sometimes got when I was doing really close work. My mum was forever nagging me about wearing my glasses more often; she said they made me look intelligent. I actually thought they made me look stupid but everyone's entitled to an opinion. It was a really hot summer's afternoon, as I recall, sometime towards the end of July. I do remember that earlier on that afternoon I'd had to open the window a little to let some fresh air into the room but there was a bit of a breeze blowing which began to agitate the newspaper on my desk and made it impossible for me to work. I rubbed my eyes and looked out of the window again. Up until that moment, I suppose, I could have easily convinced myself it was just a trick of the light or something, but the second I looked back out of the window was the precise mathematical point that my life changed forever. I think about that a lot. How cruel was God or Jesus (or maybe it was the Devil after all) to allow our two destinies to become so entwined that afternoon? I often wonder how different things might have turned out if a single element had been altered that afternoon – if, for example, it had been raining that day or I was in town running errands for Mum. But no, I looked again and I stepped onto a path from which I fear I will probably never return. I still don't think that looking is the same as doing or touching and it wasn't like I was hurting anyone. All I did that afternoon was look. But God, I had to look. It wasn't like any sort of conscious decision of mine; it was like wanting to eat because you're hungry, that doesn't feel like an option either. It didn't feel like I'd made the choice to look, more that the decision had been made for me. It was just an instinct I suppose, something I didn't have much control over. There she was and there I was and I just couldn't stop looking at her. Of course I knew who she was right away and why she was there in our neighbour's garden. Our neighbours were an elderly couple called Mr and Mrs Roderick. They were nice people and always friendly whenever you spoke to them. Sometimes Mrs Roderick used to go shopping for Mum when I wasn't around. They had a grown-up daughter who'd moved away somewhere a long time ago and a fourteen-year-old granddaughter called Lucy. From what I'd recently gathered from eavesdropping on a conversation between Mrs Roderick and Mum, the daughter was going through a fairly difficult divorce at the time and Lucy was spending the summer holidays with her grandparents. 'Just to be out of the firing line,' Mrs Roderick had said. That was why Lucy was in their garden on that hot summer afternoon and why she was sunbathing on a red and black check blanket on their patio. It's odd but the red and black blanket is still a really clear memory in my mind. I think I pictured myself lying down next to her with my face in that same blanket. I could almost taste it – it was warm and dusty and I could feel little grains of dust or sand on my cheek. I'm fairly certain there was an opened magazine or maybe a can of coke nearby but those details are less clear.

71

She was lying face down so I knew that she wouldn't be able to see me. But I couldn't take my eyes off her. She lay there still and fairly motionless although I guessed she was listening to music because she was moving her foot very slightly in a regular rhythm. She was wearing a black bikini and a baseball cap and when she moved her head I could see she had on a pair of oversized sunglasses. They didn't really suit her, I thought, and if I'm being honest I think they looked a bit cheap on her. She'd unfastened the top half of her bikini, in the way that a lot of girls do, so that she wouldn't get a white line, but it meant I had a completely unobstructed view of her back. I could even see the line of her spine really clearly from where I was standing. There was nothing between her and a star 93 million miles away and I had never seen anything so beautiful in my whole life and I couldn't even think anymore, it was like my brain had shut down and my body had ceased to function. I was simply an observer. I existed – if I existed at all any more – only in relation to what I was observing. I could see her shoulders rising and falling very slightly as she breathed in and out and then I realised I was breathing in and out in exactly the same tempo. It was like something inside me was synching with her, like there were mysterious vibrations in the air that afternoon and this made me feel very excited. I placed my fingertips in the crook of my elbow and felt the dampness on the surface of my skin. I stared down at Lucy and told myself that my fingers were actually touching the small of her back, just very gently making contact with her warm sunned skin. Then suddenly she started to move, I thought she might be preparing to turn over and so I quickly stepped back away from the window.

5

2309 First Street

Imagine a little more.

Still feeling a slight throbbing in his temples, Martin sighs loudly and continues.

Elvis Presley is remembered fondly as a dutiful son and reliable truck driver, John Lennon illustrated a handful of obscure children's books and Bob Dylan self-published a couple of slim volumes of his poetry in the late 1960s, but his quasi-beat style was rather dated and derivative and the works generated little interest. There is no Summer of Love, no Woodstock, no Sex Pistols and the world is unrecognisable in so many ways.

So imagine something else.

In this world, Tambo Bones is a colossal figure and regarded as one of the most important musical figures of the twentieth century. His work was an extraordinary hybrid that defied category and rendered obsolete the musical and racial boundaries of his era. Recognising no constraints and bringing together various genres of popular music – jazz, blues, country and folk – in a manner that had never been heard before, he wrote songs that both reflected and defined the experiences of an entire generation. Having abandoned the blackface that he'd once adopted, like so many of his contemporaries, early in his career, he became a national sensation and cause célèbre after the success of 'Georgia Blues' and the controversy that trailed in its wake. An outspoken and vocal opponent of

73

segregation, he regularly toured the South, despite fierce opposition in some quarters and frequent death threats. The darling of leftist liberals and the burgeoning Civil Rights Movement, he was once referred to by Pete Seeger as 'the most important musician in America'. His recordings continue to sell in vast numbers and his work is studied and analysed to this day. He is the subject of four full-length biographies – all currently in print – two feature films have been made of his life and a third is currently in production.

So just imagine

This is more like it, he thinks, smiling as he quickly reads through the text on the screen again. Although he's not absolutely certain what exactly he has just written; it would surely have no place in a tourist guide and it was far beyond the scope of a book simply about New Orleans. It reads like an introduction to a completely different piece. He begins to wonder if he might give Michael Barnes a couple of days off, maybe he could go for one of those swamp cruises or that ghost tour they're always plugging down on the front desk. But he likes the idea that he is attempting to put across and wonders how he can elaborate upon it. With this in mind, he expands one of the lines so it now reads:

There is no Summer of Love, no Woodstock, no Glastonbury, no Reading, no Knebworth, the electric guitar has no social or cultural resonance, there is no Jimi Hendrix, there is no Sex Pistols, no Clash, no Springsteen, no U2, no Oasis

He stops again and reads the line out loud to himself. He could really elongate such a list but speculates if the point would be better made citing fewer examples. Martin pauses at this point and decides to play track seven of the CD just one more time.

'Me try me a shotgun down in Texas. Me try poison down in Tennessee.'

The piece might have serious potential, he thinks. He could work it up a little, maybe turn it into an article. Maybe tailor it for one of those obscure little jazz or blues magazines, or those journals aimed at record collectors. He is certain of one thing; more people needed to know about Tambo Bones and this extraordinary song.

'Roll 'em, Mr Bones, Mr Bones, Mr Bones,
I say Roll 'em, Mr Bones, Mr Bones, Mr Bones!'

When the tune finishes he deletes the references to U2 and Oasis. He derives an odd sense of satisfaction from this. There is a certain truth in the observation that when you finally grow out of pop music you would really rather that it left you alone. You don't want to be constantly confronted by what you are no longer young enough to enjoy. It doesn't matter that it still goes on; you just don't want to know about it. Of course, in a sense, you don't leave pop music behind and you really play no active part in your separation. The truth is that it just abandons you and frequently does so in the cruellest and most brutal way possible. It laughs at you behind your back and talks to all your friends about you.

'There is no greater death,' whispers Martin to himself, quoting a line he recalls writing a long time ago, when he was still able to be flippant about such things.

He saves the document and glances at his watch. He is surprised to see that it is already a little after midday. He now stands up and wanders over to his window. For an idle moment or two he gazes down at the people on Gravier Street below him. Did any of them realise that this amazing city, with all its history and all the great stories that have sprung up around its streets and squares, has maybe just one more that needs to be told? Would anybody out there care to hear the amazing story of Tambo Bones?

There is something deeply comforting about this idea and anyone observing Martin at this moment might have detected the suggestion of a smile passing across his features. Then, with the very slightest shake of his head, he lifts his gaze upwards towards the clear cloudless October sky and plans the rest of his afternoon. He returns to his laptop and he is just about to close it down when he decides to reread the email from Bernice. Then, without seeming to have made any conscious decision on the subject, he begins composing an email to his daughter and spends a good five minutes labouring over the precise tone of the opening.

Dear Sally

is his first attempt and instantly deleted for sounding too formal.

Hi Sally

didn't work either; it sounded like a self-conscious attempt to sound youthful and ingratiating, which of course it was. Then there was

Hello Sally

which, for some reason, just sounded plain creepy, as though the line would continue with *you don't know me* or *no, don't turn around*. Martin manages a weak smile but is just about to abandon the whole venture when he decides to avoid using her name in the actual greeting. Thankfully, this seems to work.

Hi there,

Bernie emailed me earlier to say you'd been in touch and I gather she told you that I'm no longer living at the cottage. Long story but a bit of an over-involved one for an email! B. and I are no longer together but we're still on reasonable terms. I've been living in a flat in Canterbury.

There was no reason to expand upon the precise circumstances at this stage. Leave that for another time.

But at the moment I'm on holiday! Yes, I'm writing to you from my desk in my room on the third floor of the

Royal Crescent Hotel in New Orleans! Yes, I got here
at last and I'm loving every minute of it. I'm here for
another twelve days and I wish I could stay for longer.
I feel so at home here. Anyway, enough about me. It
was really great to hear from you. How are you? What
are you up to? How's Canada? Any plans to visit England?
Please mail me or call if you have minute.
   Love Dad xxx

Until he knows more, he thinks, it is probably best that he
makes no reference to 'Recent Events'. Although a far greater
dilemma is the issue of the three kisses; he isn't altogether
certain that they're a good idea so he deletes them. Then
after a further minute-or-so's reflection, he decides to reinstate
them. This particular debate might well have continued a
little longer, perhaps indefinitely, but it is brought to a swift
conclusion when he presses the send button. He then removes
the Louisiana Folk Songs CD and closes the laptop. Placing
both items carefully in his room safe, he retrieves his jacket
from the back of his chair and then with something which
he would steadfastly refuse to classify as a spring in his step,
he shuns the elevator and canters down the two flights of
stairs to the lobby and then out of the hotel. This afternoon's
itinerary will take him in the opposite direction to his
accustomed wanderings and he is, despite his unfamiliarity
with both the route and his destination, rather looking forward
to the experience.
   At the junction of Canal Street and St Charles Avenue he
now boards the streetcar which takes him in a roughly south-
westerly direction away from the Quarter towards what his
guide book refers to as the Garden District. Beyond the rather
curious distribution of paperback books that we have already
witnessed and a couple of trips, including the one upon which
he is currently embarked, Martin has made surprisingly few
plans for his visit. However, a ride on a New Orleans streetcar

was always one of his main intentions. Not simply because one might imagine the cars resonating with the ghostly vibrations of Blanche and Stanley but because a streetcar is generally regarded as the best method of getting around the city. With its noticeably minimal suspension and polished wooden-slatted seats, it is suggestive, on first impression, of simultaneously a fairground ride, a cable car and something vaguely military. It is perhaps not the most comfortable mode of transport in the world but after about thirty seconds of first-hand experience, Martin would happily relegate such a criticism to the level of an irrelevant quibble. Although, like so much he has encountered in this city, it is hard to avoid wondering if all this self-determining neo-primitivism is born of financial expedience or the dictates of tourism.

A quick glance around at his fellow passengers and the very briefest head count reveals a fairly even split between those he regards as locals and those he might assume to be tourists. So the question will sadly remain unresolved.

As the streetcar crawls its way further and further away from the more obvious, perhaps even over-familiar locations, the city of New Orleans takes on a totally different aspect or, to be strictly accurate, a series of totally different aspects. Block by block the whole sense of the place goes through a sequence of dramatic and then more subtle changes and mutations. It's fascinating to witness. Suddenly there are trees everywhere; there are wide avenues and large imposing detached houses. Then a block further on the houses get significantly more modest and a little less well-maintained. No doubt it will change again but as the streetcar nears First Street, Martin stands up and makes his way to the exit with an entirely different observation occupying his thoughts. According to his guide book the St Charles Avenue streetcar line opened in the 1830s, so it was well within the realms of possibility that Tambo Bones himself, as a resident of this city, had travelled this very route.

Disembarking from the streetcar, Martin walks a hundred yards or so along St Charles and then turns right into First Street. One of the travel books he'd recently read had hinted that 'caution was advisable at certain times' if you decided to visit this particular area but it seems perfectly fine to him and besides, it is a beautiful warm sunny afternoon and he imagines he is probably right in assuming that this is not one of those 'certain times' to which the writer is referring.

As he walks, he looks out for the house numbers. Some of the houses he passes are still clearly demonstrating, five years after the event, the devastating effect of The Storm. Doors and windows are boarded up and some places are still obviously unoccupied while others just seem abandoned. Some still boast the official FEMA spray-canned hieroglyphics, denoting brutally the condition of the property or the fatality of its occupants. For a moment he actually wonders if he should continue; it feels as though he is trespassing or encroaching on something but then he thinks about Mr Price. So, bowing his head now fractionally, as though demonstrating a greatly sublimated gesture of supplication, he continues walking.

Eventually, he passes a couple of men in overalls and he lifts his head to greet them with a smile and a 'good afternoon', which they both reciprocate. A small enough courtesy, he thinks, but immediately Martin's disposition takes a slight turn for the better.

Finally, after a much longer walk than he'd anticipated, he arrives at number 2309 and he checks with the folded photocopied picture in his jacket to ensure that this is the right place. For some reason he'd been imagining that there would be a few interested sightseers and tourists milling about the place, people with similar agendas to his own, but there isn't a soul around. It is not a particularly grand or prepossessing structure, it is true; a single-storey white-painted wooden-framed house with a large tree growing in the street less than a yard or so from the front stoop.

But this is 2309 First Street.

And Martin knows this is a special place.

2309 First Street was the home of Buddy Bolden, the first great cornet king of New Orleans and arguably the man who if not the actual inventor then one who helped first define the music we now know as jazz. Although there are no surviving recordings he was by all accounts a great soloist and improviser and he led one of the hottest bands of the day. Martin takes a step towards the front stoop and with an awkward almost religious reverence he looks down at the three red painted steps. On a clear night, it is said, people could hear his cornet miles and miles away, so great and powerful was his playing. He was also a drunkard and a womaniser and he spent the last two decades of his life in a mental institution but this is where it all started.

The thing with Bolden is that so many legends grew up around him; it is almost impossible to know where biography ends and uncorroborated myth begins. It is a very grey area and so few details of his life are demonstrably true. For many years it was said he was a barber by trade but that was simply inaccurate and there has never been a shred of evidence to support it. So how does this sort of information gain credibility? Does a legend begin as a deliberate falsification or is it often just a simple misunderstanding, a confusion of details? If a legend truly grows in its telling then surely the telling is always the most important aspect. Everything else is framework and background detail. The stories are what will survive. They will always have a life entirely of their own.

What is without doubt is that the stoop in front of him is the same actual stoop where Bolden used to sit and practise his cornet. All the children in the neighbourhood would gather in front of the house to listen to him. There are many reliable contemporary recollections that attest to this particular fact.

'Fucking hell!'

The expression is suggestive of wonder rather than horror and although the quiet mumbling voice is unmistakeably Martin's it seems to involve not the slightest actual movement of his mouth. 'This is Buddy Bolden's fucking stoop! This is it! The revolution starts here! Right here!'

Without lapsing too much into unnecessary hyperbole, and he would certainly hesitate before comparing it to some holy relic or a sacred site, the fact remains that this is the precise spot where a man once sat and radically altered the course of twentieth century culture. On these three little steps a musician once found a different way of communicating his ideas and in doing so he gave his country its first truly unique artistic voice.

The house itself is quiet and there still seems to be nobody around and so Martin gingerly leans forward and then gently reverses himself until he is perched on the top step of the stoop. For a moment or two the air seems unnaturally still and there is a sudden cessation in traffic noise. Under his breath, he now whispers in short emotional bursts, 'There you go, Mr Price. I said we'd look this place up. I did, I promised you, didn't I...?'

After another quick glance left and right, he removes his mobile phone from his jacket pocket. Holding it at arm's length he takes a picture of himself sitting on the stoop. The actual definition of photographs taken on this particular phone has never been great but it would be a suitable souvenir of the afternoon. Martin smiles and looks fairly relaxed in the picture. His hair, which remains unfashionably long and the only aspect of his appearance over which he ever felt any stirrings of vanity, looks a little windswept but that's OK. It was usually unkempt and in fact, on the very rare occasions that it arranged itself into an orderly fashion he almost felt obliged to offer it a biscuit. However, on this particular morning, it serves to draw attention away from other details, like the very slight reddening around his right eye – a clear indication that he has recently been crying.

'And there's the Bolden house of course.'
'The what?'
'The house where Buddy Bolden lived. Apparently it's still standing.'
'Really?'
'Indeed it is, according to the rather informative website I had the good fortune to happen upon this afternoon.'
'OK, put it on the list.'
Mr Price does as he is requested. 'Right, will do. You know, it's such a terrible shame that the old Union Sons building is apparently no more. It was pulled down to make way for some public building or another, I have just discovered. But, oh Martin, could you even begin to imagine the *vibrations* around a place like that?'
Martin still found it a little troubling when his friend lapsed into the vernacular in this manner without any prior warning. 'Union what?'
On this particular evening they are both sitting at the dining table in Mr Price's flat, something which they did infrequently and it lends their conversation an odd formality. The older man now looks at his visitor with something approaching wonder.
'Are you serious, boy? Union Sons? We're talking about the Funky Butt Hall here. The original and legendary! The venue where the Bolden Band played! Come on, Martin. The Funky Butt was the place where his reputation and his greatness were established. It's on page one in any book about jazz you might care to mention! Surely, you've heard of the place?'

82

Martin makes a face.

'And there I was thinking you were a fellow traveller,' says Mr Price with a smile.

'Anywhere else?' asks Martin, anxious to change the subject.

'Well, I thought that, with your approval obviously, it might be rather interesting to take a walk up Frenchman Street.' He points with commendable conviction at an area of the map in the guide book that lies open in front of him. 'This is again a little way out of the French Quarter, but not terribly far. I believe the district is called the...' He hesitates over the pronunciation. 'The Marigny?'

'OK.'

'The house where Jelly Roll Morton lived is still standing. Oh, sorry, I do apologise. This is presuming that you've heard of Jelly Roll Morton?'

'Oh, ha ha ha! Very funny. Put it on the list.'

'You see, your problem, Martin, if you don't mind me saying so, is that you're a sort of fundamentalist modernist. You miss out on so much.'

Martin chuckles sibilantly through his teeth. 'So what are you then?'

Mr Price reflects on the question for a moment. 'I must confess that I'm one of life's perennial agnostics. All my allegiances are strictly temporary and wavering at best. I'm quite the ideological tart, if you like. Coleman to me will always be both Ornette and Hawkins and it just depends on my mood and I don't see why I should be forced to make a commitment either way, do you?'

'Fair enough.'

'Another beer?'

'Why not?'

Mr Price wanders off to the kitchen and after thinking for a moment or two, Martin calls after him.

'But I've always hated fusion – that's modern – and anything that's even sat on the same chair as jazz rock, remember?'

But Mr Price either doesn't hear him or simply refuses to answer.

In truth they actually agreed on the music far more frequently than they disagreed. They'd had one or two noteworthy differences of opinion in the past, like the time Mr Price claimed, much to Martin's utter horror, that Sidney Bechet's genius on the soprano saxophone surpassed even John Coltrane's. Both men recall that particular evening as being slightly awkward and nowadays, as if by virtue of an unspoken mutual agreement, they usually skirt around any issues liable to bring them into conflict. Something that Martin still considers to be an almost perfect definition of a friendship.

Mr Price returns from the kitchen presently midway through a sentence. '... so in practical terms, what sort of duration would one allocate for such an undertaking? Such a *venture*, if you will?' He stresses the word as though taking some obscure personal delight in all its delicious implications.

'I've not really thought about it,' says Martin. 'A week maybe. Ten days.' He goes on to explain that based on his admittedly fleeting research on the subject, their trip would involve connecting flights and they would spend at least a day on the outward and homeward journeys. 'It probably makes sense to allow for that.'

Mr Price offers Martin an opened bottle of Old Crusty. 'Of course.'

'Thanks. It's best that this time,' says Martin, evidently choosing his words very carefully, 'that we're sort of ... more...'

'Prepared?' suggests Mr Price helpfully, offering Martin an indulgent smile, demonstrating, in doing so, a near perfect example of that particular quality to their friendship about which Martin has just been thinking. Rather awkwardly perhaps, they are both managing to avoid making any reference to their previous trip to the States. In 2007, the two of them had spent a week in New York: a visit that has remained slightly marred in the memories of both men on account of the afternoon they'd spent walking up and down 52nd Street having an increasingly vitriolic discussion about the precise location of Birdland. That particular debate has never been resolved, neither has it been mentioned subsequently. The issue still hinges to this day on whether the term 'The Jazz Corner of the World', which was how Birdland once billed itself, refers to an actual corner, as Mr Price still believes, or if the expression was simply metaphoric, which remains Martin's take on it.

'I don't wish to cast myself as a Doubting Thomas here,' is the expression that Martin remembers from that day. It seemed to be on a sort of permanent loop while his own utterances, which were probably far from charitable, he has out of expediency chosen to forget.

However, the following day they'd put aside their differences and taken a walk to Greenwich Village and found Charlie Parker's house. The fact that the property in question boasted a plaque attesting to its provenance was probably what was making both men smile so broadly in the picture they'd asked a passer-by to take of them outside the house. To this day, Martin loves that picture and it remains one of the very few pictures of himself that he allows to be displayed in the cottage. It is currently on the wall of the living room just above the CD player.

After two years, however, the memory of the Birdland incident still resonates sufficiently to ensure that all subsequent trips, like the one currently under discussion, are planned with the sort of fanatical precision that is uncharacteristic of both men.

'In terms of the actual cost,' Mr Price is now saying. 'How much more would ten days be?'

'I'd need to look it up again but I don't imagine there would be a huge difference. The flight is the most expensive bit.'

'I see.'

Martin furrows his brow in concentration as he negotiates

another mouthful of Old Crusty. 'You're still thinking about sometime around autumn, right?'

'Yes, the word is fall, actually, Martin, if you wish to be completely accurate. But all my research seems to be roughly in agreement on that particular point. March is usually Mardi Gras, hotels are usually hard to come by, I believe, or just prohibitively expensive. The summer is very hot and August is well...' he lowers his voice respectively to the point that he is almost mouthing the words. 'It's the ... er, the hurricane season.'

'Of course.'

'October by all accounts is a perfect time to visit. It's warm but not too warm.'

'OK.' Martin nods and then stealing a glance at his wristwatch, he mutters something under his breath, the general sense of which being quite discernible to the man sitting opposite. 'Actually, sorry about this but I need to make tracks in a minute. So, listen, why don't you come over to the cottage tomorrow and we'll do this online and get it all booked. I've got accounts set up with about three or four agencies; we can just pick the cheapest.'

'That all sounds rather exciting. I'd love to.'

'Bernie would love to see you and you haven't seen Wes for weeks. Come over and have some lunch.'

'Yes,' he says with a sigh, 'I have been rather neglecting my godson of late, I fear.'

Martin begins to stand up and then having failed to raise a very particular issue during the course of their conversation, decides to ask the question that has been on his mind all evening. 'Just one thing,' he says breezily, the sudden casual tone failing quite dismally to mask an underlying reticence, 'I just wondered if you found the time to read through the amendments to the manuscript?'

'Of course,' exclaims Mr Price, throwing up his hands in mock horror. 'I'm so sorry. I got so carried away with all this talk of New Orleans. I quite forgot all about it.'

Retrieving the manuscript from the bookcase, he places it on the dining table in front of Martin. Then, for no more than a fleeting moment, he places his hand on Martin's shoulder. 'Well done there, boy. I think you've done a great job. Seriously, it works so much better now.'

'Thanks,' says Martin flatly.

'You understood my point though, didn't you?'

'I think so.'

'It was just that one section. As I said, when I read it again it just didn't sit with the rest of the story. To me it just seemed deliberately titillating. Salacious, if you like. Now, Martin, I do appreciate that you once made a living writing that sort of *material* but this is a very different work.' Mr Price chuckles to himself and then with discreet familiarity he strokes the cover of the manuscript with his thumb. 'This is literature, boy, not self-pollution!'

Martin manages a smile. 'Thank you, I think.'

'But seriously, the way you've worked in the whole idea of temptation works really well and we get the moral implication of what the character is thinking and the power of the desire being experienced. That's all we need. We don't really require a detailed or graphic description of the actual fantasy or the precise details of what a person would like to do. The internal conflict works perfectly well on its own. Actually, to my mind, it's a far more dramatic device than the particulars of this character's urges. The desire is every bit as potent as the realisation of that desire. What we have left now is perfectly acceptable. It's only my opinion I know, but the reader will appreciate what is going through this character's mind without it being spelled out. You should always strive to maintain a slight respect for the intelligence of your readers, Martin.'

'So you don't think it needs any other changes?'

'Absolutely not. It was only that one section that troubled me. Although, if there was a foreword...'

At this precise point, as though a comment by some unseen

celestial agency, there is a quiet hesitant ripple of applause emanating from the corner of the room. The applause in question is actually the conclusion of the first disc of The Complete Village Vanguard Recordings by Bill Evans, which has been the soundtrack to their recent discussion.

Martin is keen to continue talking about the rewritten section of his manuscript but before he can say a single word, Mr Price is already speaking.

'You know, the funny thing about Bill Evans, seriously, his father was Welsh, did you know that? Now if you're talking about nationality strictly, you understand, in regard to eligibility for playing rugby for Wales...'

Martin almost manages a smile as he raises his eyes heavenwards. Then he opens his manuscript to the page recently under discussion.

He has no idea that this is the last time he will ever hear the story.

AN UNHEALTHY INTEREST

Chapter Seven

I don't know if it was on account of spending too much time shut indoors or too little time in other people's company (my mother, as I mentioned earlier, went through a long period of not speaking to me or to anyone), but I have never been very good at talking. I used to find it hard to make myself understood whenever I did speak to people. I stuttered and mumbled and sometimes I couldn't say the word I wanted to say – everything just came out wrong. My mum told me once I was late speaking and that may have had something to do with it. But it was always difficult for me. I used to have problems in school; I remember one of my very first teachers said I was 'tongue-tied', whatever that meant, but over time it just seemed to get worse. It almost felt like I was out of practice or something. I used to get really nervous and agitated about it sometimes and get like a panic attack. I remember one incident really clearly. I was in Woolworths one day standing in a queue to pay for one of my kits. This lady and a little boy came up to me and asked me where she could find the kits. I watched her coming towards me and I knew that she was going to start talking to me, you could just tell. I tried to tell her, I really did, but the words just wouldn't come and I felt hot like I was going to be sick or something and she just kept looking at me and asking me if I was all right. 'Are you all right, love? Are you OK?' On and on she went, just repeating it so much so that I thought that sound was coming from inside my head, like it was my brain talking to me. I tried to point to the part of the shop where they had the kits but she didn't understand and kept on saying, 'Are you all right, love? Are you OK?' I don't know how long this went on for but I remember feeling a strange sensation of coldness around my ankles and when I looked down at my feet I could see I was standing in a puddle. The lady put an arm around the little boy and they took a step away from me. She didn't ask me if I was all right after that! She just looked at me with a really angry expression on her face. I dropped the kit on the floor and ran out of the door and straight home. I didn't go back to Woolworths for ages after that.

So it all came as a bit of a shock for me to hear myself speaking so clearly that afternoon. I really thought it might have been some sort of miracle. It had been a really ordinary day up to that point, nothing to mark it down as significant or special or out of the ordinary in any way. My mum used to go to a Bible study group at her church a couple of times a week whenever she felt up to it and on that day about ten minutes or so after she'd left the house, I was sitting in the spare room as usual, working on a model. I'm absolutely certain it was a Messerschmitt Bf-110 and I remember clearly being really pleased with the way it was going when there was a knock at the door. This was strange. We never had visitors and the only people that ever knocked on the door were the postman sometimes and the milkman, but they always called at very specific times or on particular days. Occasionally, some of the local kids would knock the door and run away. Sometimes they'd shout things through the letterbox. Usually it was stuff about my mum but she never seemed that bothered by it and so I used to ignore it. The door was then knocked a second time and by this point I think I was starting to wonder if it might have been my mum coming back early. Maybe she'd forgotten something, I thought. I put the Messerschmitt down very carefully and hurried downstairs to let her in. I opened the door and after the shock of not seeing my mother there had worn off I realised I was standing face-to-face with Lucy from next door.

'Hello,' she said.

It must have been a few days after I'd seen her sunbathing, maybe a week, and I'd not seen her since then. I used to look out for her every day and had actually started to wonder if I'd just imagined the whole thing. But we'd had a couple of cloudy days since then as I recall, which may have explained why she'd not been in the garden. But the sun was shining again and that afternoon she was wearing denim shorts and a vest with a sort of floral pattern on it. Her arms looked very brown, I thought. I wanted to tell her this but I thought I should wait a bit. But then suddenly the strangest thing happened – something I would not have anticipated in a million years. I just looked at her and smiled and then I opened my mouth and heard myself saying, 'Oh, hi there.' Just like that – completely naturally and totally normal. No stuttering or mumbling, just my own voice as clear as a bell and for a second all I could think about was angels and Jesus.

'I'm so sorry to bother you,' she said. 'My name's Lucy

and I'm staying with your neighbours.' She pointed vaguely over her left shoulder at the direction of the house but only succeeded in drawing my attention to her left shoulder. It was beautiful. Perfect. There was more evidence of God in that girl's left shoulder, I thought, than in a hundred Bible classes.

'Right,' I replied as calmly as I was able. But amazingly my voice still sounded distinct and clear.

'Thing is,' she said, rocking back and forth on the balls of her feet, 'I'm supposed to meet them back here and they're not home yet. Stupidly, right, I didn't take my key with me... Yeah, I know, you probably think I'm like an idiot, right? But I'm like desperate for a wee and I can't get in the house. So I just wondered if I could like just use your loo. I'd be ever so grateful.'

'Oh right, yeah, sure thing,' I said and directed her to our downstairs toilet.

'That's so kind of you, really. I'm like busting.' She rushed quickly down our hallway towards our toilet and I heard her closing the door behind her. But I remained where I was, gripping the lock of the front door. I knew what I was doing and I knew I must not move. I knew that the door of the toilet was old and warped and that there was a about a half-inch gap between the door and the door frame at one point. If I just crept silently back up the hall and put my face near the gap I could have quite easily spied on her; she would never have seen me. I could have watched her removing her shorts, taking down her pants. I could have seen everything. She would have never known. I held onto the lock tighter and tighter as though it was the only thing saving me from stepping off into the darkness, into something unknown and terrifying, like holding onto something solid when you feel a hurricane approaching. I knew I had to hold on really tightly. If I let go for just a second there would be no coming back and I knew that. She seemed to take ages in the toilet *and I tried to think about Jesus being tempted but then I thought about her pants again and her white thighs that hadn't caught the sun. Then I thought about that thing my mum was always saying and said it out loud just so I could hear it:*

'Resist the Devil and he will flee from you.'

I said it out loud about three times and then I heard the flush. A matter of moments later, Lucy was back again, thanking me profusely and asking my name.

I must admit I did stumble a little and hesitate at that point for a moment, but I don't think she noticed. 'I'm Sam,' I said.

She smiled. 'That's a nice name. I've always liked that name.'

'Thank you.'

She stood there for a moment as if she didn't know what to say next. She looked at me and then looked down at the floor and touched the ends of her hair. Maybe I was supposed to say something; maybe I should have told her I liked her name too. But the moment had passed.

'Anyway, I'd better go and see if they're back now. Thanks, Sam, for letting me use your loo. I was like so desperate to pee. I thought I was going to have to climb over the back gate and have a wee in the garden.' She laughed at the very notion and I smiled at her as though we were sharing a joke, a private joke just between the two of us.

A moment later she had gone and the door was shut and I was back in the hall, alone with my thoughts. I stood like that for a minute and waited for the day to settle once more. Then I returned to the spare room and just stared out of the window at the garden next door. I didn't want to think about it. I tried to stop myself. I tried to think about my mum returning from her Bible class and what we would eat for our supper. But it didn't work. Nothing seemed to work. It was just I could picture it so clearly in my mind; it was like it was real to me. Over and over again, endlessly repeating, I could see her running across the lawn and darting into the bushes just beneath my window. I had a totally unobstructed view. I could almost...

'Resist the Devil, and he will flee from you.'

What happened next took me completely by surprise and I didn't really understand what I was doing. It was like I wasn't in control of my actions anymore. Something had possessed me and taken over. Everything seemed to happen at the same instant. I grabbed the craft knife from the table and I rolled up my sleeve. An instant later I was drawing the blade across the fleshy part of my arm just above my elbow. I remember that I was thinking the higher up my arm was better as there was less chance of my mum seeing it. It was a sharp stinging pain, intense at first but then oddly numb. I think I was going to do it fourteen times, make fourteen cuts, but I stopped after the first one. I could hear myself taking huge gulps of air but everything else around me was still and silent or so it seemed to me.

I looked at the cut on my arm and felt curiously disconnected from both the pain and the action that had caused it.

But maybe that was the point.

For quite a long time I didn't move; I just stood there watching in a sort of dazed stupor as drops of my blood spotted the fuselage of my Messerschmitt Bf-110.

6

The Minstrel Man From Alabam'

*But Tambo Bones and the extraordinary recording of his
'Georgia Blues' presents us with a very real problem.*

'Yeah, there's nothing like a little understatement to start
the day,' says Martin in a faraway voice.

*It is a problem which we cannot ignore or circumnavigate
yet it serves to illustrate a possibly more significant point. In
our quest for artistic or critical objectivity, can we ever hope
to divorce the art from the artist? The message from the
messenger? Surely art should be its own truth, its own reality;
it should stand apart from its creator and be judged accordingly.
One would hope that any work of art could be assessed
entirely on its own merits without any knowledge of the
artist. But can this be possible?*

Let's leave Tambo Bones for a moment and consider this point.

*Imagine you visit an art gallery, one you have never
previously visited, and you stroll into a room of early twentieth
century landscapes. You stop in front of a canvas painted
just after the First World War. The colours are bright and
vibrant in a manner that calls to mind André Derain or one
of the Fauves. It's a bold, impressive work and you decide
to check the name of the artist and you read the name Adolf
Hitler. Do you make a mental note to buy a postcard or are
you disgusted with yourself for even looking at the picture
and of course it's not like Derain at all; it's suddenly terrible,
amateurish and third rate.*

94

Alternatively, one day, you happen upon a poem in an anthology that perfectly captures the experience of a first love – all the ambiguities and the heightened emotions, every subtle detail and every nuance, every word corresponding to a feeling you felt could never be accurately expressed. This was not just the poet's unique experience but a great evocation of a universal truth. You research the poet and discover that he's a middle-aged man and the poem was written about a ten-year-old boy. You immediately...

'No, no! God, no!' Martin puts his hands over his face and shakes his head vigorously. 'Now there's one stupid fucking idea right there!' He tries to smile at the absurdity and the irony of the situation but fails in his efforts. Instead, he deletes the last paragraph and inserts the following.

You later discover that the poet had brutally raped the young lady who was the subject of the poem. He'd been tried and convicted and he'd written the poem in prison as an attempt to curry favour with the parole board.

Martin makes a low moaning sound. 'Maybe too much detail, too much like a story in itself.' He gazes forlornly at the screen for another few moments and then deletes the word 'brutally'. The word is unnecessary, he thinks, as it would be difficult to imagine a rape being otherwise. But it does give the line a better rhythm and makes it sound less cold and clinical so he reinstates it. He is just about to delete it again when his mobile phone starts ringing. This might be a slight over-simplification, as Martin's phone is not technically ringing but playing the opening few bars of 'Little Rootie Tootie' by Thelonious Monk (the original 1957 trio version, naturally) the tune that Martin still believes to be the absolutely perfect ringtone.

He removes the phone from his jacket pocket and discovering that the caller is 'unknown', he speaks in suitably hesitant tones. 'Er... Hello?'

'Hello there.' The voice is confident and male and blessed

with one of those perfect Southern accents – slow and languorous, deep and resonant – like a sleepy lion covered in honey. 'Is this Mr... Mr... *Bonny*-House, is it?'

Martin smiles at the mispronunciation of his surname. Over the years he has become accustomed to a whole variety of comments but this, he would confess, is the first time he has heard it pronounced in this manner. He toys momentarily with the idea of correcting the caller's elocution but then thinks better of it. 'Yeah,' he says instead, 'that's me; near enough anyway.'

'I'm sorry it's so early, sir. Did I wake you?'

'No, not all; I've been up for ages.'

'Oh good. I'm very glad about that and I'm pleased to make your acquaintance Mr *Bonny*-house. I'm just wondering if I can take up just a tiny minute or two of your time?'

'Er ... of course, sure thing.'

'The name is Palmer, Clayton Palmer. It seems we have a common acquaintance and I would go as far as to suggest we may also have a common interest.'

Suddenly, the walls of his hotel room tumble away, the views of Gravier Street fade and everything goes dark again. Martin feels a sharp pain in his right temple as he gasps a mouthful of air and tries to make sense of the caller's last remark. What acquaintance? What interest? What has he heard? How could they have found...?

Then suddenly he remembers the name.

'Oh yes, Mr Palmer, yes, thank you so much for calling.'

'Yeah, our friend Hugo at the New Orleans Music Company gave me your details and told me to give you call. Actually, he was very insistent. Says you were interested in the old Back O' Town Boys. That right?'

'Absolutely.'

Clayton Palmer chuckles. '*Absolutely!* Yeah, I do like that. *Ab-solutely.* So tell me, sir, why would someone come all the way from England to find out about such a funny little old thing?'

Martin takes a pause while he gathers his thoughts. 'Well, I didn't mean to exactly; I just heard the record in the shop. And "Georgia Blues" is just an amazing song. I've been playing it and playing it. Now I think that Tambo Bones was like, I don't know, years ahead of his time.'

'Yeah, Tambo,' says Mr Palmer with what Martin takes to be genuine affection in his voice. 'He's one of a kind, all right. God bless him. Well, I guess we should say God bless Oscar Oliver Brightwater, that's the man's real name.'

'Oscar?'

'That's right – Oscar Oliver Brightwater.'

'Hang on,' says Martin. 'I need to write that down somewhere. He rushes over to his laptop and types the name in bold capital letters. Clayton Palmer, meanwhile, is still talking.

'... called himself The Minstrel Man from Alabam' when he started. Can you believe that? He made a few sides under a different name with different musicians but they're nothing like those Back O' Town Boys. No, sir, I guess it's a real shame they were just a recording group.'

'Like the Hot Five?' asks Martin, re-joining the conversation.

Clayton ignores the question. 'Just the one session and the one record, that's all they left behind. But what a record, right?'

'Yeah, I mean, I was totally blown away by it.'

'But I tell you, my favourite story about him has been sort of circulating for as long as I can remember. I can't even remember a time when I didn't know the story. Well, I guess it's probably just a rumour really. You see no one seems to know who his father was but his mother was a light-skinned Creole lady who worked, they say, in one of the lesser sporting houses of Storyville. Oscar was apparently born in November 1917 and the legend has it that he was the last baby born in the district before it was closed down. That's what I've heard. Come on, it may be true, it may be complete horseshit, but it's one hell of a story.' Mr Palmer begins to chuckle again. 'Ah, Jesus, I must apologise; just listen to me going on and on. Hey, I warn you, once you get me started on all this stuff there's no stopping me.'

'No, I'm fascinated, really I am.'

'Well, it's probably a whole bunch of crap but I'm a collector, right, not an historian. Never claimed to be one neither.'

'Actually,' says Martin, feeling at this point in their conversation sufficiently confident with Mr Palmer to embark upon a small confession, 'I'm a writer and I'm intending to write something about him. I'm just getting a few ideas down at the moment but there's a lot of scope there.'

'Well, sir, that would be just grand. I reckon it's high time somebody got something into print. Don't matter to me if they're English, just so long as it gets written.'

Martin assumes this remark is intended to be jocular and so he laughs, although the laugh is rather more feeble than he might have wished.

'So, you thinking seriously about a book then?'

'Maybe, or an article. Depends how much material I can find out about him.'

'Well,' says the man on the other end of the phone, elongating the word as though it might provide him with a little more time to consider his response, 'I have to say it might be difficult getting a whole book out of the one song but, hell, I'd buy it! But to be honest, there ain't exactly a load of that sort of material about nowadays.' His voice trails off and he pauses briefly before continuing. 'You know how … how funny some people can be about all that, er … stuff?' Mr Palmer is evidently choosing his words carefully.

'Er, yeah, I quite understand.'

They fall into silence again for a moment but any lingering awkwardness is quickly dispelled when Clayton Palmer launches into another anecdote about Tambo Bones.

'Probably just another silly rumour,' he says by way of

qualification, 'but I was told a number of years ago that Tambo himself had once boasted to his band that he was the illegitimate son of Joe Oliver. Seriously, he said that was why he'd been given the name Oliver.'

Of course, it was a ludicrous claim and Martin may have made a comment to this effect but sadly he is currently thinking about polka-dot boxer shorts again.

'Can you believe it? That guy was really something, right? Maybe you can put that story in your book or whatever it is.'

'Maybe I will,' says Martin, rather pleased that the only man to whom he has mentioned the idea appears to be taking the venture seriously.

'I was told he was in an argument with the guys in his band. He was playing some show somewhere out of town with some pick-up band or another and it was just one of those nights when the musicians just couldn't get it together. Someone was dragging the beat and they started accusing each other and eventually the band got into a fight right there on the stage. It was when someone accused Tambo of losing the tempo that he made the claim about his parentage. I guess the audience probably thought it was all part of the show.'

'That's a great story; I like that.'

'Well, I agree it's a hell of a story but I wouldn't stick my neck out and claim that it's necessarily a true one.'

There is another pause in the conversation at this point, which is only ended when Martin speaks. 'The thing is,' he says cautiously, 'could there actually be any, er ... *feasibility* to such a claim?'

'Well, it was a couple of years before Joe Oliver left for Chicago so I believe he was still in New Orleans. So it's possible, I suppose.'

Martin frowns and shows his teeth. 'Actually,' he says in a tone of some delicacy, 'I was thinking more of a question of ... you know...'

'Do you mean ethnicity, sir?'

Martin smiles. 'Yeah ... that's what I mean, I think.'

'In all the photos I've seen, without his make up, obviously, Oscar Brightwater looks like a fair-skinned Creole man; Oliver was a Creole too so it doesn't automatically rule it out.'

'There are photos?' asks Martin, voicing the question as a blurred single syllable in a voice that he can barely recognise as his own.

'There sure are. Quite a few in fact.'

'And you've actually seen them?'

'Sir, I actually own them. What kind of collector would I be if I didn't own them?'

'God, I'm sorry... I didn't mean to suggest that you were anything less.'

'I appreciate that, sir, I do. I'm just having a little joke with you.'

'Do you think there's any chance of seeing your photos?' asks Martin, in a tone that successfully manages to sound more curious than pleading.

'Well, sir, this is the reason behind my call,' replies Mr Palmer, obviously enjoying the moment. 'I figured you might like to drop by and take a look at my collection. It's obviously not just relating to Tambo Bones, but I do have a few good pieces. I believe Hugo already told you I have an original 78 of "Georgia Blues".'

'Yes he did.'

'It's not bad but I'd hesitate to say "very good". It's a little flawed in places, a few nicks here and there, but I've still got a blank cheque with some faggy dealer in New York who's looking out for a mint copy for me.'

'I'd love to see the one you have anyway.'

'Sure thing. So, Hugo told me you're on vacation here. Whereabouts are you staying?'

Martin explains briefly that he's staying at the Royal Crescent Hotel and will be in New Orleans for another week or so.

'But I can be flexible,' he says by way of a fairly enigmatic conclusion.

'So are you free after lunch?'

'Oh, definitely!'

'You familiar with the Quarter, sir?'

Clayton Palmer describes in some detail his house on Dumaine Street, a process in which he takes an evident delight, and the best method of locating it. '... the block above Dauphine, on the right-hand side. Double shotgun with green shutters. You can't miss it. There's an old lamppost right outside.'

'OK, about three o'clock then?'

'Yeah, I'll look forward to it, Mr *Bonny*-house.'

'Please,' says Martin, trying his very best to smile, 'just call me Martin.'

And talking of Bill Evans...

On 19th October 2009, a recording of a 1970 concert in Finland of the late pianist with his trio is released for the first time. Issued on a small independent label, the reviews are mixed and the sound quality is often singled out for criticism. Martin will never own or listen to the record; neither will he listen to Bill Evans very much at all after 19th October 2009. For on that very same day, shortly after midday, at Kent and Canterbury Hospital, Stanley Mervyn Price is pronounced dead, the cause of death being head injuries sustained in a road accident earlier in the day. According to witnesses, the man had stepped out from behind what was consistently referred to as an illegally parked box van and right on to the road that circumnavigates Canterbury bus garage. The vehicle had obviously obscured his view although some witnesses stated that he looked as though he might have lost his balance stepping off the curb, but others made no such claim. All, however, agreed, that he'd wandered directly into the path of a National Express coach en route to Dover and that the collision was virtually instantaneous. One second either way – earlier or later – and the scenario would have been entirely different.

The driver of the coach maintained that he never saw the man prior to hearing and feeling the impact.

Mr Price never regained consciousness.

There is no simile, no metaphor that accurately captures the sense of loss that Martin experiences that afternoon when, having been listed as an emergency contact number, he receives the call from the hospital. Naturally, he'd been at home waiting for his friend to arrive for lunch and there was a lasagne in the oven and it wasn't like him to be late and his phone went straight to voicemail and they were supposed to be booking their trip to New Orleans and he'd only seen him last night and then … and then the phone call. Shock and disbelief, they say, but the term is meaningless. The shock is actually physical and your hands shake and you can't breathe properly and disbelief is not to doubt the veracity of the information; it is so often simply the inability to process that information.

Martin calls Bernice, he collects Wes from school, he repeats the news, he repeats it over and over, always in the hope that it will suddenly reveal a secondary truth, a greater truth, something which he can then understand. He holds on to the facts, the raw basic essential details in the hope that they will grow familiar to him and lose their power in time. But ten days later they haven't lost even the tiniest fraction of that power.

'Bloody hell, boy bach,' says the man in the black three-piece pinstripe with the 1970s lapels. 'That was a hell of a fucking speech you did back there, boy!' Patting Martin on the shoulder in a slightly over familiar manner, the gentleman unwittingly draws attention to how unsteady he is on his feet.

'Well, thank you. I'm glad you liked it.'

The man shrugs. 'I never said I liked it.'

'Right. Well, OK then,' says Martin, smiling hopelessly and unable to think of anything further to add.

'Bloody rubbish it was! What in God's name were you thinking of there, boy? I mean what sort of bloody eulogy was that supposed to be?'

Just as it begins to feel that he might be marooned in this particular exchange for the rest of his life, Martin catches sight of Bernice behind the two-piece greenish mohair suit with the black tie man and eventually manages to attract her attention.

'Look,' he announces to his companion in the most ebullient tones he can muster, 'why don't you help yourself to some more food from the buffet? And get your glass refilled while you're there.'

The black three-piece pinstripe man takes the hint and saunters off in the direction of the sandwiches and Martin hears him muttering under his breath, 'Bloody rubbish, bloody rubbish,' to no one in particular.

'Who the fuck is that?' he whispers to Bernice as soon as she is within earshot, inclining his head in the direction of the man at the buffet.

'Um, I'm not sure. He's Welsh I think.'

'Well, thanks. That narrows it down a bit.'

'Wait, I think he was an old school friend, somebody said. Or he might be the brother of the solicitor I was talking to earlier. Why do you ask?'

'He didn't seem to like my speech very much.'

Bernice smiles at him and gently places her hand around his.

'Well, he was probably expecting something more, I don't know ... traditional, yeah?'

'Maybe I should have prepared something. Quoted Dylan buggering Thomas or something. But he used to absolutely hate that sort of stuff.'

'I know. Don't get upset.'

'It was something improvised on the spot. It wasn't disrespectful. It was fucking jazz!'

'Well, I thought it was really good anyway.' She kisses him fondly on the cheek. 'But I really need to go and sort out some more plates and bring the rest of sandwiches in from the kitchen.'

Martin watches Bernice picking her way carefully through the couple of dozen people currently occupying the two smallish downstairs rooms of their cottage. There are a couple of familiar faces but these are greatly outnumbered by the guests he does not recognise. Disregarding the slim possibility of mass formal introductions in the very near future, he assumes that he will simply continue to identify the anonymous mourners only by what they are wearing. He stares vaguely at some indeterminate point on the carpet and once again, as has happened so many times in the past week or so, he finds himself completely drained of all human emotion. His responses still feel automatic; nothing seems to involve feeling anymore. It is all just a physical electrical reaction.

He looks up and does another quick head count and a voice from somewhere deep within him says, 'A good turnout.' It says it again a few more times but it doesn't say anything else. It is not what it's saying, rather it's the voice it has chosen to speak with. He turns around and the shiny silk suit and Ascot hat lady smiles at him again and he smiles back. He is sure she is familiar somehow but can't remember the circumstances under which they might have met. As she passes she brushes her hand down his arm affectionately but says nothing. He simply assumes that she is another of Mr Price's old acquaintances from the little village in Powys where he'd been publican at the Star of Wales for so many years.

The black tailored dress with lace detail and the silver brooch lady who'd been sitting at the front during the service wanders over and explains in a small voice frail with emotion that she needs to be on her way very soon. Then, with little or no warning, she throws both her arms around him. The gesture is more comradely than affectionate but it is certainly heartfelt and the initial awkwardness Martin experiences quickly dissipates as he reciprocates the gesture. At its conclusion he feels his shoulder being rather vigorously tapped and the navy blue blazer and black shirt man with the red face is asking him where the toilet is.

'Top of the stairs on the right, mate – can't miss it.'

'Must have been quite a shock for you.'

Martin now turns in the direction of a very different voice and finds himself face-to-face with the two-piece charcoal business suit and Hermès scarf lady. Once again he can claim no prior acquaintance, although the lady's opening remark betrays no suggestion of a Welsh accent.

He smiles politely. 'Yeah, it certainly was. It still hasn't sunk in. I'm still not ... you know.'

'I know, I know.'

'Did you know him long?' asks Martin, once again seeking any available opportunity to talk about the man.

'A good few years now,' says the lady with the sort of expression that betrays nothing and everything at the same time. 'I live in the same block of apartments in Canterbury. I used to often pop in for a chat with him. He was such great company. He was always talking about you.'

'I don't think I'll ever get used to him not being around. Seriously, we were in Sainsbury's earlier in the week buying all the drink for today. We got to the checkout and Bernice had to send me back because I'd put six bottles of Old Crusty in our trolley. It was just ... automatic, I suppose.'

'He was a bit of a devil for the ale wasn't he?'

'You know, I met him when my grandfather died and now this and I can't help thinking that there just seems this terrible awful logic about it all.'

The lady smiles in a manner which suggests a certain level of discomfort. 'You must have loved him a great deal.'

'I suppose I must have.'

'Anyway, I'm going to help myself to a vol au vent or two. Nice talking to you.'

'OK.'

'I did like your, you know, that whole thing you did at the crematorium by the way.'

'Thanks,' says Martin and wonders if she is just being polite.

The speech to which the two guests have been referring took place about an hour and half ago. It had certainly not been Martin's intention to actually speak at the service and by his own admission he had not prepared anything but he'd been urged to do so by the priest taking the service. During their earlier meeting there had been several references to the fact that mourners usually prefer 'the personal touch', and as Martin had taken the responsibility for the funeral arrangements upon himself, he remained the most obvious candidate. To be truthful, there weren't many arrangements when it comes to the internment of a 'lapsed Baptist'. As Martin has recently discovered, it was mainly just the service at the crematorium and 'some food back at the cottage'. This is the phrase that Martin has expediently adopted, fearing that most alternatives had some underlying religious significance.

For the first twenty-four hours after he'd heard the news, Martin had actually wondered if he could get a traditional jazz band to play at the service, like an old New Orleans second line, but there wasn't enough time to arrange it. Then he'd hoped he would be able to play some music at the service and he'd brought a couple of CDs with him, having narrowed the choice down to either 'West End Blues' by Louis Armstrong's Hot Five or 'Goodbye Pork Pie Hat' by Charles Mingus. But the CD player at the crematorium wasn't working and so the idea was abandoned. Yet Martin has remained reticent about the whole idea of a speech, considering the service to be something of an ordeal in the first place and that anything that secured its prolongation was to be avoided at all costs. But Bernice had finally managed to convince him, although he is extremely dubious about the whole idea.

'Now I believe Mr Bonehouse is going to say a few words.'

There is no avoiding it now. He stands up and, walking past the coffin with the sort of determined stride that highlights rather than masks any apprehension, he makes his way to the small plain wooden lectern. He does a quick head count. Roughly thirty, thirty-five at a push. He puts his hands in his jacket pockets and then he takes them out again. He clears his throat. He doesn't need to; he just feels the situation warrants it.

'There is a ditch somewhere,' he begins tentatively, as if uncertain of how loud he should be speaking. 'Nobody actually knows where it starts or where it ends, nobody has even seen it yet it runs alongside every single road, street, lane, crescent and cul-de-sac the length and breadth of the entire country. This is the ditch that we have all heard about and indeed many of us have spoken of. For it is the very same ditch in which every teenage boy and teenage girl will one day be found lying at the end of most cautionary tales. This metaphoric ditch into which we hurl all young adults negligent of public transport common sense and mobile phone etiquette has much in common with the equally allegorical bus that, as we all know, could kill us tomorrow. So I admit that maybe this is why I'm having such a problem coming to terms with the death of my dear, dear friend who as we all know was actually run over by a bus. Losing someone so close is always such a difficult thing to accept and process but in this case I really think that the manner of his death is equally difficult to come to terms with. It seems perverse and totally unnecessary. Of course we all know that there isn't really a ditch and so surely by extension there can't really be a homicidal bus either. So everything is wrong about it. It is just some glib device we throw at each other whenever the situation warrants;

it doesn't really happen to real people – people we know and people we ... people we love.' Martin briefly attempts to make eye contact with Bernice but her face is momentarily turned away. 'I don't really know ... well, I can't really speak about his background in Wales or his family, although I do know he remained close to his sister until her death a couple of years ago. I have known him... No, I apologise; you must forgive my tenses this afternoon... I *had* known him for the past – what is it? – fifteen, sixteen years and so I can only really speak with any authority about the man I know ... *knew*. But he was so many things to me: the supportive parent, the best mate, the older brother, wise to the ways of the world, the kindly indulgent uncle, the grandparent with the wicked gleam in the eye, the one to whom you could tell all your secrets.'

At this point, Martin glances towards the coffin in a manner that suggests that, beyond simply acknowledging its presence, he is also actively seeking its approval.

'We made friends because amongst other things, we both had an interest in jazz, but over the years I realised that it was never just about the music with him. I think, at heart, Mr Price was an idealist, a utopian, and I'm pretty certain this was just another connection to a world he believed to be noble and lasting and where artistic innovation is still rated far above commercial success. As long as there was music somewhere in a world that was so emotionally and intellectually uplifting then it gave him some small hope for the future of that world. I like to imagine that it was this same belief in a better world that lay behind his lifelong support of the Labour Party.' Martin wonders if he should stop at this point as he fears he might have drifted off the point somewhat. He returns to his subject. 'There were always so many different facets to the man; whatever you wanted him to be, he was that person. Endlessly patient, never judgemental and utterly unshockable. I always felt that he wasn't a man of his time, rather he was a man for all times who recognised no constraint on aspiration or endeavour or ambition. He was constantly developing new interests and continually surprising me; he had the sort of enthusiasm it was impossible or just useless to resist. He had wisdom with no pretence to authority; for knowledge without awareness, conscience or empathy is no longer knowledge.'

Martin pauses at this point and scans in vain the thirty or so faces in front of him for some discernible trace of a reaction. Undeterred, he continues. 'When he settled in Canterbury, he was getting on for sixty and moving away from Wales for the first time. It is hard not to have a great respect for any man that can do that. He never looked back because he was the sort of person who, certain noteworthy tastes in jazz aside, saw no virtue in looking back and he was always on the lookout for the next new horizon. I don't know if this is common knowledge but he was actually on his way over to see me that fateful terrible day and we were planning to book a holiday to New Orleans together, somewhere he had always wanted to go but had never been. He'd just popped into HMV to pick up an iTunes voucher for my son, Wes, and was returning to his car when, as many of you will already know, he walked out into the traffic and was hit by a bus. Perhaps it's the trite easy everyday symbolism of it all, but it still doesn't seem real to me. Maybe that's why I'm trying to read it rather than just accept it. I'm too cautious in my thinking maybe, too reticent, perhaps we all are, every one of us. Maybe I need to be bold and hurl caution to the wind. You see, you never know what might be in store for us tomorrow, how easily it could all be taken from us. Mr Price was never cautious or reticent, was he? Right, you see, I get it now; I've learned my lesson...' Martin narrows his eyes and instinctively bites his bottom lip. 'So can you come back now, please, Mr Price, and I'm sorry but you'll always be Mr Price to me, never Stan or Stanley, and that's maybe one of the few certainties I have left. He gave me so much over the years and I learned so much from the man. I just feel so saddened that I will never now repay the debt and even in his death he has left me with an allegorical fable that I can selfishly continue to learn from. It is something, perhaps, that we can all learn from and in that respect he will always be with us. To say he was like a father to me would be unfair; I never knew my father but somehow I think I know in my heart he could never have been as kind or as generous or supportive as my dear Mr Price. I never knew anyone quite like him and the only other certainty I now have is that every time I draw breath I will think about him and every time I think about him I will miss him.' Martin now casts his eyes downwards. Everything else is private. 'I can't think of anything else to say.'

Martin looks again at the second photograph. It is a formal studio publicity shot taken, he would guess, to promote the record, as the group never actually performed on a stage together. The four men are posed awkwardly around a bass drum on which is written *The Back O' Town Boys – New Orleans, LA.* They smile vacantly and perhaps manically and might be taken for prisoners or murderers rather than entertainers. These are the details you notice when you finally get past the blackface makeup. Reading about it is one thing but seeing it right in front of you like this is very different and as Martin can now testify with little fear of repudiation, it still has the capacity to shock.

Aware that the silence between them is extending to the point where it might become noticeable, Martin suddenly asks, 'So, this group never actually performed together outside the studio?'

'That's right. I suppose if the record had been a success they would have carried on. It's one of those great "what ifs", right?'

110

'I'll say. So who's the guy at the back, just above Tambo there?'

'Let me have a look. Oh yes, that's Bent Chesterton.'

'Ben Chesterton?'

'No, sir. Bent, with a "t". Damn *fine* piano player.'

'Bent?'

'Yip.'

'*Bent*?'

'What I said.'

Martin thinks for a moment. 'Is that like a Danish name or something?'

'No, sir, it was a nickname.'

'Bent?' Martin looks uncomfortable. 'Uh, I have to ask,' he smiles with some difficulty. 'Was he ... er ... gay or something?'

Clayton Palmer straightens his back and looks momentarily confused. 'You mean was he a fag? No, poor man had polio or something; his back was all twisted and so forth, had a great big hump there or something. So they called him Bent.'

'I suppose it makes a sort of sense,' says Martin, managing a weak smile and recalling that Mr Price once told him that 'Dodo' Marmarosa who played piano on many of Charlie Parker's Dial recordings was thus nicknamed, perhaps cruelly, on account of his having a rather large head.

'Sad really,' says the older man reflectively. 'Bent Chesterton was a great piano man, one of the best; really, I'm not lying to you. A bit later the man played on so many of them great sides in the fifties and sixties. Never got no credit neither. He liked a drink, true enough, but basically he never played much away from the recording studio. Man looked kind of gimpy with his hump and that. People are funny about that stuff. But I'm telling you he was the go-to guy for a long, long time. Had that whole New Orleans left hand thing going on.'

It is another beautiful October afternoon and Martin has

been, for the past hour or so, a guest at the home of Mr Clayton Palmer of New Orleans. The two men are currently drinking Coors Light and sitting at a table in the small courtyard at the rear of the house as Martin looks through the pile of documents and photographs that Mr Palmer has scanned for him. The earlier humidity has lifted and it is warm and balmy and Martin can hear insects.

Clayton Palmer is a genial, red-faced man with a dignity to his bearing and conduct that possibly suggests a military background. He speaks in a clear, very deliberate manner as though he has no intention of ever repeating himself. From their conversation so far, Martin has learned little about the man's background beyond the fact that he is not a native Louisianan and was originally from Texas and that he'd worked in television until he'd retired a couple of years ago. But he has the most impressive shock of thick white hair and the frankly enviable talent of looking utterly at ease in a bootlace tie and cowboy boots.

'So,' he says, raising his can towards Martin as though proposing a toast, 'you reckon you got enough stuff in that one song there for your ... book or piece you're gonna write?'

'I think so,' says Martin with trepidation. 'I, er ... certainly think it's an interesting story.'

Clayton leans forward in his chair. 'It is that, sir. It's another one of those great stories that attaches itself to this amazing city, am I right? Damn right I am! That's what New Orleans does best! It takes you in and turns you into a story, makes you immortal – a story that will live forever! When you hear some news report or read about some recent crime statistic that's what's going on. This city isn't constructed out of bricks or timber.' He bangs his can on the table for emphasis. 'No, Martin, it's entirely built on stories – its own stories. Our stories! One day, maybe a long, long time from now, we'll get over The Storm but the stories about it will be around forever. Stories matter and sometimes they're the only things that matter. Nothing endures, nothing survives, nothing remains, just the stories we tell about ourselves.'

Mr Palmer, concludes Martin, is either a gentleman who aspires to profundity or one who should consider avoiding any sort of alcohol in the afternoon.

'You wanna know something?' Clayton continues. 'If this place was hit by one of those big meteorites that flattened all those forests in Russia that time and there was nothing left but some great big crater, people would still come here every year just to look at the crater! It's true, man. They'd bring picnics and sit around just to be near the crater and then all the stories would start. There was no place on earth ever like it, they'd be saying. And before you knew it there would be bonfires and a couple of tents, then more tents, then a couple of houses would go up and then a couple more and before you knew it...' Clayton's voice trails off and he chuckles to himself feeling that his point has been well made.

Martin now sees an opportunity to return to the obvious key issue that they have thus managed to avoid. 'So how do you feel about the whole, er ... blackface aspect to all this? Does that ... pose a problem to collectors?'

Clayton considers the question and chooses his words carefully in a manner that suggests a certain level of prior experience in dealing with this matter. 'It's extremely *complicated*, Martin; there's not a simple right or wrong, good or bad button we can push here. As you know, I collect items of historical and social interest from the era of the medicine shows – recordings, printed items and ephemera – and as you may have already discovered in your research, those particular travelling shows lasted well into the 1970s. I've got a big collection of Emmett Miller, Leaky Adams, Freeman Davis, Scat Henderson and the like.'

Martin nods but feels disinclined to actually interrupt.

'And the blackface tradition lived on in the medicine shows

and of course it will always be a problem to a collector like myself. But I'm not condoning it, Martin, or agreeing with it or celebrating it in any way. If you collect this sort of stuff it's an unavoidable historical reality. The medicine shows were always tarnished by their association with minstrelsy and by extension, Jim Crow and I doubt that will ever change. But, as I say, it's complicated.'

'In what way?' asks Martin, managing to sound curious rather than accusatory.

'Well, as an example, take our friend in the picture there, Oscar Oliver Brightwater: Tambo Bones to you. A Creole gentleman who performed in blackface and there were a great many like him. Jelly Roll Morton was one and the great Bert Williams of course, a man who Booker T. Washington once praised as having done more for the black race than himself. He performed in blackface. Also you must remember down in the South here back in the thirties, the only way that a black musician could get on stage with a white musician was if they were both in blackface. It was a terrible and stupid situation but that's the way it was.'

Martin looks once again at the photograph of the Back O' Town Boys and struggles for the right words. 'But it's morally so ... demeaning. It's just...'

'I agree but some regard it as a theatrical tradition rather than social or political one. The primary intention being to entertain not to demean or dehumanise.'

Martin shakes his head. 'I'm not so sure about that.'

'OK, so what are those ridiculous shows they put on for kids at Christmas in England when the men dress up as ugly old women?'

'Oh, you mean pantomimes?'

'Yeah, that's just a different tradition you got right there. I saw one of those shows when I was in London with my kids years ago. Those men aren't celebrating women or empowering them; they're degrading and demeaning them, right? People might object but there are those that say it's fun or it's traditional and blah, blah blah.'

'Fair enough,' says Martin sheepishly.

'So what if you got a lady to play the part of the ugly old woman, would that be subversive or sexist or would she be ... you know?'

'Betraying her gender?'

'Yeah, exactly. Or would the whole thing be missing the point? Is the humour not based on the fact it's obviously a man pretending to be a woman? You see, it's so complicated. You can see similar contradictory elements in the shows which involve similar theatrical traditions. You could argue that alcoholics should be pitied rather than laughed at, right? But where would vaudeville be without the comic drunk? Look, I'm certainly not saying blackface falls into that category, Martin, but I am saying I'm not a racist, OK, just because I collect this stuff, and that I imagine is the answer to your actual question.'

'OK,' says Martin, smiling with some difficulty but happy to leave the subject alone at this point. 'So who is this guy in the other picture?' He holds up the photograph in question. It is a sepia-tinted full-length portrait of another blackface performer leaning against a prop lamppost and dressed rather theatrically perhaps as the aforementioned drunk character or as a tramp. There is a signature across the bottom of the photograph which Martin is still unable to decipher. 'I can't read the name at all.'

Clayton smiles broadly. 'That, my friend, is Sweet Papa Stalebread!'

'Sweet Papa who?'

'Sweet Papa Stalebread. The one and only!'

'And who's he?'

Clayton now takes considerable delight in informing Martin that the man in the photograph is also Oscar Brightwater and that he had adopted that particular stage name in his

115

late teens when he'd first started out. 'Look a little closer and you might be able to recognise him. I think that picture must be from the late thirties. It was roughly the same time that he started using the tagline The Minstrel Man from Alabam' and it kind of stayed with him even after he dropped his original stage name in favour of Tambo Bones.'

'But why Alabam'? He was from New Orleans; you'd think that would have meant something amongst entertainers back then.'

Clayton looks vaguely amused by the suggestion. 'But Minstrel Man from Alabam' is catchy and it rhymes. It ain't about geography! Like it or not, Martin, that's the business we call show!'

Feeling suitably rebuked, Martin concentrates on the photograph again. 'Anyway, what sort of act was it?'

'It was mainly a comedy act; he worked with a lady called Bunny Yum-Yum and they used to do a bit of slapstick and a few novelty songs. Very, very unlike the Back O' Town Boys, you understand. But there are a couple of recordings that survived, including his theme song, and legend has it there is, in a vault somewhere, about ten seconds of silent film of the two of them on stage. I've never seen it but I have it on good authority that it exists.'

Martin isn't certain he likes the idea of Sweet Papa Stalebread; it all sounded a bit too much like music hall for his tastes and he is keen to return to the subject of Tambo Bones.

'Do you think,' he asks quietly, 'I could have another look at the original 78?'

'Of course you can; let's go back inside.'

Back in Mr Palmer's palatial living room, which he'd only fleetingly glimpsed on his way through to the courtyard earlier, Martin positions himself at one end of the white leather sofa, an item of furniture so preposterously large that he is probably occupying the area known as the Northern End. He wonders if he should vocalise this particular observation but decides against it. The whole room, he concludes after a further moment's appraisal, has a sort of conspicuous opulence that perfectly complements its owner.

Clayton returns from another room holding the original 78 recording of 'Georgia Blues'. The record is in its original brown paper sleeve and protected in a transparent plastic cover. He hands it to Martin with all the necessary reverence and ceremony that one might expect from a true collector. 'There you go.'

Martin takes the record but says nothing. Instead, he studies the details on the label. 'Georgia Blues' by Tambo Bones and His Back O' Town Boys – not *The* Back O' Town Boys as the Louisiana LP erroneously has it. As Martin is currently discovering, this is precisely the sort of detail that matters enormously to collectors; the focus is always on the artefact and not the art. The disc was issued by the Hi-Tone Recording Company with the catalogue number 14910, but there is no date on the label. There is no date on the B side either, just the title 'Back O' Town Boogie Woogie', which Clayton described earlier as a fairly undistinguished instrumental.

'So you think this was issued early forties, right?'

'1941 or early '42, thereabouts. There was that notorious American Federation of Musicians recording ban that started in August 1942, so it had to be before that. If you asked me to stick my neck out, I'd say about late 1941. He'd have been a fairly young man at the time too, maybe twenty-three or twenty-four, not much more than a kid, but he'd already been in the business ten years by then. We weren't quite so hot on schooling back in the twenties and thirties I can tell you.'

'1941?' repeats Martin reflectively if not incredulously. 'That is extraordinary. Can you imagine the effect a song like this could have had if it had been sung by Big Bill Broonzy, or Josh White say, or Woody Guthrie and not ... not...'

'"The Minstrel Man from Alabam"?' offers Clayton helpfully.

117

'Exactly.' Martin shakes his head in disbelief. 'I mean, this is just such a remarkable record, right?'

'You'll hear no argument from me, sir, in that regard.'

The smile suddenly drains from Martin's face and when he speaks again his voice is calmer and more measured. 'So, Clayton, what is *your* actual take on this record? Do you share my view that it's some brilliant but overlooked protest song? A great civil rights rallying call about two decades too early?'

Clayton considers the question. 'To be honest, Martin, I always thought it was just a sort of bad, even tasteless joke. But, it's not really my field and you do make a very persuasive argument in its favour.'

'Thank you.'

'Who knows, maybe it's exactly what you say it is.' Clayton pauses for a moment to gather his thoughts. 'Or else it simply is an attempt at comedy; maybe it's just supposed to be a funny song. Maybe the guys in the band were goofing off in the studio and the engineers just carried on recording.'

Martin looks a little crestfallen. 'But surely the humorous aspect would only work if you had the visual joke of the man being in blackface. That sort of comedy simply wouldn't work on a record. Besides, the words are too literal and too specific and Tambo is not mocking or making light of the black man's plight; he's identifying with it. Remember, underneath all that cork, the man was still a Creole! No, Clayton, I can't go for that. I still think it's the rough and ready, less sophisticated rural cousin of "Strange Fruit".'

'OK, then, Martin,' says Clayton indulgently, 'we'll go with your version. You've talked me into it. But you know what they say: judging a man's actions are always far easier than determining his underlying motives.'

'True enough,' says Martin, happy to let the subject rest there.

When Clayton retrieves the record he bemoans the record-buying habits and the poor musical judgement of his fellow countrymen in the early 1940s. Sadly, The Back O' Town Boys' contract with Hi-Tone was strictly a one-shot deal and when the record failed to sell in any significant quantities outside of Louisiana, they were immediately dropped. Besides 'Georgia Blues' and its B side, Oscar Brightwater's recorded legacy remains solely the discs he made under the name Sweet Papa Stalebread.

'So what are they like?' asks Martin, feeling a slight throbbing in his left temple, an early indication that a migraine might be fairly imminent.

'You can judge for yourself; I've copied them on to a CD for you. It's in the file with the scans of the photos I gave you earlier. Not great quality I warn you but you'll get the general idea.'

Martin is unable to contain his enthusiasm and blurts in a sudden flurry, 'God, is there anything else like "Georgia Blues"?'

Clayton takes a breath. 'Well, you'll need to find that out for yourself, Martin.'

'Fair enough.'

This seems to be a natural point in their conversation for Martin to think about leaving and so he gathers together the various scans and files that Clayton has given him and stands up.

'I'm not going to take up any more of your time, Clayton, but you have been so helpful. I can't ever thank you enough.'

'Maybe a credit in that book of yours would be nice.'

'OK, you got it.'

'You know,' says Clayton, 'it seems Oscar never had any formal musical training, which was rare in those days. He was largely self-taught.'

'Good for him.'

Clayton looks unconvinced. 'Well, maybe. You English people have much higher regard for self-education than we do.'

119

Martin frowns. 'Do we?'

'Yeah. I guess I always kinda think self-educated people are like people who cut their own hair!'

Martin braces himself. As someone who would place himself in both categories, he awaits the witty rejoinder with mounting unease. *You can always tell, they always leave bits out, the result is never as good as they think it is...* But thankfully nothing further on the subject is forthcoming.

The two men shake hands and walk through Mr Palmer's study towards the front door. Martin looks at some of the framed posters on the wall, further evidence of the man's defining passion, as they pass.

His interest is observed by Clayton. 'You see, Martin, the medicine shows never actually went away; they just mutated a little. Evolution, they call it or a bit of that old voodoo shape-shifting went on.'

Martin smiles nervously. 'I'm not with you.'

'Look around you, sir.'

'I'm not sure what you –'

'Think what was on the wall of the living room, just now, just to the right of where you were sitting.'

Martin instinctively glances over his shoulder. 'Er ... do you mean the TV, that big screen TV there?'

'Yeah, that's right.'

'The TV?'

'Well, not actually the TV – more what is actually shown on the TV: the whole format of television itself.'

'OK,' says Martin, uncertain if he is following correctly this particular train of thought.

'Come on, now, think about it. Think about TV as we all know and love it. Free, deliberately low-brow, plebeian, puerile entertainment interrupted at regular intervals by people earnestly trying to sell you things that you didn't know you actually needed or wanted until that moment! Sound familiar? It's a medicine show, baby, pure and simple! Remember, I worked in TV all my life and so I should know! Believe me, it's no different today!'

Martin shakes his head. 'I never really –'

'Yeah, I know.' Mr Palmer smiles and pats his guest on the back. 'So here's to goddamn progress, right?'

Martin, perhaps wisely, declines to comment.

'By the way, Martin, there's just one thing. This morning after you'd told me you were a writer I looked you up on the internet. I tried to get one of your books off Amazon but it kept showing up as unavailable. Everywhere I tried – unavailable, unavailable. So what's going on there?'

'Well, Clayton,' says Martin, fixing his host with a final broad smile. 'It's complicated.'

7

Sweet Papa Stalebread

As one might possibly imagine, the remarkable story of Tambo Bones began at the precise moment of his birth. For, according to local tradition, he was the last baby born in Storyville before it closed for business in 1917.

Storyville. There it is again. It is corny and predictable but, despite his better judgement, the word still resonates with him. Of course the district was named after Alderman Sidney Story but, recalling Mr Palmer's earlier remarks, he can now almost convince himself that Storyville was simply an ancient local colloquialism that applied to the entire city. The town of stories. Perfect.

Martin smiles. Amongst his possible readership, might there be anyone unfamiliar with Storyville? It was unlikely but not wishing to take any chances he amends the line as follows:

For, according to local tradition, he was the last baby born in Storyville, the legendary red-light district of New Orleans, before it was closed down in 1917.

He doesn't like this very much; it's clumsy and dilutes the impact somewhat but he decides to ignore these misgivings and continue.

Tambo entered the world as Oscar Oliver Brightwater, the son of a Creole mother and an unknown father. His mother worked in one of the less opulent bordellos in the District, one source locates the premises on Bienville Street, but we have no record of her profession or if she was actually a prostitute. She could have equally been employed as a housekeeper, a cook, a maid or in some other menial capacity. The rumour that Oscar was a 'trick baby' (i.e. the consequence of an unwanted pregnancy arising from unprotected sex with a client), a rumour supported mainly by there being no record of his father's name, may have some veracity. However, at this distance, we are unlikely to know the truth or to ever discover the name of his father.

Oscar grew up without a father

Martin pauses for a moment and manages a rather lopsided half-smile. Now he begins to ponder the virtue of mentioning the King Oliver rumour and quickly decides against it. The two paragraphs he has just written seem to be composed almost entirely of conjecture and hearsay. Even the bit about the bordello on Bienville Street, which he found in one of the clippings Clayton had copied for him, appears to be very little beyond guess work. The writer of the article in question had concluded that because all the grandest sporting houses of Storyville were on Basin Street then it followed that Tambo's mother must have worked in premises located some distance away. Glancing at a map and setting Basin Street as the boundary marker of the District, he probably came up with Bienville Street simply because it was a few blocks to the west.

In truth, he is finding it all rather difficult.

This whole anecdotal backstory on Tambo, although fascinating in its own way and a prime example of Clayton's theory was not what really interested him. In his keenness to get through this section he worries, with fair cause, that he might be rushing it. Feeling more than a little disenchanted with the tone and the whole approach to his opening, he turns away from the screen and reaches across the desk for the CD once more. Deciding on little more than a whim to give it another hearing, he inserts the disc into his laptop. The CD is recognised only as Unknown Artist and Unknown

Album, a situation from which Martin secretly derives a sort of quiet humanistic superiority.

This is the CD that Clayton had given him earlier in the afternoon of the only known recordings of Oscar Oliver Brightwater in his earlier incarnation as Sweet Papa Stalebread. Under that alias he had toured the South with Doc Harmon's Original Gypsy Oil Medicine Show for a couple of years in the late 1930s, during which time, according to one clipping, he appeared alongside a performer named Chinny Chin-Chin. There were no further references in the notes to any person of that name – a cause of considerable relief to Martin.

He concentrates his attention again on the music. Upon the first couple of listenings, Martin would have to concede to feeling something perilously close to disappointment. He is no musicologist and apart from the most basic chords on the guitar – just enough to accompany himself on 'Go Tell Aunt Rhody' should the need arise (which was frankly unlikely) – he was no musician either. Therefore, he was reduced to describing music by comparing it to other music, which was far from ideal. Sweet Papa Stalebread's music *reminded* him of the sort of hokum songs that Blind Boy Fuller or Tampa Red might have sung. Hokum was a hybrid, largely vocal genre that flourished in the 1920s and 1930s, a blend of blues, ragtime and jazz. It was good-time music and usually featured upbeat catchy choruses and lyrics often loaded with innuendo. 'They're Red Hot,' the one Robert Johnson song that still puzzles many of his listeners, is a fairly good example of the type. Hokum was hugely popular with African Americans at the time, although it remained largely ignored during the great resurgence of interest in blues amongst white audiences in the 1950s and 1960s. An apposite example of this particular trend is present in a recent jazz study in Martin's possession, which refers to hokum as 'hokum' throughout the text, as though the writer sought either to question the credibility of the genre or was simply using the quote marks to distance himself from such a musical aberration.

For the duration of a heartbeat, a shiver now passes the length of Martin's spine as he recalls the spoken introduction to 'Georgia Blues' and the reference to white people only wanting to hear the sounds of 'pain and damn helplessness'. Sweet Papa Stalebread was definitely drawing on aspects of the hokum tradition but there were other influences at work, too. In fact, his self-titled recording actually sounded, in truth, a little like an old-time minstrel song but that was a word that he wanted to avoid as much as possible. According to Clayton, the two recordings (there are rumours of alternative takes but none have survived) were made about 1940 in Little Rock, Arkansas, a year or so before he recorded as Tambo Bones. While you could instantly recognise the singer as the same man, the manner of his delivery was very different. Although the exaggerated pronunciation was similar to what he would use on the later recordings (the substitution of 'dee' for 'the' and 'ah'm' for 'I'm', etc.), this was evidently a man desperate to wring every last drop of comedic potential from the lyrics. Sadly, it was precisely this same ebullience and enthusiasm that left the listener with the distinct impression that they were intruding on someone's private joke.

But Martin now feels prepared to give the music another chance and is more than open to the idea that he might have missed something earlier. The CD features two songs and he selects the one his laptop has designated Track 1. After a lengthy instrumental introduction played at a tempo that seems at times to almost defeat the band and during which he is still almost certain he can hear a kazoo being played, the singer starts to catalogue his various euphemistic virtues before concluding:

'Can't go fishin' without no pole
And you cain't go a day without ma Jelly Roll!'

Then the band kicks it up a couple of notches as the vocalist begins the chorus.

'They call me Sweet Pa-pa Stalebread, sweet Papa Stalebread
Ah'm der one dey all approves
Ah'm der one with all dee moves
They call me Sweet Pa-pa Stalebread, sweet Papa Stalebread.'

It would be difficult after seventy years to ascertain if the song had provided the young Oscar with his stage name or if the reverse was true and it had been composed on behalf of the character. But speculation on this matter made very little difference to Martin, who was already of the opinion that he would remain permanently unimpressed by either.

The music continues in a similar vein for a couple more minutes but Martin has ceased paying attention. Sadly, it still qualifies as something of a let-down. It was probably a good song and better than many; it just wasn't earth-shattering. It wasn't amazing. If anything, he should admit to feeling slightly baffled and confused by its apparent ordinariness. He'd initially been entirely and perhaps delightfully uncertain what to expect from the song but in some way he was confident that it would startle, seduce, confuse, alarm, inspire and excite in the manner of all great music. Precisely in the manner of 'Georgia Blues', in fact. After the second chorus there begins an instrumental passage, at the point one would imagine there being a solo of some kind, and once again the band struggle to keep pace with the tempo.

Martin now turns his head away, like a man not unacquainted with the underlying principles of sulking, and rummages again through the top couple of documents in Clayton's file. He looks again at the photo of Tambo as Sweet Papa Stalebread. He stares at the smiling face and wonders if it is now simply an expression of mockery or disdain. He places it face-down on the desk and picks up another document.

This evening he is beginning to feel far safer with facts.

According to the photocopy he now holds in his hand,

126

there is a record of a Rose Brightwater in the 1920 US Federal Census living Uptown in New Orleans on Palmyra Street. She is listed as living with her three-year-old son, Oscar, and a man named Tolliver or Tulliver. Her occupation is stated as seamstress while Mr Tolliver, as well as being designated the head of the household, is listed as being a laborer. In the *Personal Description* column under the heading of *Color or Race*, Tolliver is categorised by the single letter *B.*, while Rose and Oscar are identified as *Mu*. Mulatto in 1920 seems to be the only option available to census-takers when denoting a person of mixed race.

This is, however, the one and only time that the name Rose Brightwater shows up on any Louisiana or federal records. Although there is a single police record from that period noting that a Rosy [sic] Brightwater was once cautioned for *lewdness and public drunkenness*.

'Good for you, Rosy!' he mutters under his breath and registers with some relief that Ms Brightwater's son and heir has finally concluded his rather irritating song. The few seconds of silence that follow are blissful, uncomplicated and absolute.

Now he feels ready for Track 2.

According to Clayton's notes this song was originally pressed on the B side of the 78 of Sweet Papa Stalebread's eponymous theme song. 'What You Wanna Do That For?' is again an up-tempo number with both its great leaden boots still firmly rooted in the world of vaudeville. This time the listener could clearly make out the sound of an accordion which gave the arrangement a sort of Cajun feel and Martin now wonders if the kazoo he thought he could hear in the earlier song might have simply been a badly recorded accordion. The simple, slightly diluted ragtime feel and the chord changes of 'What You Wanna Do That For?' sounded like the tune might have shared some common ancestry with one or two of Blind Willie McTell's songs. The lyrics, however, were hard to decipher; the poor condition of the original disc was also a factor and it is only now on about the fourth hearing that Martin begins to make out what Sweet Papa is singing about.

It seemed that he was trying to convince his ex-girlfriend or perhaps his current girlfriend not to marry somebody else. The verses follow the same pattern:

'*I came a-knocking on your front door,*
Say what you wanna do that for?
I knocked all night and the night before,
Say what you wanna do that for?'

Then there is a brief four-bar bridge over which Martin can now make out

'*All I can do is sing this song*
Until you see you're doing wrong.'

Then the verse concludes each time with the same refrain:

'*You say it ain't against the law,*
But what you wanna do that for?'

Thankfully, on this occasion, Mr Stalebread appears to be singing straight – without affecting his usual vocal mannerisms and accent. Sweet Papa sings the second verse and now Martin finally notices the very slight but significant modification in the arrangement. When the song returns to the bridge section the band plays in stop-time – playing only the heavily accented first beat of every bar in unison. This gives the lyrics a far greater impact.

'*It makes me sad, I must confess,*
To see you standing there in that long white dress,'

As the song continues, Martin notes that the band reverts to playing in stop-time exclusively when the singer refers to this 'long white dress'.

Aside from the second verse, this occurs in verse six:

'*It makes me sad it makes me blue,*
That long white dress looks so right on you.'

And again in verse nine, the final verse:

'*Say Holey Moley and say God Bless,*

128

But you won't catch me in a long white dress.'
This arrangement obviously gives those particular lines far greater clarity and emphasis. This was the part of the song that the singer really wanted us to hear. So why did Sweet Papa wish to focus our attention on the long white dress? Martin's initial instinct was to wonder if the singer, particularly in verse nine, was wrestling with temptations of transvestism. Not such a ludicrous notion when one considers Kokomo Arnold's legendary 1935 recording of 'Sissy Man Blues', which features the refrain, 'Lord, if you can't send me no woman, please send me some sissy man.'

Perhaps the colour of the dress was symbolic in some way. It could mean so many things. Was it death maybe? Was it a reference to drugs – a white powder? Heroin? Cocaine? Was that a problem down here back then? Did it have a religious significance? What exactly was the implication here? Was it being used as a method of representing purity? Was it some sort of code?

That word seems to trigger another and then another and now Martin finally stumbles on to the truth. The actual meaning is so obvious. How could he have missed it?

At precisely the same instant as this sudden revelation, he hears once again Thelonious Monk negotiating his classic introduction to 'Little Rootie Tootie'. Fumbling to liberate his phone from his jacket pocket, he blurts a hurried, breathless, 'Hello.'

'Martin?'

'Hi, Clayton. I'm so glad you phoned.'

'Thank you, sir. That's most kind of you to say.'

Martin is far too agitated to respond to the pleasantry. 'It's not a dress he's singing about, Clayton – it's a robe, don't you see? It's a long white robe! What was I thinking? It was right there in front of me. It's not difficult, it's just totally ... you know ... *there* ... self-fucking-evident!'

'I think you have the advantage of me, sir,' says Clayton

with the slightest suggestion of a chuckle in his voice. 'What are we actually talking about here?'

'Sorry, Clayton, my fault.' Martin's voice now drains itself a fair measure of its gushing over-enthusiasm. 'It's just that I've been listening to the CD you did for me: the songs of Sweet Papa Stalebread.'

'Oh yeah?'

'Well, it's the second song in particular – "What You Want To Do That For?"'

Clayton groans. 'Oh yeah. Not one of his finest I fear.'

'I agree totally but he's singing about this long white dress, makes a real point about it, emphasises it all the way through the song. But I'm convinced he's not singing about a dress, Clayton; I'm positive he's not – he's talking about a robe! A long white robe. Don't you see? It's obvious. He's singing about the Klan.'

'That's very interesting,' says Clayton, utterly unconvinced by the notion but not wishing to offend, 'and it's quite a theory too.'

'You see, he says it makes him sad and makes him blue that the long white dress looks so right on you. That's what the song is about. He's addressing a member of the Ku Klux Klan. Maybe this person was a friend and he's become alienated from him and so he's asking him, "What you want to do that for?"'

'Well, like I say, Martin, it's a theory.'

'Look, the song was recorded in Arkansas, yeah, and the Klan was once pretty strong up there; am I right?'

'Whoa there, Martin, you might want to hold on to your pecker there for a moment or two! I know that a lot of people over there in Europe and Britain know a bit about the Ku Klux Klan and believe me, it's like some terrible stain on the South that we'll always have with us, but to be truthful with you, Martin, and you can check on this yourself, the Klan pretty much peaked in the twenties and by the early forties it was dying out. So maybe you'll want to bear that in mind?'

The tone of Clayton's slight rebuke renders the question rhetorical and when Martin continues his manner has become noticeably more reticent. 'OK, but I think it's definitely a possibility, bearing in mind the sentiment of "Georgia Blues" which was, after all, only a fairly short time afterwards.'

'I agree with you, Martin. Absolutely. But what can I say? It's an interesting theory. Although maybe, just maybe, you might be hearing things you want to hear and making connections that aren't really there.' Clayton falls silent for a moment as though waiting for some sort of response from Martin. When none is forthcoming he continues in significantly more jovial tones. 'But, hey, you're the writer, not me, right? If you think there's a story then there's a story. What do I know?'

'Thanks, Clayton.'

'Anyway, the reason I'm calling is that I had a bit of a think after you left and there's another chap in the Quarter here that I think may possibly be able to help you.'

'Really?' asks Martin with the tone of interest now returning to his voice.

'Yeah, there's an old fellow who busks on Royal Street with his grandson. He's got a big white beard nowadays and he usually wears some kind of wide-brimmed hat. You can't miss him. They play old blues tunes – not my kind of thing but the young guy plays a decent enough guitar and the old chap blows into that ancient harmonica of his. They usually set up outside that little supermarket they got there. You know the place I mean?

'Yeah I do, I know exactly the place you mean.'

'I'm sure you do. They're usually there around lunchtime. You see them there most days. Anyway, go and chat to the old fellow, buy him a beer maybe, tell him I sent you if you like.'

'OK, will do.'

'Fellow goes by the name of Juju Jones nowadays. You know, the tourists eat that sort of stuff up.'

'Thanks,' says Martin with a dry, mirthless laugh.

'Oh, present company excepted obviously.'

'You're too kind, sir.'

'Anyway, I don't remember what Juju's real name is but I do recall that he's some kind of kin with Bent Chesterton, maybe a nephew or a cousin, I'm not sure, but the two of them are definitely in some way *related*.' He stresses the word oddly as though there is something deeply suspicious about such things.

'I see.'

'They did work together back in the sixties I believe and I know Juju spent a couple of years touring with one of the very last medicine shows. So I'm pretty sure he'd be worth you talking to. If Tambo Bones left any more stories behind him then, believe me, Juju has probably heard every last one of them.'

Martin thanks Clayton for his call and promises to update him after he's spoken to Juju. He returns to his laptop and jots down a few more thoughts on 'What You Want To Do That For?'

It is not theory or interpretation, he thinks, it is meaning, and based on 'Recent Events' he would certainly cast himself as one who recognises the difference.

'You sure you're ready to do this?'

'Yeah, I think I am.'

It is two weeks after the funeral and Martin prepares himself to finally open the email that Mr Price sent him the evening before he met his death, probably no more than a couple of hours after the two men had parted company. He'd not checked his email inbox the following morning and only discovered it after he'd heard the news. He'd pushed the whole matter to the back of his mind and promised himself he would deal with it when he felt he was able.

This morning he has decided to keep his promise.

The cursor hovers over the envelope icon, where it has remained for a good five minutes, as he continues to regard the screen with a combination of fear and a sort of suspicious reverence. Bernice stands over him with both hands placed firmly on his shoulders, as though the anxiety of the moment might induce a state of sudden weightlessness in her partner, and Wes loiters nearby.

'Go on, Dad,' he mutters impatiently.

Bernice turns and frowns admonishingly at the boy who shrugs his shoulders with all the characteristic intransience of his generation.

'Look, if you don't feel up to doing—'

'No, I'm fine,' says Martin as he clicks decisively on the icon and the page loads instantly on the screen. He reads the email two or three times in complete silence.

Hi Martin,

Very excited about New Orleans I must say. Although I stoop to flatter myself I do believe I've just had a bit of a brainwave! I confess that since you left I have been indulging in a little sleuthing and have discovered that there are couple of music festivals on in October in New Orleans! Now I'm sure you would concur that it would be a singular treat to attend such an event. Perhaps we should modify our itinerary accordingly. You might wish to peruse that link I sent over yesterday for further information.

Oh, and here's another one for you to think about!

Just imagine you had to pick a letter of the alphabet and from that point onwards you are permitted to only listen to jazz that had been recorded under the

*leadership of a musician whose name began with that
particular letter. After making your selection, you can
never listen to anyone else ever again! It's a permanent
condition and there will be no further modifications
whatsoever.*

*Say you went for A, you can have Armstrong and
both Adderleys, Albert Ayler, Albert Ammons, Gene
Ammons, etc. You can't have M because I've already
chosen that for me! See, I've got Monk, Mingus, Mobley,
Morton, Montgomery, Morgan, McLean, Mulligan, Blue
Mitchell. I've got the whole history of jazz right there!
I could even go really modern with a bit of Marsalis
and Metheny!*

*Anyway, have a think about your choice and I'm sure
we'll have a frank and forthright discussion over lunch
tomorrow!*

See you then.

S.

*P.S. Will pick up some iTunes vouchers for Wes on
the way.*

There it was.

There was no great truth, no final revelation; it was not
a lasting testament and it did not translate easily into eulogy.
There was nothing you could read into the text that would
elevate it to the level of conclusion or summation. Its significance
was only that it was not in any way significant and yet
Martin finds something akin to a real sense of joy as he
reads again phrases like 'stoop to flatter', 'a singular treat'
and particularly 'indulging in a little sleuthing'. Like the tone
of a great tenor saxophonist, like Lester Young or Sonny
Rollins, there was in Mr Price's expressions something instantly
recognisable, reassuring and comforting in its own way. Part
of the skill was always to make such things sound deft and
natural and not the consequence of force or deliberation.

Such phrases, Martin decides, might also be regarded as the equivalent of a signature riff. All great jazzmen have signature riffs – little easily recognisable musical motifs they often work into their solos. Even a master improviser like Charlie Parker had a few he would use from time to time; he would often end a song by quoting, for reasons that remain obscure, the theme from 'Country Gardens'.

Buddy Bolden too had a particular phrase that he often played: a sort of *be* dah *be*-dah *be* dah *be*-dah and … and…

And now Martin feels more alone than ever.

Nobody will now have the remotest idea what he is going on about or exhibit the slightest interest in his drawing parallels with jazz or jazz musicians. Of course, Mr Price would have understood and would have immediately chimed in with some suggestions of his own. Jazz provided them with almost all their points of reference; it gave their lives some sort of meaning and permanence. You might have stood there in horror and bewilderment as troops were sent to Afghanistan and then Iraq but there was always 'Fables of Faubus', 'Blue Train' or 'Cool Struttin'' that took you somewhere else – somewhere far, far better. Love fades, people leave, children grow up but 'Straight No Chaser' will always sound like 'Straight No Chaser'.

But in 2009 the romance of jazz, like the romance of socialism (and anything else he had once believed to be blessed with roughly the same ideological purity) felt as though it belonged to some distant bygone era. Now he must resign himself to the fact that in the music there will be memory and pain. Indeed, there will be a sadness that he will only ever experience at that intensity in the music. Yet, strangely, he will ultimately find something approaching comfort in the very permanence of this condition.

Somewhere a voice is shouting.

'Phone!'

The voice is ignored but not easily deterred.

135

'I said, PHONE!'

Martin turns away from his computer screen and calls over his shoulder, 'Who is it, Wes?'

'A lady who wants to speak to you.'

'Thanks, kiddo, that's unbelievably helpful.'

Martin hurries out into the hall and takes the phone from his son, who glowers at him in the traditional manner. 'Hello,' he says in the most engaging tone he can muster.

'Good morning. Am I speaking to Martin Bonehouse?' The lady's voice is clear and measured with every syllable carefully stressed.

'Yes, that's me.'

'Is this a good time to talk?'

'It's fine,' he replies with a certain caution, acutely aware that in all probability the next line will be an inquiry about his internet provider or his gas supplier.

'That's great, Martin. Can I call you Martin?'

'Of course.'

'Well, my name is Angela Bingham-Hogg and we have actually met. In fact, we met quite recently, although I don't believe we were properly introduced.'

Martin's surprise at this statement is evident. 'Really?' he asks in a hurried gasp.

'Yes, we met at the funeral. I don't know if you remember. I complimented you on your speech and you told me about putting beer in your supermarket trolley.'

'OK,' says Martin, recalling vaguely the conversation.

'I told you that I was Stanley's neighbour and that I live in the same apartment block.'

'Oh yes, of course, I remember now. Lady with the ... the scarf, right?'

'Oh good I'm so glad you remember. Well, Martin, I'm calling because I need to make an appointment for the two of us to have a little chat. You see, Martin, you should know I was more than just a friend to Stanley.'

'Right,' says Martin slowly, the word deliberately drained of any hint of emotion.

'No, no, no, it was nothing like that. I merely mean that for the past couple of years I have also been acting as his solicitor.'

'I see,' says Martin, altogether uncertain if what he is now feeling is somehow related to disappointment. Very odd.

Ms Bingham-Hogg continues, 'So it is in this capacity that I need to see you. There's no great urgency but if we could make an appointment today for some mutually convenient time that would be very helpful.'

'Of course,' says Martin and then adds cautiously, 'What is all this actually about?'

'Naturally, I will explain the matter in greater detail at our meeting but rather than leave you worrying unduly I will simply state that it is regarding Stanley's estate and the will he recently altered. There is absolutely nothing for you to be concerned about but there are things we need to discuss.'

'I understand.'

'Now, we can arrange to meet at the office. I'm a senior partner here at Cartwrights. You might know us; we've got premises in Castle Street, on the same side of the road as that little gallery and opposite the big music shop.'

'I know the place.' Martin smiles privately to himself. Cartwrights is actually located next door to the kebab shop – a detail that Ms Bingham-Hogg seemed reluctant to mention.

'We could meet here or if you prefer we could meet at Stanley's flat. I recall him telling me that you had a spare key.'

'Yes, I did. I mean yes, I have.' Tenses again – God, how long does this normally last?

'So, we'll arrange a meeting at the flat then. Would that be OK with you?'

Martin is slightly taken aback by the suggestion but hears himself saying, 'I don't know. I suppose so...'

'Good. So how soon would we be able to meet up? I can do any evening this week.'

Martin thinks for a moment. 'Tomorrow? Or is that too soon?'

'No, tomorrow is fine. I'll be finished here by five at the latest and so shall we say six? Would that be OK?'

'That's fine.'

'I also have a key so if I'm there before you I'll let myself in.'

'Right, I'll see you tomorrow.'

Angela Bingham-Hogg hangs up without saying goodbye, which Martin regards as a trait of her profession rather than a singular indication of impoliteness. He pays the matter no further mind and returns to the computer to read his email again.

At just after six o'clock the following evening Martin is leaning against the wall in the hallway opposite the entrance to Mr Price's flat. After giving the matter some consideration he has eventually decided on his dark Levi's, a jacket and a collarless shirt. This would hopefully convey the idea that while he fully appreciates that the meeting might be a casual, informal affair there are certain conventions that should also be observed. He has remained in roughly this same spot for about ten minutes. He'd arrived a little ahead of schedule and had got as far as taking the front door key out of his pocket. He'd been about to put it in the lock when he noticed his hand had started shaking again. Mr Price was not behind the door, he couldn't hear him moving about, Mr Price wasn't in his kitchen getting beers out of the fridge and he wasn't going through rows and rows of CDs looking for that one track he so urgently wanted to play.

There is just space now.

Too much space, too much air, too much silence, too much oxygen and Martin doesn't feel able to proceed any further on his own.

Finally, at about ten past six, he hears footsteps on the

staircase drawing nearer. Instinctively, he places his left hand over his right.

'Hello, Martin. I'm so sorry to have kept you,' says Ms Bingham-Hogg. 'My conference ran over a little. I do apologise.' She is a little shorter than Martin recalls and prettier too. 'Did you forget your key?'

'No, I thought I'd ... wait for you.'

'Well, that's very gallant of you, I must say,' she says in a tone that might have teetered on the flirtatious.

At the third attempt she manages to unlock the door and Martin follows her into the flat.

'I popped down last night actually to drop all the files off ready for us. I put the heating on as well and gave the whole place a bit of an airing.'

'Good idea,' says Martin vaguely. Once he is over the threshold he suddenly feels as though some great burden has just been lifted from him. Glancing around the flat, which is somehow both strange and familiar to him today, his mouth contorts into an awkward, almost apologetic smile. There is space and silence here but that is only part of it. Far beyond anything that he might have hastily dismissed as bereavement or even nostalgia, Martin can only liken the experience to one of suddenly feeling 'safe'.

'Would you like some tea? Coffee?'

Actually, what Martin would really like at this precise moment in time would be some loud, angry John Coltrane blasting out of the speakers. One of his classic Impulse recordings, something like 'Chasin' the Trane', maybe – something to fill the space. Instead, he hears himself saying, 'Yes please, a coffee would be nice.'

Angela Bingham-Hogg is evidently not someone who believes in the value of small talk or the conversational advantage of the preamble, for as soon as she hands Martin his coffee she opens the larger of the two files that are currently sitting on Mr Price's dining table with a pragmatic, 'Right then.'

It is an action that Martin regards with a sudden sense of vague trepidation. 'Is that *all* to do with Mr Price?' he asks timidly.

'Oh yes.'

'Is it terribly complicated?'

'Not complicated as such – rather, it is very carefully detailed.'

'I see,' says Martin, gradually moving his right hand away from the table and out of sight where the trembling might be less observed.

He listens as Ms Bingham-Hogg explains that Mr Price had regularly updated his will, making changes a couple of times every year as his circumstances altered or modified. The most recent update had taken place a few weeks prior to his death. It was something, she adds, over which he was always particularly meticulous. It was demonstrably extremely important that his affairs were always kept in order and up to date.

She now asks Martin if he knows about Sarah.

'His sister?'

'Yes.'

'Of course. I met her on several occasions. I even went with him to her funeral a couple of years ago.'

'Well, up until her death Sarah would have been the sole beneficiary from Stanley's will, there being no other surviving relatives.'

'That's what I would have assumed, probably.'

'As it was, she predeceased him and he inherited from her.'

'Really?' asks Martin in a tone that manages to bypass surprise and arrive instead at a sort of affronted cynicism. 'I never knew that. He never mentioned anything.'

The solicitor smiles knowingly. 'No, Stan absolutely hated talking about money, didn't he?'

'Yeah, yeah, I'll say.'

'So, in addition to the original estate, there is also this additional inheritance from his sister, which I believe he never touched. It represents quite a large amount of money in fact.'

Martin nods to indicate that he's paying attention but can think of absolutely nothing to say.

'Sarah owned a couple of properties in South London, in the Streatham area I believe. They generated a tidy sum as rental units but after her death, Stan realised that he was sitting on some very valuable real estate. There was also the additional burden of managing and maintaining the properties and so within six months of inheriting them he'd sold them.'

'So this would have been fairly recently, right?

'I can find the exact date if you wish?'

'No, no, that's OK.'

'As you know, he had one or two very small vices but on the whole he lived very modestly. The flat was paid for and he just left all the money from the property sales in a high interest account and as far as I'm aware he just forgot about it.'

'I didn't know about any of this.'

'I know you didn't,' says Bingham-Hogg, pausing briefly before adding, 'He didn't want you to know.'

Martin's eyes flash while the rising pitch of his voice betrays panic rather than anger. 'Why didn't he want me to know?'

'Because it's all yours now.'

'What?'

'All of it. Everything. This flat, all the financial assets and the entire estate. He left it all to you. After his sister died, we rewrote his entire will and he named you as the sole beneficiary.'

Martin covers his face with his hand as though attempting to mask his expression. 'Fucking Hell! Oh, I'm so sorry.'

'Don't apologise. Under the circumstances it's a perfectly reasonable response.'

Martin sips his coffee medicinally but without recourse to further expletives he can think of absolutely nothing further to say.

'There are, as I mentioned earlier, a number of details and

conditions in the will that you need to be aware of. He did leave very precise instructions.'

As though feeling the need to reacquaint himself with his friend as he recalls him, Martin glances around the room and eventually he allows himself a brief smile. 'Yeah, I can believe that.'

'OK, I'll try and make this as brief as possible as I know it's a lot to take in.' She opens the smaller of the two files and scans the top document. 'Right, Martin, just out of interest, are you in full-time employment at the moment?'

'Not really. I do a few articles now and then. Mainly features and magazine work but it's not steady employment any more by any means: certainly nothing like a regular income. For a long time, I stayed at home looking after our son while Bernice, that's my partner, went out to work. The arrangement has sort of just carried on after the boy started school.'

'A house-husband? Do people still use that expression nowadays?'

Martin manages a reflective chuckle. 'Well, I haven't heard it in a long time.' However, he can assert with reasonable authority that, following a public humiliation over breakfast earlier in the day, no one in the whole, hip, happening world refers to headphones as 'cans' anymore.

'So, Bernice is a teacher, isn't she?'

'That's right. At a primary school in Dover.'

'And your son is, let me see, I've got it down here somewhere. Yes, here it is ... Wes? Is that right?'

'Yes.'

'What a charming name. Anyway, in this clause here, Stan refers to him as his Godson. Is that correct?'

'Yes, that's true.'

'OK, so is he a bright boy, Wes? Does he do well at school?'

'Yeah, he's pretty smart. He's usually in the top stream.'

Ms Bingham-Hogg smiles and looks unduly pleased with herself. 'Oh good, because there is a clause in the will that sets aside £50,000 in trust for Wes to pay for his further education or for a deposit on a house if he chooses a different path in his life.'

'I'm sorry,' says Martin, pressing his hand into his chest and gasping in a series of short rapid bursts, 'but I don't know if I'm actually taking all this in.'

She leans over the table and brushes his arm with her fingertips. 'You're doing very well, Martin. It won't be long now.'

Martin can still taste salt in the back of his mouth and so he reaches for his coffee once more.

'Now, when he last revised his will, which was, let me see...' She turns over a couple more documents. 'Here we are – the start of last month. Anyway, during that last revision he inserted a clause at the start of the will. Apparently, you have written a book, is that right?'

'Yes, well, I sort of... It's just a manuscript at the moment.'

'Now this is important. This book has never been published, is that correct?'

'No, like I say, it's just a manuscript.'

'Did Stan ever read this manuscript?'

'Yes, he did, a number of times actually.'

'Well, he must have thought very highly of it because he has made it a condition of the will that if the book has not ever been published you withdraw funds from the estate as soon as possible and get your book into print. What's the name of it, if you don't mind me asking?'

'An Unhealthy Interest,' says Martin automatically.

'I see, well, that's quite a catchy title I must say. So what's it about then, this book of yours?'

'Um... It's a sort of love story I suppose.'

'That sounds very *interesting*.' She smiles awkwardly as though taking private delight in her own inference. 'You must make sure you send me a signed copy when it's finished.'

143

It is roughly at this moment that, having experienced the entire range of human emotions in the past half an hour, Martin descends into a kind of disconnected numbness. Mr Price, Wes, his novel, all the things that matter to him, all the things in his life that were organised and certain have suddenly broken free of their moorings to revolve and spin in the light and the space above his head. There was no logic, no reason, no order now, no obvious narrative, no beginning and no end, not linear but circular. Spiral even. He pictures comic strips and paintings by Chagall, panels on a medieval stained-glass window – a story built around a central figure. But the central figure is no longer constant! It keeps shifting and moving, not contained anymore within its own form or boundaries. The landscape is dark, then it's light, now it's dark again – flashing like a warning sign. He feels his eyes flickering – an indication that a migraine is probably imminent. Somewhere in a different room in a different town Ms Bingham-Hogg continues to talk and at some point, he hears something about how he will have to attend a further conference at Cartwrights sometime in the next week or so.

'Yeah... I understand,' he says eventually.

'Actually, you may be interested to know, this whole evening constitutes one of his requests too. He asked that the solicitor handling his will should offer the benefactor the opportunity of having the will read at the flat. He thought the whole business would probably be stressful enough anyway.'

It is only when a tear falls down his cheek and onto the table in front of him that Martin realises he has been crying for the past few minutes.

Ms Bingham-Hogg gathers up her files and stands up. 'I'll give you a moment, Martin. I'll be out in the hall.'

'OK... Yeah... Thanks.'

The most curious thing occurs about five minutes later. Ms Bingham-Hogg is still outside in the hall checking her Blackberry for messages when she hears what sounds like one half of a conversation coming through the open door to Mr Price's flat. She is not altogether certain about what exactly she is overhearing but she hears quite clearly a faltering male voice saying precisely the following:

'It's got to be B. hasn't it? You had to get the best for yourself, didn't you? You old sly fucker! But I'm going to go for B. You know why? I'll tell you. Check this out – Basie, Kenny Burrell, Donald Byrd, Bechet, Beiderbecke, Clifford Brown *and* Art Blakey. Not bad, right? OK, it leans a little towards hard bop maybe but that would suit me just fine. I can even throw in the perennially underrated Tina Brooks! And of course if I need to go really modern I've got Braxton too, so that's pretty much covered.'

Not wishing to intrude any further, she turns and steps quietly away.

AN UNHEALTHY INTEREST

Chapter Nine

For the rest of that summer I wore long-sleeved T-shirts, the things that my mum used to always buy me but which I never used to wear. They were stupid awful things with pictures on which she used to buy for me from that catalogue that raises money for her church. They were always in these foul bright colours like orange and turquoise – the colours you wear when you're a child! I used to like to wear dark colours. I thought they suited me; I used to like black or dark brown or navy blue. I didn't like her buying clothes on my behalf but it was something I was never interested in doing myself. So I let her do it, I suppose, only because it saved me the aggravation. I absolutely hate shopping for clothes; I hate the way people in those shops look at you. Like they're so much better than you or just better looking than you! To be honest, I've never been that concerned about what people wear – people think it's so bloody important what shop you bought something from or how much your shoes cost, but it just seems like a stupid waste of time to me. You could do so much more with your time. Think about it! Just imagine one day you'll be dead and all you'll have to show for your life is a big pile of shoes. Shoes that no longer matter to anyone – just like you! Anyway, I used to wear the same old things until they fell to bits and that suited me down to the ground. Often, I'd wear clothes that were dirty because I used to hate it when my mum washed my clothes. She'd always say that she'd seen disgusting filthy stains in my pants and that she'd tell the minister at her church all about me. I'm not sure if she ever said anything but it wouldn't surprise me if she did. She was always threatening to do things like that. Some days, during the winter, when she went out to one of her Bible classes, I would wash my clothes by hand and dry them on the radiator before she got back. In the summer, because the radiators were turned off, it wasn't as easy so I usually didn't bother trying. It was actually easier during the summer I'm talking about because I started wearing all those long-sleeved T-shirts that had been piling up and I seemed to have loads of them in my wardrobe. She never asked why I'd suddenly started wearing them and to be honest, I don't think she actually paid much attention to stuff like that. She was always much more interested in Jesus than in me. Actually, I wonder what Jesus would have said if I told him what was happening. Jesus, I'd have said, there's this girl who's moved in – well, actually she's staying next door at the moment – and she's fourteen and every time I see her in their garden I have to watch her. It's not always easy because my mum is often gardening out at the back of our house and I have to make sure she doesn't glance up towards the spare bedroom and see me standing there right up tight next to the curtains where I usually stand. I'm sure she'll catch me one day and then that will be the end of everything. Lucy is so beautiful and funny and she has these freckles just here on her nose and on her cheek and sometimes she pops in for a chat and I know it sounds really trite and pathetic, but it just makes me feel so happy. I mean really happy, a sort of deep, deep contentment that I've never known before – like it's the best thing that's ever happened to me in my whole life and it's as though suddenly I forget all the sadness and all the pain; like all that happened to someone else, someone I've heard of but don't really know that well. But then it happens. Then I start to think what I'd like to do to her and it's like so vivid in my mind I can feel the warmth of her skin beneath my fingers, I smell her hair and almost taste her mouth. It just takes me over and I know it's wrong and I know she's only fourteen and I know it's forbidden but I can't help myself. I thought you'd understand, Jesus, because aren't you supposed to know all about temptation? Maybe you can sympathise? So, I just have to touch myself; it's the only way I can cope with all the things that are going through my mind but it's wrong; it's so wrong but I can't overcome any of it. So that's when I get my craft knife and I cut myself. It's always somewhere on my left arm but it's been going on for a few weeks now and it's been happening a lot and to be honest, the arm is a bit of a mess and one of the cuts looks like it might be infected; it's oozing pus and everything. Maybe one day I'll have to have the whole arm amputated. Recently, I've started to really think sometimes that's probably how it will all end. But can't you see that I have to do this? It's not as if I have any choice. It constantly reminds me of those urges and it helps me to understand. Didn't people do things like that in the Bible? Now I have to wear long-sleeved T-shirts so my mum can't see my arm. Is this my punishment, Jesus, or is it more like – what's that word that people like my mum say? – atonement? I don't know anymore, it's all

147

got really confusing now. Is this how it's going to be for the rest of my life? Sometimes, I actually wondered if I would have been happier if I'd never set eyes on her. I used to tell myself this and then she'd come to the door and it was like she always came in the afternoon when my mum was at her Bible class and just for a moment I'd think about pretending to be out, but I'd know she was there just the other side of our front door, just a couple of feet away from me and that she was just so beautiful. And I always found it easy to talk to her and she really seemed to enjoy chatting about stuff and sometimes she asked my opinion about things. Sometimes she actually asked me for advice and nobody had ever done that! She was talking to me about school and her GCSE choices one day and then she started asking me about the school I used to go to. I told her I didn't remember it clearly but that one day I'd just decided the whole thing was a massive waste of time and I just stopped attending. She thought this was funny but it was the truth as I recall it. The school didn't seem that bothered and probably just assumed there were problems at home and that I'd be back again when they were sorted out. I do remember a couple of phone calls, maybe a letter or two, which my mum tore up without reading, but nobody at the time seemed to be all that concerned to be honest. The truth is that I was never any good at learning and used to have real problems paying attention. I could follow what was going on for about ten minutes but then I'd just let my mind wander and just think about all the stuff I had in my head so I'd lose all sense of the lesson. I would just be thinking about all sorts of things and sometimes I can actually remember falling asleep on my desk! What did the teacher say? Get this! Nothing – never said a word! But I always hated every single one of my teachers; they were all absolutely useless. But I think they probably all hated me, too. I didn't exactly make their jobs easy for them! For some reason she found this extremely

*amusing. She did that little laugh she does that shows off
those brilliant dimples in her cheeks. But then I warned her
that she shouldn't make the same mistake as me and that
school was actually important. I told her she was a bright
girl and she must study really hard. She smiled at me as
though she agreed with me and then she leant forward and
I could see she wasn't wearing a bra under her vest. I caught
a glimpse. I hadn't planned it; it just happened. I don't think
she noticed me looking but it started me thinking about it
again and I couldn't stop myself. You see until I met Lucy
I just didn't really think like that. In fact, the idea of sex
had always made me feel sick. I used to have some of my
dad's old magazines hidden under my bed and I used to look
at them at night or when my mum was out. They weren't
those really bad, really rude ones; they weren't men and
women and stuff – just women on their own. I think they
must have been from a few years back. All the women in
the magazine would always look slutty and mean and they'd
be naked and just lying on the floor with their legs wide
open and all I could ever think about would be how disgusting
they would smell. I imagined a horrible acrid sweaty smell
coming from their crotch region and I would just want to
throw up. I would never want to touch anyone like that and
the pictures used to put me off the whole idea. Lucy was
different; she wasn't like that. As soon as she left, I told
myself I wasn't going to touch myself and so I just got
undressed and looked at myself in the hall mirror as though,
by watching myself, it was like my mum watching me and
I'd be able to stop myself doing anything. I just felt stupid
and disgusted that the only function of my body was to
emphasise the impurity of my thoughts. I thought about the
moment when she had first leant forward and imagined how
the situation could have developed from there; she could have
taken my hand and made me touch her. I turned away from
the mirror and it was like I could actually feel her skin and*

suddenly everything was beyond my control. That was the worse one ever! Roughly at that moment I heard my mum's key in the door. I ran upstairs, took my craft knife and cut deeply into the already infected wound. It really hurt. It hurt far more than all the others and that's what I'd wanted. Then I rummaged in my drawer for a plaster and took another long-sleeved T-shirt out of the wardrobe.

8

JuJu Jones

In the persona of Sweet Papa Stalebread, he had, in 1940, already recorded a song that seemed to suggest a certain awareness of race issues. Whilst lacking the overt and unequivocal message of 'Georgia Blues', it does hint that he regarded music as a means of putting his particular message across. In the tune 'What You Want To Do That For?' the singer makes a series of references to a long white dress, which, in context, appears

Martin looks at this final word and wonders if what he still rather fancifully terms his author's voice is beginning to sound tentative and uncertain. Maybe he should be more assertive in his speculations?

the singer makes a series of references to a white dress, which, in context, could only refer to the white dress(code) of the Ku Klux Klan.

Although it was true that he'd found nothing on the internet to support this hypothesis, searching for 'Ku Klux Klan' and 'white dress' generated surprisingly few hits and most of these were links to a painting by Norman Rockwell entitled *The Problem We All Live With*. Although Rockwell was not an artist one would automatically associate with the civil rights struggle, his painting makes its point clearly enough as it commemorates the day when a five-year-old girl became the first African American pupil to attend a white elementary school in the South. However, the letters KKK are clearly

151

visible at the far left of the picture on the wall behind the girl and there are four US Marshalls flanking her front and rear. The Marshalls are depicted with their heads cropped out of frame and this has led some commentators to speculate that it was the artist's intention to suggest that the four men are all members of the Klan and we are simply not seeing their hoods.

Furthermore, this historic moment took place at the William Frantz Elementary School right here in New Orleans.

While none of this could be read as an actual confirmation of the 'white dress theory' he was seeking, he was left feeling that, on some level, his ideas were somehow coalescing with other ideas, sharing a wavelength and harmonising with some great essential truth.

And that was good enough for him.

Sweet Papa Stalebread's lyrics are possibly too ambiguous or too covert to warrant prolonged attention. In fact, they may only be considered relevant in the light of the later recordings. 'What You Want To Do That For?' is a simple song, very clearly in the hokum tradition and consequently, it is easy to overlook; yet it has a certain period charm. It reminds the listener

'Shit!' Martin jabs the delete key with a sudden angry relish. The gesture is a timely interruption and serves as a sort of personal declaration and confession that he is just about to lapse once again into writing about a piece of music by likening it to another piece of music – something he is still keen to avoid if at all possible.

As though seeking alternative inspiration, he rummages once again through the folder of Clayton's original notes and having found a short paragraph that refers to Tambo working as a caretaker at a school during the early 1960s, he abandons the previous paragraph and tries a different approach.

Hokum as a musical genre has suffered from a decline in interest in the past sixty years. Partly, one imagines, this stems from its association with minstrelsy and other archaic musical traditions. Furthermore, with rare exceptions, comic or funny songs are rarely durable and seldom have any life beyond their moment. However, had there been a revival in interest in hokum music in the sixties, alongside the folk and blues booms, it is fascinating to speculate upon the fate of Oscar Oliver Brightwater, if he'd started appearing at festivals and begun playing his music to a whole new generation – one that surely would have fully understood and appreciated 'Georgia Blues'. So picture him without his burnt cork makeup, as an older man on stage at Newport, alongside Pete Seeger or in a cramped cellar in Greenwich Village with the young Bob Dylan. It is a powerful image and it's very sad, therefore, that having abandoned music entirely, he ended his life in such obscurity. As far as we know, he made

Martin stops suddenly and turns his attention once again towards the open folder on the desk; there is an uncertainty in his expression now or maybe a mild confusion. He scans a couple of pages then a couple more but his search is a fruitless one. Subtracting six hours from the time on his laptop would make it currently 07.26 and he makes a mental note to call Clayton in an hour's time when he is more confident the man will be awake.

Martin now gets dressed and makes his way downstairs to the dining room where he eats his breakfast with uncharacteristic solemnity and reflects upon the apparent oversight that has recently been brought to his attention. How the fuck has he managed to overlook something like that? How can he even entertain the notion of a biography without being in possession of such a fundamental fact? Was he really just *that* desperate to throw himself into a new project? There is some truth in this, certainly.

'Idiot,' he says by way of conclusion. He sips his coffee and repeats the word to himself. 'Idiot.'

Now he is shaking his head indulgently as though finding

his own weaknesses endearing in some way. Fortunately, he is unobserved.

Ten minutes or so later, Martin is back in his room again. With his phone now firmly clasped to his ear, he paces the perimeter of the small rug at the foot of his bed.

'Come on, Clayton, pick up.' The words are forced through clenched teeth and to a person unfamiliar with Martin's current situation there might be the suggestion that this is a man perhaps trying a little too hard to enjoy the drama of the moment. Of course, there would be a degree of veracity in such an observation and Martin would certainly concur that dramas of one's own creation are infinitely preferable to the kind forced upon the unsuspecting and unprepared.

'Come on, Clayton, pick up the – oh bollocks!'

'Hi there. You're through to the voicemail of Clayton Palmer...' On the telephone, his voice is warm and even-toned, genial even, with just a vague hint of the mildest self-assurance. 'If you'd like to record a message...'

Martin thinks about hanging up but changes his mind at the last moment.

'Hey, Clayton. It's Martin. Um... I've come across a bit of a problem here. I'm going to need some more, er ... information from you before I can carry on. So, I'm heading over to the Quarter now to see if I can grab a few minutes with this JuJu Jones fellow. I'll call you later or I'll drop by if that's OK.' He then adds apologetically, almost as an afterthought, 'Er ... bye then.'

At a distance of about 200 yards, the riff begins to reveal itself for the first time. He walks a further 50 yards up Royal Street and the riff is now unmistakable. It is 'Dust My Broom' (or one of its dozen or so variants) as originally recorded by Elmore James. 'Dust My Broom' is one of the undisputed classics of post-war blues and a virtual cornerstone of the repertoire. Ubiquitous is probably the word. In fact, you can postulate with near certainty that in all likelihood there is a band playing it tonight at a pub or a bar or a club that's within walking distance of wherever you are. For an apparently simple song, 'Dust My Broom' exhibits a great inherent paradox – namely, it is almost impossible to play badly, yet it is incredibly difficult to play well.

At a distance of about 70 yards, however, Martin is reassured that he is currently experiencing one of the better interpretations as the singer repeats that he *'don't want no woman who wants every downtown man she meets'*.

According to tradition, and this is confirmed by his own personal observations, the Quarter is not generally known as an early riser and habitually prefers to slumber until lunchtime. So, on this particular morning, as he nears the junction of Royal and St Peters, he is surprised to see a dozen or more people watching this oddly matched pair of street musicians blasting out Elmore James covers. Not simply the loose coalition of the curious or the collection of passers-by or tourists he had envisioned; there is immediately the sense that this is a genuine audience and everyone appears to be completely engaged with the music. This is precisely the moment when another basic, fundamental aspect to New Orleans reveals itself to Martin. One would imagine in such a place where there is so much music to be heard that people would inevitably become blasé and bored with it all. But the absolute opposite is true and, be they tourists or residents, they all seem to share that same passionate enthusiasm to absorb every last available little riff.

As he joins the crowd, Martin can now see that the musicians are set up in the road a few yards away from the entrance to Rouse's Supermarket who, judging by the numbers of open cans and bottles in evidence, are doing a brisk trade this morning.

Matching might be overstressing the point, but the two musicians are dressed in *complementary* blue denim dungarees, a detail which makes Martin feel slightly uncomfortable. This morning, after a few days' involvement with the subject, he finds that he regards their sartorial choices as ambiguous at best. He can't help it; the dungarees remind him of plantation songs and whether intentionally or ironically, it could be argued that the duo were in their own way directly referencing aspects of the minstrel tradition.

He pushes the idea out of his mind and concentrates on the music instead.

'...*and my friends can't get in my room*,' sings the guitarist.

He is by some considerable margin the much younger of the two men and at this point, as though seeking confirmation, instruction or approval, he glances sideways at his companion. The two men make fleeting eye contact and then, perfectly on cue, there is one of those classic Jamesian turnarounds and the song concludes.

'Thank you very, very much,' the young guitarist says. 'That was an oldie by the late, the great, Elmore James.'

Martin joins in the applause which, considering the hour, seems boisterous and entirely genuine. The singer then reminds everyone that they have their CD for sale but Martin is no longer looking at him; he is instead staring at the older man, the one with the bashed-in fedora and the white beard. The man who, until a matter of seconds ago, had been blowing into a harmonica. He looks around randomly at the faces in the crowd, there in his expression the sort of vague disinterest that teeters on condescension, but then he breaks into the warmest of smiles, revealing a few missing teeth in the process.

'We'd now like to play for you a song that is a particular favourite of ours...'

Putting a precise age to the man would be difficult, he thinks, sixty-something? Certainly no younger.

'...and we do sincerely hope you enjoy it too.'

Perhaps nearer seventy? Or even older? He has never been very good at guessing approximate ages, particularly of those older than himself. On this particular morning this is all it takes; the connection is quickly re-established and he finds himself thinking once again about Mr Price. Meanwhile, the guitarist and the old man exchange a sequence of mysterious gestures and nods that conclude when the younger man strums a single open chord of E major and begins to sing.

'*Bay ay ay ay ... bee...*'

And then, right on the beat, the duo are straight into their reading of Sonny Boy Williamson's 'Bring it on Home'. Again they stay pretty close to the original recording and the old man's harmonica is therefore given far greater prominence. The song remains to this day one of the genre's quintessential train songs and the locomotive pulse of the guitar and harmonica is as irresistible as it ever was – if the reaction of this particular audience is anything to go by.

Martin looks at the old man again. How many times has he played this song? Hundreds probably, maybe thousands? Yet he is still so involved with the music, so focussed on his art, playing as though every memory, every feeling, every moment of his life was being dragged out of him and then channelled through that tiny instrument. He stands for a moment, hardly daring to move, let alone breathe, as the guitar and the vocals fade into the slight morning chill until all that remains is that single sound – beautiful and essential and pure.

'Thank you very much; you're very kind,' says the singer at the song's conclusion a couple of minutes later. 'You're a truly great audience, seriously! We love y'all. So please give generously. Remember, the more you pay the better we play! My name is Little Vee and this fine gentleman on my right is Mr JuJu Jones.' A single loud cheer goes up at this point and a number of heads turn in Martin's direction.

'Thank you for that, sir! Well, we're going to take a fifteen minute break and then we'll be right back with you. So don't y'all be going no place!'

The audience now begins to disperse and Martin chooses

his moment carefully. As soon as the guitarist abandons his seat, he steps forward and dropping a couple of ten dollar bills into the bucket marked *Tips*, he helps himself to a CD entitled 'Little Vee and JuJu Jones – Wheredeyat!!!' Then, after placing the item carefully in his pocket, he asks tentatively, 'Mr Jones?'

The old man is currently preoccupied examining his various harmonicas. 'That's me,' he says without looking up.

'I er ... really enjoyed the music,' says Martin clumsily.

This prompts a nod but still he doesn't look up. 'That's good.'

Martin shifts his weight from one foot to the other. 'I wondered if I could possibly talk to you about something for a couple of minutes?'

A pair of dark brown eyes, unequivocal and intense, now burn into Martin's face as JuJu Jones looks up and acknowledges the man standing in front of him for the first time. 'And what might that be regarding?'

'Well, I was given your name by Clayton Palmer.'

The harmonica player suppresses a chuckle. 'Y'mean Clayton sent you?'

Martin smiles awkwardly. 'Yes, that's right. You ... er ... know Clayton then?'

He throws his head back in a gesture of disbelief. 'Everyone knows Clayton, man!'

'Really?'

'Yeah, that cat's strange even for New Orleans, man! When they need to raise the bar on crazy, Clayton's your man.'

Martin chuckles, mainly out of politeness, uncertain if the remark is intended to be taken literally or otherwise. 'Well, he speaks very highly of you,' he says for want of something to say.

'Is that so?'

The old man's question does not seem to require an answer and furthermore it would appear to signify the end of this particular exchange – a point that is not lost on Martin.

'Clayton says you knew a piano player called Bent Chesterton,' he announces in hurried, nervous tones. 'Is that right?'

JuJu Jones takes a deep wheezy breath. 'Shit, is that what this is about?'

'Well, partly,' says Martin.

The old man pauses and appears to be appraising the situation for a moment or two. 'Tell you what then, you go into that store there,' he gestures with his thumb towards Rouse's. 'You get me a pack of Marlboro and a couple of bottles of that Abita Golden. Bring 'em back and I'll tell you what you want to know.'

Martin does as requested and returns a few minutes later. 'There you go,' he says, handing over the brown paper carrier with minimum ceremony as though anxious to dispense with this tedious diversion as quickly as possible and pick up their conversation.

The old man opens the bag and peers at its contents suspiciously. 'You took your time.'

'There was a queue, all right?'

'Yeah, yeah, there's always a damn *queue*...' JuJu's voice trails off into a belligerent mumble and Martin seizes the opportunity.

'Anyway, sir,' he says, adapting to the formality of the local vernacular with relative ease, 'you were going to tell me about Bent Chesterton.'

'Well, firstly we don't want to be going around disrespectin' the deceased and all that. Poor man is dead now so be grateful if you call him Gus Chesterton, that's the man's name and he never cared much for that nickname when he was alive. So it's proper to show some manners here!'

Martin holds up his hands up in an instinctively defensive gesture that could be regarded as either interruption or surrender. 'OK, I understand perfectly. I apologise. So tell me about Gus.'

'Yeah... Gus was kin on my mother's side. His brother was actually married to one of my cousins. Gus was maybe ten years or so older than me but I knew the man pretty well, y'know? The man was a great musician, played all kinds of instruments too.'

'But he was mainly known as a piano player, right? Clayton reckons he was one of the best.'

The old man finally manages to locate a bottle opener in one of his ample pockets and opens one of the Abitas. He then carefully returns the bottle to the paper carrier. 'Clayton might be a fool but he's not stupid,' he says as he takes a long reflective swig from the bottle. 'Yeah, Gus was the finest I ever heard; he could play any music in any style. Seriously, you could drop him into any old session and no matter what you be playing, straight jazz, blues, country, rock 'n' roll, anything you can think of, Gus would instantly put his mark on it and make it a hundred, maybe a thousand times better. Heard it happen so many times. The man never got the credit he deserved.' He pauses for a moment to add emphasis to his sneering conclusion. 'He never got no damn money neither!'

'That's really sad.'

'Yeah, well, show me a musician with a happy ending and I'll show you a white boy!'

This is not a turn in the conversation that Martin particularly welcomes and he is keen to change the subject. 'Did you ever do any recordings with him?'

JuJu takes another gulp of his beer. 'Oh shit, yeah! We played on dozens of records together over the years. Back in the... Well, it must have been the late sixties we played together on a few of Alligator Red's records. I tell you, that was one fine little combo. They called us The Swamp Boys back then – Alligator Red and the Swamp Boys – and you know something? All those records we made, they all sound pretty damn good even now! Mainly because of Gus's playing. I'm telling you that man used to play his ass off and if you were in the same room as him he'd somehow make you play your ass off, too!'

'Yeah, he sounds amazing,' says Martin, subtly glancing at his watch, 'but I know you'll have to start playing again in a few minutes and there's another person I'm really interested in who played with Gus back in the forties.'

JuJu snorts derisively. 'That's well before my time, son. Just how old do you think I am?' he asks without humour or flippancy.

'No, sir, I understand that, really I do. I just wondered if you'd heard of him. He used a number of different names. His real name was Oscar Oliver Brightwater.'

'What was that?'

'Oscar Oliver Brightwater.'

JuJu shakes his head. 'Sorry I don't –'

Having come this far, Martin is not about to be deterred. 'Like I said, he used a number of names, like Tambo Bones.'

This time the name registers with the old man. 'Tambo Bones, you say?'

'Yes, so you know the name?'

''Course I know the name!' He breaks into a chuckle which soon transforms itself into a cough. 'Although to be truthful with you,' he says after regaining his composure, 'I ain't heard it for a while.'

'He was a singer and composer...'

JuJu takes instant offence to this remark and makes no attempt to disguise it. 'Yeah I know who he is, son. You don't need to tell me. I ain't that far gone yet, y'know!'

'I'm sorry I didn't mean to –'

'And why exactly would you be interested in old Tambo? It was that funny, hokey, old-timey kind of music.'

'I realise that, but Gus played with him, didn't he?'

'Yeah, he did a couple of times. In fact, I'm pretty sure the first time Gus made it onto a record it was one of Tambo's.'

Martin's eyes widen. 'Yeah, absolutely; it was the 78 of "Georgia Blues".'

'Well, there you go.'

Martin now notices that the guitarist is making his way towards them. 'Did you ever see Tambo perform?'

'Oh yeah, a few times but this was much later. Maybe in the seventies sometime? I saw him playing at some barbeque thing once near Lawrence Square on Magazine, I think it was. He was playing in a sort of Cajun band and he was using a different name.'

'You don't recall...?'

'No, I'm sorry, son. I can't help you there. But it was definitely him because I was with Gus and he introduced us. He always seemed like a fine, straight-up kind of feller to me!'

At this point the guitarist joins the conversation. 'Hey, Jay, you ready to start again?'

'Yeah, I guess so, just 'bout.' He turns to Martin. 'I reckon we're near done here, son, that right?'

'Of course. I'm sorry I took up so much of your time.'

'That's fine. Anything else you need you know where I am.'

'Thanks.' Martin leans over and shakes the old man's hand and then as he is turning to leave, he freezes for a moment. 'There's just one tiny thing you might be able to help me with. I've been trying to contact Clayton but maybe you know the answer. It was a really stupid oversight on my part; I mean I know he was born in 1917 or thereabouts. Apparently, there is some local legend that he was the last child born in Storyville...'

'Yeah, I heard that,' says JuJu, interrupting. 'Ain't no rumour neither. Just because it's a good story doesn't mean it has to be a lie, right?'

'Yeah, but ... OK...' Due to constraints of time, Martin feels that he should let the subject drop. 'Anyway, I just really need to know what year, approximately, did Tambo die?'

Judging by the rather hearty chuckle, JuJu Jones evidently finds the question amusing. 'When did he die? When did he die?' he repeats in vaguely mocking tones. 'What exactly did that cracker, Clayton, tell you?'

Martin attempts to withdraw even further into his linen jacket but can think of no suitable reply.

'What are you talking about, son? Who told you Tambo was dead? Man, you should really do your research a bit better!'

'What!?' asks Martin, as amazement amplifies his voice to fractionally below a shout. 'What are you saying?'

'I'm saying he's not dead. Why is that a problem?'

'It's no problem.' Martin shakes his head in a gesture that highlights rather than masks his sudden confusion. 'But he must be in his – what? – he must be almost ninety-three now?' Martin gives the figure incredulous emphasis.

'So, my mother passed last year, God rest her soul. Lady was ninety-six!'

'OK, so let's be absolutely clear here; you're saying Tambo Bones is alive?'

'As far as I'm aware. But I haven't heard that name in a long, long time. He was going by the name of Washington Adams last I heard.'

Finding an old napkin in one pocket, Martin now begins frantically searching for a pen.

'Never heard of no Oscar-whatever-you-said.'

'Oscar Oliver Brightwater.'

'Nah, that's a new one on me.'

Finally locating a pen, Martin now writes WASHINGTON ADAMS in large capital letters and underlines the two words emphatically.

JuJu continues, 'I hear he's a bit frail nowadays. He lost his house and all his possessions in the Storm and like so many of us, I don't think he ever fully recovered. I think he was living somewhere over near Bywater. Been there a long

163

time too, I believe. Anyway, I'm not sure if this is true but I heard he left the city and was living in Houston with some relation or another. Then, a couple of years ago, they managed to get him a place in a retirement home, one of those so-called assisted living places back here in New Orleans. As far as I know he's still there.'

The guitarist sits down next to the old man and picking up his guitar, he plays a brief variation on the riff to 'Smokestack Lightning'. The point is thus clearly made and Martin's interview with JuJu Jones is now at its conclusion.

'So he's still around here somewhere?' he asks in anxious, hurried tones.

'Well, I suppose you could say that but it's out of town a bit. Never been there myself but it's a really nice place I'm told; it's over on the West Bank, other side of the river, down in Timberlane. Place is called Maison de Belle Vie, big place too I believe. Down there on Lapalco Boulevard.'

Martin exhales noisily and shakes his head. 'I can't believe Clayton didn't say anything about all this.'

'Well, to be fair to the cat I doubt he knows shit about it. I only found out myself talking to some dude from the Musicians Union one time. Besides, that ain't Clayton's thing, you know?'

'Yeah, maybe...'

Just at this moment, the guitarist reaches across the old man to shake Martin's hand. 'You have a nice day now, pops.'

The subtext of the gesture is not lost on Martin. 'Thanks. You too. Good luck with the rest of your set.'

It is only when he has walked about 20 yards back up Royal Street and he hears Little Vee and JuJu Jones locked into their version of Jimmy Reed's 'Big Boss Man' that he becomes aware he is carrying a screwed-up piece of paper in his hand. He quickly concludes that the only satisfactory and logical explanation for this is that the guitarist passed it to him moments earlier as they were shaking hands.

Carefully opening the crumpled document and deciphering the small neat handwriting, Martin is now presented with a name and an address.

A. C. Monroe

649 Barracks Street. Ramp.

Martin's pace increases slightly as though he now has some subconscious desire to suddenly be as far away as possible. As he walks, the music grows ever quieter until it is a whisper and then a memory. The only subjects that occupy his thoughts as he reaches Canal once more are the two names.

Washington Adams. A. C. Monroe. Two names. Twenty-three characters. One name of fifteen and the other eight. Nine vowels. Fourteen consonants. Simple.

Martin crosses the busy thoroughfare and heads back towards Gravier Street. Except nothing is simple anymore. Firstly, Washington Adams was such an obviously fake name one is forced to speculate on its author's intention. Martin's knowledge of North American history remains fairly sketchy prior to the dawn of the twentieth century, yet he is sure that most Americans would know that Washington and Adams were the names of their country's first two presidents. So what exactly was going on here? Of course, Mr Brightwater had used many names in the past. Tambo Bones was an assumed name but it was also ironic and possibly intentionally subversive. So why had he started using a name that was so unimaginative and obviously fake? Even Sweet Papa Stalebread showed greater flair.

Unless...

He stops walking for a moment and takes out the napkin on which he'd written the name. He stares at the two words for a few minutes and then starts writing. On his first attempt he manages to find in Washington Adams an anagram of *Sad Man Saw Nothing* but this doesn't appeal to him as much as his second attempt which he writes on the reverse of the napkin: *Sad Giant Showman.*

As a general rule, Martin considers himself fiercely opposed to all forms of orthodoxy. Yet he finds, despite this, there is sometimes a certain pleasing order to the world. One needn't speculate or meditate any further on this fact; it is just one of those things. It doesn't signify anything in particular but on those rare occasions when it occurs it improves the quality of his day quite considerably. Discovering this anagram in Tambo's most recent alias, shortly after learning that the man is still alive, qualified as just such a moment.

Sad Giant Showman.

Martin puts the napkin back in his pocket and begins walking again. Reaching the junction of Gravier Street, having decided there is nothing at all significant in the fact that A. C. Monroe is an anagram of Cameroon, he now ambles towards the entrance of the Royal Crescent Hotel. Thinking about JuJu Jones and Little Vee again an idea now comes to him that he feels is worthy of exploring in Tambo's story somewhere, and he feels a sudden urgent need to get back to his laptop. He now recognises it as one of those great truths, hidden yet somehow obvious, of the type that only reveals itself somewhere like New Orleans. He begins to quicken his pace once more.

He also now has the most overwhelming urge to listen to 'Georgia Blues' again.

When he passes over the threshold it is shortly after midday and based on his admittedly limited familiarity with the hotel, he would still cheerfully declare that he has never seen the lobby look so busy. Evidently, a coach party has just arrived and the staff on the front desk are struggling to cope with the influx. The new guests look old yet extremely well-maintained with their pastel shades and lightweight fabrics, but they are not happy and they seem quite determined to give voice to their displeasure. Martin smiles politely and attempts to navigate his way between groups of people and luggage in the vague direction of the elevator. It is, he thinks, rather like stepping through a half-remembered dream about a shipwreck.

The noise is indescribable: a rising crescendo of animal discontent and frustration. People wanting to get things straight, those demanding *just one* moment of someone's time and others declaring that this isn't what they had been led to believe. On top of all this, a young woman is calling for her father. He manages to take a couple of steps towards the elevator but the woman's voice seems to get louder.

'Dad...! Dad...! DAD!'

Martin finally manages to press the button to call the elevator, a gesture that is quickly followed by a loud involuntary sigh. Peace and sanctuary are now but a moment away.

'Dad...! Dad...! Oh, for fuck's sake!'

At this precise moment, Martin feels someone tugging his elbow and he turns around.

'Are you ignoring me? I mean, your memory can't be *that* bad, can it?'

He can think of nothing to say; he simply repeats her name twice – once as a question and once as confirmation. 'Sally? Sally!'

'You see, I knew it was in there somewhere! How are you, Dad?'

'I'm ... OK. But where...? I mean ... why are you...?'

'I think this is the moment when we, like, do that hugging thing, Dad. Remember?'

'Of course.' Martin puts both his arms around his daughter. 'I'm so pleased to see you,' he says but these are the last words that she is able to make out. When he finally pulls away from her she notices that he seems to have been crying.

2.14.

Just a bit longer now. OK, try again.

He opens his eyes.

2.14. Fuck. Again.

2.15. At last!

He can now present himself with a simple and quite satisfying calculation; for it has been precisely twenty minutes, according to the digital bedside clock, since he first woke up. Twenty minutes during which he's been at no time in any real danger of falling back to sleep. The sensible thing would have been to switch the lamp on and read for a while but he'd not wished to disturb Bernie, who remains deeply asleep in the bed alongside him and entirely oblivious to the situation.

But he's been using this time positively and amongst other things, he has finally worked out why he hates atheists so much. Actually, it wasn't their paradoxical piety and general smugness and to be truthful, it wasn't really hatred after all – more a sort of raging jealousy, a grand self-defining envy. For, in the past ten minutes or so, he has discovered, with the sort of irony that is enormously pleasing at two o'clock in the morning, that the thing he envies most about atheists is precisely the same thing he envies most in devout Christians. Namely, it is their absolute *certainty* – that all-absorbing, complete, 100% conviction in a single central idea, whatever that idea might be.

That must be a wonderful thing, he concludes, not to be eternally mired in all this doubt and confusion.

Here lies Martin – not dead yet. But even his shoelaces are agnostic.

Shortly after this mild revelation he'd returned to closing his eyes and trying to accurately count minutes in single-second increments. Currently, however, his mind is entirely occupied in recalling various anatomical details of his ex-partners. The specific details are sadly predictable as is the resulting slight stirring of an erection. Instinctively, out of shame, prurience or expediency, he now cups his hand over his penis. He often thought about things like this when he couldn't sleep and would inevitably ponder the same question: is there a lady from his past who has ever thought about him in a similar way?

Where are you tonight, Martin?

An urgent voice whispers from a dark corner of the bedroom, a face obscured by shadows and the frailty of memory.

I am here, my love, my one and only love.

Do you remember me, Martin?

Of course I do.

Do you ever think of me?

I think about you all the time.

I wish you could just touch me, touch me here, just one last time.

Oh God, so do I, so do I . . .

One day, he will write a story about a man who made a point of choosing friends who he considered his intellectual inferiors. Then one day he realises he has no friends anymore and he hasn't learned anything.

Sleep is no longer an option and at precisely 2.17 he finally accepts the fact. Gingerly and with the sort of poise that might be considered impressive given the hour, Martin manoeuvres himself from under the quilt and gets out of bed. Bernice stirs slightly but doesn't wake up and so he slips quietly out of the bedroom and makes his way downstairs.

Entering the small living room at the front of the cottage, he wanders over to the table and switches on his computer. He opens the curtains fractionally and stares out into blackness. On balance, Wickham is probably still there but it is too dark to be absolutely certain and any alternative hypothesis will have to wait until morning. He thinks about making himself a coffee but that would suggest he has completely abandoned any notion of going back to sleep and he doesn't feel quite ready to make such a commitment. Instead, he goes into the kitchen and makes himself a piece of toast and an instant hot chocolate.

Returning to his computer, he notes with some excitement that he has received an email from Authorland.

Dear Mr Bonehouse,
Thank you so much for your recent enquiry and the
upload of your manuscript. We would be delighted to
work with you towards the publication of your novel
entitled AN UNHEALTHY INTEREST.
Please download the attached information PDF and
familiarise yourself with our various publishing packages
and select the one that you feel most suits your needs.
In the meantime I would be grateful if you could
provide me with a brief synopsis of your novel entitled
AN UNHEALTHY INTEREST. This would be used to
form the basis of a press hand-out and be used on our
website to promote the book. So please include the details
you feel that are important to your novel entitled AN
UNHEALTHY INTEREST.
I look forward to hearing from you.
Dan Matheson
Authorland Publishers

Well done there, boy.
This time the voice he hears is as familiar as sunlight and
as safe as the ages.
Did well there, didn't you?
'Well,' says Martin with a self-conscious shrug, 'we're not
quite there yet.'
Well, if I may be so bold as to pass comment from an
alternative viewpoint, I think your reticence is ill-founded. The
evidence is frankly irrefutable; your novel is going to be published.
'Not exactly "published" in the conventional sense...'
Of course, I readily accept that this might represent your
interpretation and in its own way I'm forced to concur that
your reading is not without some validity. However, I do
think you should allow yourself a certain sense of achievement
at this point.
'Should I?'

Yes, you should and you should also be a bit bloody happy about it all.

'I think I am happy. Look!' Martin turns away from his monitor and smiles rather hopelessly in a manner that suggests sudden panic rather than contentment.

Well, you must forgive me if I sound a little cynical in this regard. Now just you get on with it and write that sodding synopsis they're asking for!

'OK,' says Martin blandly as he turns back towards his computer and opens a new document. 'Look, I'm doing it, all right?'

The decision to submit his manuscript to Authorland had been taken directly after his meeting with Angela Bingham-Hogg a couple of weeks earlier, although he still does not actually recall making any such decision and the whole process seemed to be one of those oddly detached mechanical activities that occur during periods of bereavement – when ghost-like you wander through days and weeks and observe with a vague passing interest as your life becomes something that happens to you rather than something in which you take any active part. Bernie had urged him on several occasions to submit the manuscript to an orthodox, mainstream publisher but Martin had refused to listen. He cited Mr Price's wishes and usually that curtailed any debate on the subject.

The fact that Authorland promoted itself as a publishing service rather than a conventional publisher and the author paid for publication in advance did substantially reduce the possibility of rejection – something that has always appealed greatly to Martin. However, it has been a few days since the last communication and if forced to be completely honest, he would confess to a certain apprehension on the subject. He is therefore anxious to respond to their request as soon as possible.

Noisily, he slurps a mouthful of hot chocolate and gathers his thoughts.

AN UNHEALTHY INTEREST
SYNOPSIS

An Unhealthy Interest is, at its heart, a love story, although it is also a study of obsession and longing and the sort of destructive passion that destroys

'Yip, that's what destructive things generally tend to do.' Select, delete.

It considers the conflict between pure basic desire and the recognition of the abnormality of that desire. It is about the demons that can overwhelm a person and the lengths that person must go to defeat them. It is a story about desire and the age-old conflict between conquest and capitulation.

Martin yawns and shakes his head. 'That's a fucking boring book you've got there, boy,' he says in an accent intended as tribute rather than parody. Delete.

An Unhealthy Interest is a novel about human weakness; it is about obsession and judgement and the ease with which we can sometimes find ourselves slipping into either.

Written boldly in first person, An Unhealthy Interest invites the reader to see the world through its central character's lusts and obsession. The 'I' in the story makes model aeroplanes and lives in a house with only a dominant and religious mother for company. We are invited into this small cramped world and challenged to make some sense of it when the protagonist begins to wrestle with the improper feelings that arise from a chance meeting with a fourteen-year-old girl. The cycle of lust and shame, of urge and denial, culminates in bouts of self-harming.

The book does not shy away from depicting the daily realities of forbidden desire and it approaches its subject and the surrounding issues in a frank yet sympathetic manner. There is, however, a major twist at the end of the book which changes the entire meaning of the story and readers will find that their perspective on the character will change radically.

172

Although it is not the author's intention to court controversy
'No, no, no,' says Martin a little louder than the situation
may have warranted. 'I don't think we really want to get
into any of that nonsense.' Select, delete.
Maybe, on reflection, he thinks this might not be the best
time to be doing this. He saves the email as a draft and then
glances around the room half-heartedly in the vague hope of
locating a magazine or a newspaper or anything he could
gaze blankly at for a few minutes. Usually, there would be
one or two lying around but sadly, Bernice must have been
in there earlier in the evening and tidied up. At this particular
moment, the only available reading material within easy reach
is the biography of Bix Beiderbecke, the early jazz cornetist,
which has occupied a particular space next to his computer
unopened and untouched for many weeks. The book had
been lent to him by Mr Price a few weeks before his death.
In fact, he'd insisted that Martin read it declaring it a
'fascinating new study'. Beiderbecke's music had never really
been of even passing interest to Martin but he'd politely
accepted the offer. He has browsed the biography a couple
of times but has not even touched it since the funeral. But
the book has remained on his desk and when sitting there
he will still glance at it every few minutes.
The fact that Martin never got around to reading the book
should not be taken as a reflection on either his friend or
the subject of the study. For Martin's approach to biographies
has sadly been the same since adolescence. Ignoring the usual
conventions, he will generally restrict himself to simply scanning
the index and looking for any items of a vaguely salacious
or titillating nature listed next to a subject's name. Anything
that might catch his eye: *bizarre sexual practises of, anti-
social behaviour of, racist outbursts of,* etc. etc. and immediately
he will turn to the relevant page.
It is essentially the fast-track tabloid approach to biography
but it remains a very hard habit to break. He tells himself

173

it is because most people's lives are boring and meaningless with only the odd flashes of some essential truth and purpose, but he knows this argument to be flawed and largely unconvincing.

Thus, beyond the fact that Bix was the first white jazzman of any standing and he died tragically young at the age of twenty-eight, which he already knew, Martin had gathered very little further information from studying the index. There were, however, as he recalls, two entries of some interest. The first referred to an image reproduced in the book and believed to be the last photograph ever taken of Beiderbecke. Despite the fact that Martin hasn't looked at the book in weeks, the memory of the picture remains vivid. Perhaps because we know it is the final photograph of a man we invest it with a certain resonance, yet it is an arresting image, nonetheless. It is actually rather peculiar. As Martin recalls it, two young men, smartly attired for the period, are shaking hands in what appears to be a stretch of featureless, deserted countryside. The man on the right in the lighter suit is Bix while the man in the darker suit and the hat is his friend and fellow musician, the saxophonist, Frankie Trambauer. There is a formality about their postures that suggests they are meeting for the first time (or perhaps saying farewell). One does not get the sense that this is a spontaneous gesture, but rather one that has been posed for our benefit: a painstakingly composed tableau intending to reveal something of significance to the viewer or some visual joke, some great clue, some great explanation or final denouement, something that was once obvious but has become over time fractionally beyond our grasp.

Then you pick up another detail: Bix seems to be standing lower down than Trambauer as though he is in a ditch. Then we suddenly find ourselves in the realm of a Manet or a Courbet and the image now seems to symbolically represent the consequence of human folly or more specifically,

Beiderbecke's descent into the alcoholism that will finally kill him – the metaphoric ditch from which Trambauer had often tried to rescue him. Is this what we are seeing then, the final offer of help and friendship? A hand offered to one in such desperate need? The rural landscape provides no reference points, no context, nothing to distract the eye away from a final gesture of compassion and love.

Something in the memory of this picture has provided Martin with a measure of comfort of late. For it somehow seems to encapsulate something of him and Mr Price. There was between them something enigmatic and unspoken but there was also something that he knew beyond any doubt to be good and kind and pure. Thus, the book with its picture remains on his desk next to his computer and Marin can think of no single reason why he will ever wish to move it.

The other item of interest that Martin discovered scanning the index related to the story that during high school, Bix had once been accused of behaving in an improper manner towards a young girl. The girl was apparently five years old and although he was never charged one is left wondering if there was more to the story at the time than just local hearsay and gossip.

Martin grimaces at the irony. Bix and the Unhealthy Interest. *Now, that might be a real page turner!*

'Yeah, no doubt.'

Martin manages something not unlike a smile as once again he forces himself to concentrate on his PC monitor. Minimising his email browser, he now scrolls through his documents until he finds AUHfinaledit.doc. He clicks on the file and the final draft of *An Unhealthy Interest* now fills the screen. He scrolls down to the start of chapter 10 and begins to read. His eyes begin to close as he deletes an exclamation mark and replaces it with a full stop. He doesn't like exclamation marks particularly; it always feels as though you are attempting to point out to the reader that this bit here is important or funny so pay attention or find it amusing. He's never liked exclamation marks. He used to get very upset whenever there was old newsreel footage of the war on TV. Particularly he hated those clips of bombs being dropped from planes. They always made him think of exclamation marks. He always thought a bomb sort of looked like an exclamation mark, actually if you thought about it for a moment it was a sort of exclamation mark and a pretty fucking final one too.

Something else now drifts into his mind. Something that used to happened a long, long time ago. When he was young his mother used to send their bed linen and towels to the dry cleaners every week – God, that sounds so Victorian. Do people still do that? They took the laundry away and they returned it wrapped up in a brown paper parcel tied up with string. He used to wait for the van every Wednesday afternoon and then watch the man walking up their front path with the package. He used to pretend it was a present addressed to him and it was going to be a fantastic surprise and, and ... and...

The page with its amended punctuation is still on the screen the following morning when Bernice discovers Martin fast asleep in the living room, his head resting partially on his desk and partially on his keyboard. His hand, however, is draped over a hardback book, as though guarding it from whatever terrors are haunting his dreams.

9

Beignets, Coffee and Pralines

The blues has remained the common currency in virtually all popular music for the past century. It is an undeniably durable format. It fed directly into early rock 'n' roll and every subsequent development. The Rolling Stones, Jimi Hendrix, Led Zeppelin grew out of the blues as much as Count Basie did. Jazz sadly has not proved so resilient. In fact, jazz is increasingly looking like just another offshoot, albeit a fascinating one, that also developed out of the blues. The blues is permanent and always current and it will always adapt itself. It is more fundamental even than a common language – the blues is the great common alphabet.

He said five minutes to Sally and he really doesn't want to keep her waiting.

We are almost fifty years away from the Stones' first recordings, yet the average twenty-year-old can still relate to their classic early singles. As a seventeen-year-old in 1977 I must confess I could find no such affinity with the Hot Five at half a century's distance.

He just wanted to jot this down quickly before he went back down to the lobby. It was roughly what had been running through his mind ten minutes earlier as he made his way back to the hotel and he was worried he may well forget it.

Young musicians continue to reinvent the blues and adapt it to every generation. The White Stripes play Son House and

Leadbelly but who will process 'Struttin' With Some Barbeque'
and put it on stage at Glastonbury this year?
  The Blues is the universal
  At this point, the telephone on his bedside table begins to
ring and having a better than reasonable idea who might be
on the other end, he saves the document and then rushes out
of his room and down the corridor in the direction of the
lift.
  Between the third floor and the lobby, Martin muses on
the nature of coincidence. He'd always been slightly fascinated
by the whole concept of coincidence or rather he was fascinated
by how coincidence seemed such a potent force in certain
people's lives. It was a very powerful idea and seemed in the
minds of so many to be in some way connected to fate and
destiny. People *believed* in coincidence and this was a curious
yet highly revealing choice of word – as though it was a
declaration of faith. It existed (if it could be said to exist)
beyond the boundaries of science, mathematics, religion and
just about everything else and there are those that seem to
regard it as an invisible energy or some sort of naturally
occurring phenomenon: the point at which our dull little lives
connect for a flashing moment to something greater or
something we simply consider to have more meaning.
  There were theories and entire books on the theme of
coincidence and there always would be but Martin would
simply claim to be a curious observer, albeit one who nowadays
regards the whole concept as a sort of 'low-fat chaos theory',
rebranded for people who believe in horoscopes.
  The world is anomalous – that's what it does best. It's had
a lot of practice. Ignorance, he maintains, is often a major
factor in many of those episodes that we might fondly attribute
to coincidence. The more information one gathers the less
one is inclined towards the phenomenal. Meeting his daughter,
who he hasn't seen in a number of years, in a hotel lobby
4,000 miles away from his home is, at first glance, a fairly

extraordinary coincidence. However, the actual facts in this particular case are a little more mundane.

Martin dimly recalls a note from Sally with her previous year's Christmas card during which she mentioned she had recently started dating 'an amazing guy called Stefan'. She then went on to list Stefan's qualities in considerable detail and made reference to his suitability as possible 'husband material'. Martin might well have lost interest at this point for he has no memory whatsoever of a subsequent paragraph in the note that referred to Stefan being a couple of years older and a qualified dentist with a small family firm in Montreal. Stefan has taken a week off work to attend the convention in New Orleans and when Sally read Martin's email stating that he was also in New Orleans she thought it would be such a great opportunity to surprise Stefan and to also catch up with her father. She quite literally threw some things into a bag and made the three-hour flight the previous evening.

So was it then a coincidence that Stefan *just happened* to be a dentist and *just happened* to be at a convention in New Orleans when his girlfriend's father also *just happened* to be there?

'Oh, fuck it,' says Martin quietly to himself as the brief 'ting', like a distant evening bicycle bell calling him from the great collective childhood consciousness of all men, alerts him to the fact he has arrived on the ground floor.

The lift door opens to reveal that the lobby has now returned to a semblance of normality once more and Martin smiles sympathetically at the desk clerk who returns the gesture. He quickly spots his daughter sitting in a quiet corner next to a potted fern. Evidently, lost in thought, she is staring at some indeterminate point in the middle distance and doesn't notice Martin's approach. For a fraction of a second, looking at her again after all this time, she reminds him of her mother but then that connection thankfully vanishes as he notices she is sitting terribly upright with a straight back and one foot resting on top of the other – just how she used to sit when she was little. She also has that same slightly bemused expression on her face. You never knew what Sally was thinking when she was young. She'd lose herself in some reverie and when asked what she was thinking about, she would smile and say 'nothing much'. But Martin wasn't fooled.

She was always profound.

But all fathers like to believe their daughters are profound.

'Sorry about that,' he says through a hastily assembled smile. 'I was putting my laptop in that, er … little combination safe thingy in my room.'

Sally rolls her eyes but feels that any comment would be entirely superfluous.

'So, do you fancy getting some lunch, then?'

'Yeah, something like that.'

'Well, what do you want to eat, then?' he asks in a manner that misses the intended ebullience by some margin and instead sounds brusque and impatient. 'Any preferences?' he adds hastily.

Sally gets up slowly from her chair and yawning rather flamboyantly, says, 'Oh, nothing too much; Stefan and I had breakfast at our hotel this morning.'

'OK, right.'

She puts her arm through his as they walk towards the exit. 'You decide, Dad.'

'What about beignets?'

'Yeah, beignets is cool.'

They walk around the corner and turn into Magazine Street.

'So, was Stefan pleased to see you?' Martin asks and again, for the second time in as many minutes, his tone belies his original intention. Failing to sound genial and interested, he manages to sound cynical and over-protective. It is simply nerves, he tells himself and satisfied with this conclusion, he lets the subject rest.

'Kinda pleased,' she says slowly, 'but mainly kinda surprised, y'know?'

Despite the obviously American syntax and rhythm to her speaking voice, Martin can still detect the vaguest hint of something South London in some of her vowel sounds. It is something he immediately finds rather endearing.

'I'll bet.'

'You know I really hope we can, like, meet up while we're all here. He totally wants to meet you.'

'That would be good.'

'Oh, Dad, I really *really* want you to like him. Mum thinks he's a bit, I don't know, kinda *geeky*. But you know what she's like, right?'

'Oh yeah,' says Martin, enjoying the frisson of an unexpected shared confidence.

'She's like totally up herself nowadays.'

Martin nods reflectively. 'Yeah, I can believe that. Besides, there's nothing wrong with geeky.'

'Exactly! Anyway, he totally loves music too and he's got, like, a billion records or something. All sorts of stuff. He listens to, like, *everything*. He was actually in a band too when he was in college.'

'Really?' says Martin, measuring his response more carefully this time. 'What sort of music?'

'Don't know if it would be your sort of thing. Sort of acoustic but still indie I suppose, a bit rootsy and country, too. They had a couple of singles out, too.'

'Sounds interesting.'

'Yeah, Go Pookie!'

'What?'

'That was their name – Yeah, Go Pookie!'

'Er ... catchy,'

'Before that he was in Devilish Anagrams and they actually supported the Dirtbombs once.'

'Right,' says Martin, smiling in the manner of a man who

has had quite enough of devilish anagrams for one morning. Then he thinks for a moment again about coincidence.

'So where are we, like, actually going?' asks Sally as they reach the pedestrian crossing on Canal Street.

'Well,' says Martin, taking all too evident delight in the question, 'the Café Du Monde will be absolutely heaving at the moment. It's always best to get there early and I think we've missed our chance today.' Trying not to enjoy himself too blatantly, he then adds, 'But there's a nice little place over in the French Market. I think we'll go there.'

The lights change and they cross the road in silence as Sally regards her father with a series of suspicious sidelong glances: a particular mannerism she mastered at a very early age.

'So,' she says as they reach the kerb, matter-of-factly but not entirely without kindness, 'you're, like, getting to know your way around a bit then, are you, Dad?'

Martin nods and smiles to himself. He could never keep secrets from Sally. Similarly, any lapses into lofty self-aggrandisement are unlikely to pass without comment. It is truly a beautiful day, he thinks. He is currently sauntering up Decatur Street in the city that he's fallen in love with and at this precise moment in his life he cannot think of a single living person with whom he would rather be sharing this day more than Sally.

The smile falters a little but for once Sally doesn't notice. He recalls that in pursuit of some half-formed idea he'd once had for a novel, he'd scribbled some notes somewhere about the 'ambient desperation' and 'background sadness in all human lives'. There was something to the effect that *isolation is ultimately a desired condition; for it is the final consolation of separation.* The novel had progressed no further than a few sketched-out ideas as he realised that, despite any loftier claims otherwise, he was actually attempting to write about his feelings for Sally after the divorce.

Some things, he thought at the time, were best left unspoken. But now she is here again and they both understand that there is so much that is missing from their lives, times, places, incidents: the fabric of a lifetime, of a generation. But somehow that is less important now and while they are together, if it is only for an afternoon or for a couple of hours, his life will be enriched by this simple contact alone. The past is immense, unassailable, colossal, but under the right conditions it can be reduced to little more than setting or background. So while they inhabit this small afternoon together, neither will feel the need to confess to past failures or ancient disappointments and Sally will simply want to talk about Stefan while Martin will be desperate to tell her all about Tambo Bones and Storyville, 'Georgia Blues' and JuJu Jones, Sweet Papa Stalebread and Clayton Palmer, then finally, Sad Giant Showman and Assisted Living. But there is no rush. Not this afternoon.

'So how is your mother, then?' asks Martin as they take their seats at a table in the open-air dining area of the French Market. It is fairly busy but finding a table has not proved difficult. They have bought beignets, coffees and a couple of pralines – the popular local variant being a fudgy, sugary confection that Martin is anxious to introduce to his daughter.

Sally takes a slow, deliberate mouthful of her coffee. 'I don't know really; I don't see her very much anymore to be honest. Seriously, when I first moved onto campus, I was still, like, going back home every weekend but we were, like, always arguing and stuff.'

'Really?' says Martin, suppressing an overwhelmingly strong urge to smile.

'Oh yeah, it was terrible. She just used to pick on me, like, constantly; I could never do anything right in her eyes. I was untidy and scruffy and my grades were never good enough –'

'Well, I can *totally* sympathise there,' says Martin, interrupting (her syntax was irritating but it was clearly infectious). 'I used to get the untidy and scruffy speeches too.'

Sally smiles. 'Yeah, I'll bet you did! She just turned into a real super-bitch and so I started staying on campus at the weekend, hanging with friends and all that. I did a bit of waitressing, that sort of thing. Now I spend most of the weekends at Stefan's place. She might text me or email me sometimes and we drove out to see her a few weeks ago, but I think we've totally drifted into our, you know, "sporadic contact" phase.'

'That's too bad,' says Martin without conviction. 'You really should try a praline.'

'What are they like? I'll bet they're like a billion calories or something?'

Martin ignores the question. 'Is she still with, you know, *whatshisname?*' he asks, investing the word with an almost adolescent disdain.

'You mean Peter?'

'That's him.'

'Oh, Dad, keep up! He left, like, absolutely *ages* ago, before I even finished high school. I wrote to you and told you.' She then adds uncertainly, 'Didn't I?'

'Maybe. So is this final then?'

'Yeah, they're like totally divorced now and everything. Mum bought a dog, called it Bovary and, like, how totally predictable was *that*, and took up yoga. Then she started blaming me for everything. F.Y.I., these pralines are, like, totally amazing. I'm definitely going to buy some for Stefan. So what happened with you and Bernie then?'

Martin shifts his weight slightly in his chair as he realises he has no prepared set of responses or any simple, glib answers to such an enquiry. In fact, apart from a couple of predictably difficult conversations with Wes, this is the first time anyone has actually raised the subject with him. 'Oh, you know, it was just the usual ... you know ... *stuff.*' If he stayed vague on the subject he would avoid having to tell any blatant lies. 'It was the age difference thing, maybe, I don't know. I'll tell you all about it another time.'

Sally seems satisfied with the answer and is happy to let the subject drop. 'Listen, I was so, so sorry to hear about Mr Price.' She reaches over the table and touches his hand. 'I know how much he meant to you.'

'Yeah. Thanks.'

'You know, I really would have liked to come over for the funeral but Mum didn't tell me about it because I'd just started my second year at university and she didn't want me missing any of my seminars. And there you go again! Thanks so much, Mum!'

'So how is university anyway?' asks Martin, seizing the opportunity to shift the conversation slightly. 'What is it called again? Con-something?'

'Concordia University.'

'You see, I do pay attention,' says Martin, affable rather than assertive. 'So you're still doing ... it was a humanities course, wasn't it?'

'Yeah, communication studies.'

'Enjoying it?'

Sally nods her head emphatically. 'Like, totally. It's completely brilliant.'

'What do you –?'

'Oh wait, wait, hang on,' says Sally, suddenly animated and rummaging under the table for her rucksack. 'You just reminded me.'

What happened next took Martin completely by surprise and lent the afternoon a sudden resonance, something that a man with his limited powers might be reduced to describing as 'dreamlike'. These are the confines of our tiny worlds, he thinks; these are the boundaries we set for ourselves, the point beyond which everything blurs, mutates and reassembles itself. He is holding her as a baby in his arms and marvelling at her ability to breathe through her nose and her mouth simultaneously – a skill all babies possess and lose shortly thereafter. But she was four days old and already she was a more evolved species.

Already she had surpassed him!

Then he remembers watching her as a child, recalling how she could, like all children, so effortlessly slip from crying to laughing without a tangible transition; as if every possible human experience was so new and overwhelming and she hadn't yet developed the method by which she could rationally order or moderate her feelings; as though laughing and crying were simply different manifestations of the same emotion. But what emotion exactly? Did they explain that to you? Probably a variation on precisely the same emotion that Martin is currently experiencing: not crying, not laughing but just the overwhelming urge to do both, as he looks down at the table in front of him and finds himself gazing at a point in space left of his praline and to the right of his coffee, the point where there currently lies a fairly tatty copy of *An Unhealthy Interest*.

He says nothing for a few frozen moments.

A fly settles on the corner of their table and a woman laughs somewhere nearby. There were no great themes or adventures anymore; there were only details, leftover scraps of other people's lives; all their regrets and misfortunes. Passing his hand over the cover of the book as though seeking some sort of instant physical or tactile confirmation, he finally asks in a low voice, 'How... How do you know about *this*?' Intentionally or otherwise, he invests the word with the suggestion of conspiracy and intrigue.

This was most definitely not the response Sally was expecting and she is slightly confused by the question. 'Er ... well, I didn't think it was, like, a big secret or anything. I got it on Amazon ages ago, like the day it came out or something.'

'But how –?'

Sally furrows her brow in disbelief. 'Oh come on, I'm your daughter; I like to know what you're doing, OK? So bite me, sometimes I Google your name to see if you're on Facebook or if any more of your articles have been posted online. Actually, there was a really good one about Whitstable that I read recently. Anyway, that's how I found out about the book.'

Martin manages a weak smile. 'I was going to send you one, of course I was ... but then one day it just didn't seem like an appropriate thing to do anymore and I suppose I could imagine how your mum might react.'

'Will you sign it for me?'

'Er... Are you sure about that?'

'Of course I'm sure. I thought it was a great book. I've read it about four times! I actually used it for one of my assignments.'

Martin shakes his head. 'Sorry, I don't understand.'

'It was one of those mid-term things; the whole class was told to select a non-mainstream book, something totally obscure that didn't have, like, a broad readership and as few reviews as possible. The idea, they said, was that our interpretation would be an entirely personal response and not influenced by any external sources. We had to write a full critique and deconstruction of the text and set it in a cultural and political context. So I did your book.'

'Really?'

'Yeah and guess what, I got a fucking A!'

Martin puts his hand over his mouth and feels his teeth digging into the fleshy part of his palm. Removing his hand he looks over at Sally and attempts a smile but he says nothing.

'Mr Gotterher – that's the guy who set the assignment – was so impressed he asked to read your book and I'm like that's a bit of nerve, right? But he really liked it, too. He tried to get his own copy but he said it was, like, not available *anywhere* online anymore so he passed my copy on to a few people and another few people and I only got it back last week. That's why it looks so fucked up. Everyone thought it was totally cool, Mr G. told me. I mean they liked it a lot.'

'Are you serious?'

'Of course I'm serious. It's a great book, Dad. You should be really proud of it.'

'You think so?'

'Well, as I put in my remarkably incisive critique, and I quote' – Sally now extends her right arm theatrically and lapses into her best baritone news anchor voice – '*at a time when aspiring to liberality is considered a noble calling the author turns that idea on its head by exposing so many of our deep-rooted prejudices. The book is not comfortable reading but the author forces us to hold a mirror up to our assumptions and our bigotries and thus this is a courageous and important book.* Well, what do you think?'

In the wake of 'Recent Events', it had become too easy to lose sight of the fact that he'd once done something as mundane as 'written a book', and Martin at this moment is experiencing a sensation which he can only liken to a vague combination of mild tinnitus, vertigo and motion sickness. He struggles to find the words. 'It sounds ... great. Well done.'

'I wanted to post some of it in a review on Amazon but for some reason the site wouldn't let me.'

Martin grimaces but refrains from commenting.

Sally now delves into her rucksack once more and eventually finds her pen. 'So will you sign it, then?'

Martin turns to the title page and writes in a shaky, fairly eccentric hand the following message.

To SALLY,

Who can probably still breathe through her nose and her mouth <u>at the same time</u>!

BEIGNETS, COFFEE AND PRALINES

Thank you so much!!
With all my love
Dad xxx
New Orleans October 2010

It would be pointless to deny it.
He is disappointed with the cover. It is his only reservation.
In a period of his life that will be fraught with uncertainty,
it is perhaps the only thing about which he will remain fairly
confident.
The single constant.
So, if he is to be totally honest, he is actually very disappointed with the cover. It looks cheap and garish with its
handwritten title and hastily composed illustration. He'd also
had it in his mind that the background tint would be a dull
sort of ochre colour, whereas the finished item seemed to be
more of an unpleasant shade of orange.
When he'd been sent a single copy for his approval last week
it had not seemed quite so, well ... mediocre was probably a
fair description, and at that time it was possible he'd simply
been overwhelmed by holding in his hand the *first* copy of his
first novel. Now there are fifty of them in five neat piles of ten
on the kitchen table alongside the sturdy cardboard box in
which they have just arrived and he's beginning to think that
his approval might have been granted a little hastily.
In fairness, Authorland had sent him a few dozen stock
covers which they claimed they would then adapt for the
specific needs of his book and Martin had chosen the particular
layout in question. They had only done exactly what they'd
promised. So he has no legitimate grievance. But it is tarnishing
a moment that Martin has been anticipating with a mounting
sense of excitement for a number of weeks.
Once again, he tells himself that he is not going to let this
dampen his morning and he simply promises himself that

189

he'll be more vigilant in the future. Besides, with the right sort of encouragement he could almost believe it was crass and vulgar in an intentionally ironic or subversive way. On the positive side, Mr Matheson at Authorland had told him that it would be two to three weeks after approval before his author's copies would arrive. However, when the Parcelforce van drew up outside the house earlier that morning it had only been ten days.

Although Mr Matheson had been keen to stress right from the start, even before Martin had signed his contract, that Authorland was a publishing service and not a conventional publisher, Martin had been consistently impressed by their efficiency. Admittedly, under this particular arrangement, the author is significantly more involved with the whole process of publishing and during the past month or so Martin has been responsible for the typesetting, layout, spell checking and editing of his own manuscript prior to its submission. Anything therefore that was libellous, offensive or illegal in the text was entirely the author's problem. Similarly, the author was expected to design or select a cover of the book. That was the problem, of course; he was a writer and not a designer or an artist.

He reassembles the books so that there are now ten equal piles of five copies. Then he reinstates the original arrangement. Shortly after completing this process he is startled by the sound of the phone ringing in the hall. In a curiously paternal manner, as though fearing the possible effects of this sudden intrusion, he continues to scrutinise the piles of books as he reverses himself quietly through the kitchen door.

'Hello?' he says in a fairly cautious tone as he picks up the receiver.

'Hi there. It's me.'

'Hey, Bernie. What's up?'

'Well?' she asks in an excited tone, the single syllable thus rendered as neither a prompt nor an enquiry.

'Well what?'

'You sent me a text,' she says slowly, 'about the books...?'

Despite his single lingering reservation, Martin now finds himself breaking into a broad smile. 'Oh yes, they arrived an hour or so ago. They're all on the kitchen table.'

'Oh baby, that's great. What do they look like?'

'Well, they ... they look like ... my books!' he says, choosing his words carefully.

'Oh, I'm so excited. I can't wait to see them. But listen I've got some more news. Actually, this is really, really good news! I couldn't wait until tonight I had to call you now during my lunch break.'

'OK,' says Martin in a drab tone that fails quite spectacularly to complement his partner's mounting enthusiasm.

'You remember I told you about Jason, one of the little boys in my class? That his father worked in Canterbury Waterstones and I had a chat to him the other day about stocking your book? You remember?'

'Yes, of course.'

'Well, I saw him this morning again when he dropped Jason off and he said that they'd definitely order a few copies of your book and do a sort of local author display.'

'Oh God, that's amazing! Well done, Bernie and thank you so much for doing that. I really –'

'But no, wait! That's not all – here comes the best bit! Turns out that Jason's mum is a producer on Thanet FM! Can you believe it? I had no idea; I've never really spoken to her that much. Apparently, she reckons she can easily get you a slot on one of their afternoon shows. They have a sort of current affairs programme that usually features inter-views of local interest. It's called Thanet Talk Radio. They've had a couple of writers on the show in the past and she seems to think she can get you on in a couple of weeks. I mean, come on, how brilliant is that?'

Unaware that he has been holding his breath, Martin now

exhales loudly. 'I'm ... stunned! I really don't know what to say. That's just about the best news I've ever had!'

'I said it was really good, didn't I?'

'You did. But why are they being so helpful?' Martin frowns and then adds as an irreverent aside, 'You're not sleeping with them, are you, Bernie?'

'Of course I am. I degrade and debase myself regularly on behalf of you and literature! But seriously I think Jason had a few problems with his old school and they're just grateful that he's settled now and making progress. I always said I was a good teacher!'

Martin takes the implied flippancy as an invitation to ignore the remark. 'But this is just so brilliant, Bernie. God, have you any idea what this might mean?'

'Oh yes, I've got a pretty good idea. Anyway, she'll call you in a week or so and go through a few possible dates with you.'

'Yeah, sure thing,' says Martin vaguely, his sudden nonchalance a consequence of assimilation rather than disinterest.

'Look, I've got to go now, baby. I'll see you later.'

'Yeah sure, OK, bye then.'

Martin wanders back into the kitchen on legs that feel less steady now, less confident somehow. Without any apparent conscious will, he leans over and grabs the edges of the table. Staring once again at the cover, he discovers he no longer feels quite the same level of revulsion. Instead, he hears a voice in his head repeating the same line.

So, Martin, tell us about your book... So, Martin, tell us about your book...

He takes the top copy from the pile nearest to him and opens it at random.

So, Martin, tell us about your book...

AN UNHEALTHY INTEREST
Chapter Twelve

When you're young it's just so easy; it's all done for you –
you're instructed who to love. You must love your parents
you must love your granny and all that. You never question
it; it's just a word you use: something you get used to saying
but you don't really understand it. Then one day you fall in
love and you realise you can't control it, you can't make it
happen, it doesn't occur when you want it to or when it's
convenient it just hits you like a punch in the face and you
can't ignore it or pretend it's not happening. Maybe, like me,
you think it will never happen but then suddenly out of
nowhere it falls into your life and nothing is ever the same
again and nothing is ever as important. It's something that
stays with you for always – I can still feel it even now as I
write this. You can't prove it or touch it or see it. It's the
most invisible thing in the world apart from God. Except, I
don't believe in God. I never told anyone this but I had
never felt anything in my life as strongly as the feelings I
was soon developing for Lucy. Suddenly I was able to
understand those stupid, silly songs they play on the radio
all the time: love makes me feel like this and that and how
much I love someone or another. Finally, I could make sense
of them! It was like I'd stumbled upon a phrasebook for
some obscure ancient language and finally I got it! That is
not to say those sexual feelings weren't still as powerful as
ever but there were other times too when I just wanted to
be near her so I might take comfort from her mere presence.
I suppose I could divide them into my body moments and
mind moments and I would probably experience both many
times during the course of a day. Sometimes when we were
together I would try to stand as close to her as I could
without her knowing just so I could brush my hand against
her arm. Other times I would lean towards her claiming I

had water in my ears and so I couldn't hear what she was saying properly then I might be able to smell her or feel her breath on my face. Sometimes that was all it would take to make my day perfect. I'm not ashamed to say I started to fall deeply and secretly in love with her. That was probably the worst part of it all – that I couldn't speak of it for fear she would run away from me. I wanted so much to share my feelings with her but I knew I never would. I wasn't sure she'd understand and it might frighten her or turn her against me. I suppose we were sort of friends but I hadn't had any friends for such a long, long time – probably not since I was in school – so I can't really speak with any confidence. But I saw her most days if only to say 'hello' or to wave to her from my window. When we did have a few minutes together we would talk about things and pick up conversations that we'd started the previous day. I felt very relaxed with her and I think she felt the same. In the beginning, I used to make sure that it always appeared we were meeting by chance; I'd watch her in the garden sunbathing and as she gathered together her things to go back indoors and knowing that she'd use the back door at the side of their house, which was directly opposite our back door, I'd rush downstairs and take a bag of rubbish out to our bin. I'd say 'hello' and pretend to be surprised to see her and then we'd exchange a few words. As the summer wore on, however, we'd actually arrange to meet up. She'd say something like, 'Are you in later? I thought I might pop over,' or 'I'm so bored – what are you up to today?' We started to spend more time in each other's company and I got the impression that she was starting to like me. One day I even told her that I made model kits and she asked to see one. I swear to God no one had ever asked me that before! I showed her my Junkers Ju 87 and she said I was very clever and that she would never have the patience and she laughed but not at me and I wanted her to have the kit and to keep it forever but I stopped myself. I don't know why. It was like I could always feel my mum watching me all the time – even though I knew she was out. I don't think they actually spoke to each other all that summer but my mum made no secret of the fact she didn't much care for Lucy. She would use words for her. Not nasty, dirty words, but old-fashioned words like 'flighty' and 'fast', and she'd never use her name only 'that little missy from next door'. It wasn't long before my mum started telling me I was disgusting for trying to consort with someone like that. She always said that Jesus was the only person I should be trying to get to know. She kept saying that she knew what I got up to and my thoughts were lewd and impure and that I was being tempted by the devil. She said she could smell the devil on my bed sheets and on my clothes. I wanted to tell her that if my thoughts were lewd and impure then it was God that had planted them in my head and not me and she should save her lectures for him! One day I came close to telling her that I genuinely loved 'that little missy from next door' and therefore there was nothing lewd or impure about my thoughts. Also, I might have actually briefly thought that if I announced that I was in love with Lucy my sense of shame and disgust would somehow leave me, that love would instantly absolve, cleanse and save me. Sadly, I knew this to be just some twisted variation on a great ancient lie and my mum always knew when I was lying. By that point I had cuts all the way up both my arms and I suppose that was my great confession to impurity. After a couple of weeks' practice, I'd started holding the craft knife in my left hand so I could make cuts on my right arm. I'm very right-handed and I found it difficult at first but eventually I got the hang of it. It was obviously really important that my mum never saw them. Sometimes there would be blood; sometimes I'd have to take a really messed up T-shirt and sneak it into a rubbish bin a few doors down in case my mum found it. Sometimes I'd have to use sticking plasters to stop the bleeding so I started hoarding boxes and boxes secretly in one of my desk drawers. I didn't question my actions; it wasn't right or wrong – it was just something I did. It didn't stop me touching myself and in a funny way, it actually became part of the process, the finale or the final act. Apart from the long-sleeved T-shirts, I did have to make certain other adjustments to my daily routines to make sure I wasn't discovered. For example, for as long as I can remember, my mum always came into the bathroom when I was in the bath – presumably to check I wasn't doing anything sinful. It was just one of her habits that you had to get used to. There was no bolt on the door and she would just suddenly walk in on me. She'd look at me for a moment but say nothing. Then she'd just walk out again. Since I had fairly deep lacerations on both arms, I couldn't let her see me in the bath so I started having a shower first thing in the morning before she was awake. She never said anything about this. Who knows? Maybe she felt that showers were less likely to promote sinful thoughts; I really couldn't say. Then one afternoon that I would guess was during the third week of August, something happened and the whole course of my life shifted once more. Like it had happened that first time I caught sight of her in the garden. Similarly, on this occasion, I was also in the spare room looking down at the red and black blanket on the patio – she always laid it out in exactly the same manner in exactly the same place and this in itself I felt to be a strong defence against my mother's allegations of flightiness. There was an unopened magazine and a water bottle but there was no sign of her. This wasn't unusual; she would often arrange her blanket in that very specific way and then disappear for a while. I was in no hurry; I could wait all afternoon if I had to. I'd done it many times in the past. But then, like I said, something happened and to this day I'm confused by my memory of the events of that afternoon. Something really bad happened, I know that, and

I knew instantly that everything had changed. I remember the water bottle and the blanket and I know that part of the memory is real but then it gets confused. Sometimes I have an image in my mind of Lucy walking onto the patio with a young boy who is wearing shorts but no shirt; they are laughing and touching and being sort of disgusting and intimate with one another. I can smell their sweat and it's dirty and disgusting. After that it's all a sort of a blank. At the same time, I have a vivid memory of my mum returning from her Bible group early and running up the stairs looking for me at almost the precise same moment. In my mind I really don't know which is a dream and which is real. I think I can recall someone knocking at the front door and my mum being on the landing outside my room. I'm sure that they are not just knocking; they are also calling through the letterbox, too. I can picture my mum with her hands shaking and looking at me as if she expected me to do something. I remember wondering if maybe my mum had told someone about me. But then the knocking and the shouting stops and I'm sure I have some memory of a door slamming and a car driving off. Then it all goes blank again. The next memory about which I'm really certain is of sitting in the kitchen with my mother a little while later. I'm drinking tea and she's shouting at me. I can clearly recall her calling me names and quoting the Bible and telling me that I'd brought all this upon myself. Stuff like, 'You're such an idiot. How many times have I warned you about this? Oh yes, much too proud, too full of yourself to listen to your own mother! Well hear this! Proverbs 11, verse 2, when pride cometh, then cometh shame. Who does that sound like? Proverbs 16:5. Everyone that is proud in heart is an abomination to the Lord. Does that sound like anyone you know? I knew this would happen one day. People who conceal their sins will not prosper. Proverbs 28:13!' She went on like that for a bit but I stopped listening. Whatever happened that afternoon things were noticeably very different around the house. I didn't actually see Lucy for a couple of days. There was no sign of her and she didn't knock on the door and I wondered if she'd started avoiding me. I still thought about her and I carried on touching myself whenever I did. I still wanted to do all the things to her I kept thinking about. All those things... I just couldn't help myself and it wasn't something I could ever get any control over. Love was on the side of the angels, lust on the side of the Devil. My mum didn't say that; I worked it out for myself. But you soon learn that the Devil is actually on both sides and that's his greatest trick. I thought I'd learned to deal with lust and its effects. But lust never made me cry, never kept me awake all night and never made me feel that my whole reason for being alive had just been taken away from me.

10

The Left Hand of Daddy Rice

Obscurity is the final, irrefutable damnation of posterity. It is cruel, lasting, absolute and merciless. It is also the blank page or blank canvas onto which we can project any number of our own fantasies. But we must bear in mind that obscurity can also be a defiant gesture on the part of the artist. As a deliberate denial or a rejection it becomes in itself an artistic art, a personal statement, a means by which the artist's integrity and ideology remain

Martin emits an involuntary groaning animal noise. 'Oh Christ!' he growls through his teeth. 'Stop right now, before you start babbling on about fucking Rimbaud again!'

Tambo Bones last made music, as far as we are aware, in the 1970s and since then has drifted into forty years of silence and obscurity. He is currently a resident in a home for assisted living in Timberlane, New Orleans.

While there are still those who regard an early demise as the sole guarantee of continuing credibility, longevity in an artist will remain a perplexing issue. In considering an artist's survival into their eighties or their nineties, one is often confronted with details that appear, on first reading, anomalous or even paradoxical. Picasso, for example, could have met Rimbaud.

'*And* there it is!'

Picasso, for example, could have met Rimbaud but also watched Hendrix at Woodstock. Similarly, Tambo Bones could have watched Louis Armstrong boarding that train at New

Orleans Union Station in 1922 that took him north to meet up with Joe Oliver in Chicago and then made a reference to this very event earlier today on his Facebook page.

Martin stops writing at this point and saves the document. This morning he feels for the first time that he is actually struggling with his topic. The ideas are not flowing as naturally as they have been and the whole tone seems forced and uninspired – what he used to call 'writing for the sake of writing'. He would return to it later.

Then, as though suddenly self-conscious, he smiles guiltily to himself and opens a new document. Ever since his lunch with Sally the previous day and her enthusiasm for *An Unhealthy Interest*, a very strange thing has been happening to him. Every so often, at the oddest moments, a series of vaguely related thoughts and themes have begun forming in his mind. It is a familiar process yet it is one he has not experienced in a very long time. The Facebook reference had brought it back to mind again.

He begins to type quickly.

OEDIPUS NET

Woman indulges in torrid explicit online 'relationship' with much younger man. Daily, they exchange photos and films but never of their faces. It's exclusively a masturbatory affair but we also follow both parties in their otherwise dull lives, their evening encounters being the only exciting aspect of their days. (Work in the following somewhere: Note to all international internet smut pedlars – whenever I see the term 'hairy twats' I can only picture Free at the 1970 Isle of Wight Festival playing 'Mr Big'; you may wish to bear this in mind for the future.)

They use aliases whilst online and enjoy the anonymity and delight in the possibilities. 'Madame X' claims an entire erotic history on her behalf, as a young girl she'd lived in France and North Africa, starred in a few porn films which got her expelled from the UK, etc. etc. and she claims to be currently living in Provence (?).

'Boy1993' is 28 and married but claims to be 17 and a virgin and at some boarding school in the South East he refuses to name. We follow how their dismal lives contrast with the erotic liberation of those couple of hours every evening when they step into their fantasy world. Boy1993 actually works in local government and spends the weekends with his dull sexually inhibited wife and tends his garden. He visits a local art show and buys a painting for his father for his birthday – a landscape in oils painted by a local artist – and it is the picture that he sees upside down on a chest of drawers behind Madame X one evening.

So, is Madame X his mother?

Or the artist?

What does he do next? No idea.

It would in all probability progress no further than this but these 285 words represent something of unparalleled significance to Martin. It is an idea for a novel. It is nothing more than this and if questioned at any length on the subject he would be the first to admit that it is probably a rather weak idea and it would make a similarly feeble novel. However, it is the first time in over a year that he has even thought about writing any sort of fiction again. He saves the document, aware that he may never even do as much as glance at it a second time. In itself, it would never be important or memorable, yet at this precise moment that is hardly the issue.

He could make a good case for attributing this sudden burst of inspiration to the great lost gods of New Orleans, a credible enough argument, but he strongly suspects that it is more directly connected to his conversation with Sally. He adds the date to the foot of the page, saves it once again and finally closes the document.

Now he stands up and wanders over to the window, then, craning his neck, he looks up and scans the early morning sky for clouds. It is another beautiful clear morning. It wouldn't be a good book, he thinks, on reflection; there are major problems with the plot – prior to seeing the painting, how come the man fails to recognise a room in his own parent's house? Furthermore, did he really want to get involved again with anything with a vaguely sexual theme?

There would be other ideas. Better ideas. One day.

Feeling the need to focus his mind somewhat on more pressing matters, he returns to the laptop and scanning the files on the CD currently in the drive, he automatically selects track 7. Attired still in his comically enormous Foot Locker T-shirt and like some satirical portrayal of a drunken medieval monk or a novice shaman, he is soon dancing around the room in a very personal and slightly unorthodox manner and singing along to the music.

'So *now ah'm gwine down to Georgia – kiss de first white woman I see.*

Yes sir, ah'm gwine down to Georgia – kiss de first white woman I see.'

Sally had said she'd be interested in hearing the song and was keen for Stefan to hear it too. These might have been sentiments expressed entirely out of politeness but he would like her to give it a listen. It is important to him and he wants to share it with her.

'*Roll 'em, Mr Bones, Mr Bones, Mr Bones,*

I say Roll 'em, Mr Bones, Mr Bones, Mr Bones!'

After they'd left the French Market the previous afternoon, they'd walked around the Quarter for an hour or so and Martin had told her the whole story of Tambo Bones and gone into some detail on the subject of the book he was intending to write about him. Sally had listened intently and said 'awesome' a few more times than was strictly necessary, which might have suggested to the uninitiated that her mind

THE LEFT HAND OF DADDY RICE

was otherwise occupied. This would, however, be unfair to the young lady as she did ask a number of relevant and pertinent questions and when Martin told her he was intending to pay a visit to a certain A.C. Monroe on Barracks Street the following morning, she'd immediately volunteered to accompany him.

He continues to sing while at the same time he discards, with very little grace or poise, the voluminous T-shirt. He achieves this objective roughly in the manner of a man casually disposing of a parachute.

'*Roll 'em, Mr Bones, Mr Bones, Mr Bones,*
I say Roll 'em, Mr Bones, Mr Bones, Mr Bones!'

Then he hears it for the first time. It is as though he is subconsciously seeking to reinforce his earlier assertion that the criterion for any great piece of music is its capacity to continually sound fresh or to reveal new details on every hearing. There it is again and now he can clearly hear in the instrumental passage of 'Georgia Blues' a faint, oddly discordant, piano riff. Naked now apart from his boxer shorts, he is rooted to the spot, frozen again in space and time – his heart and respiratory rate locked in common time with the rhythmic pulse of The Back O' Town Boys.

There it is again. It is playing against the rest of the band, jarring slightly and ignoring the usual conventions of key and tempo. It sounds like modernist bop pianist Bud Powell has just stumbled into the studio. Or Thelonious Monk. Actually, it sounds a bit like Little Rootie...

Martin eventually locates his phone in a jacket pocket.

'Hello,' he says cautiously.

'Hi, Dad, it's me.'

His face breaks into a broad and genuine smile. 'Oh, good morning, Sally. How's things?'

'It's all good. Everything's fine. What about you?'

'Yeah, yeah, same.'

'Just wondered what time you want to meet up this morning.'

Suddenly aware of his semi-nudity, Martin takes a moment to reflect on the question. 'I don't know.' He sits on the bed and acting without any apparent conscious will, he gingerly pulls a corner of the quilt over his lower half. 'In about an hour or so? What do you reckon?'

'Sounds cool. Where are we going again?'

Martin picks up the piece of paper from his bedside. 'Um, here we are. Barracks Street. That's on the edge of the Quarter over towards The Marigny. It's not far. We need to find number 649. It says "Ramp" here on the note so it's probably at the Rampart Street end.'

'OK. Say, have you had breakfast yet?'

Martin shakes his head. 'No, I don't think I'll bother. I've gone off granola. I just can't eat it anymore.'

'Hey, I got an idea. Why don't I, like, grab us a couple of beignets on the way over to the Omni Royal Crescent and we'll eat them on the way?'

'That would be great. Anything but granola.'

'OK. I'll see you in an hour. Bye.'

'Yeah, see you then.'

Martin ends the call and begins to get dressed. His problem with granola is in fairness only a couple of hours old, but he feels no shortage of passion on the subject. He doesn't have a problem with the food itself, although he still maintains that it is difficult to have particularly strong positive or negative feelings on the matter; it is just the word *granola*. He really doesn't like it and can stay silent on the subject no longer. They should just market it as 'Breakfast Stuff' – that would be better. Catchy, too. Anything please but *granola*!

But the main problem is that it has started to sound too much like some tiny little Pacific island that America bombed to smithereens under Reagan. That was a very different America and it was one he didn't want to think about anymore.

*   *   *

'What was the number again?'

'649.'

'Are you sure?'

'That's what it says here.'

'And are you, like, totally certain that's Rampart Street, right? Because it says North Rampart Street on the sign.'

'No, there's only one Rampart Street and this is it. It turns into South Rampart Street as it crosses Canal Street.'

Sally sighs theatrically. 'Ladies and gentlemen, give it up! My father, the New Orleans Nerd!'

Martin takes his daughter's comment in the jocular manner it is intended. He does, however, experience a certain frisson of something like pride in being so categorised. 'Well, you know me . . .'

It is just after eleven o'clock and it's already warm. They cast with their stick-like shadows, the shapes of ancient statues on the roads and sidewalks, upon which one senses one is constantly stepping on a terribly fine layer of sand. Or dust. Or bones. They have just spent a confusing and frustrating few minutes looking at house numbers, a point which Sally feels is worth making once more.

'All these houses are, like, eleven hundred and something, there's 1119, 1121. That's, like, a boundary wall or something and that's definitely a car park.'

Martin rubs his eyes. 'OK, let me think . . .'

'Yeah, I definitely know, like, a car park when I see one.'

Martin points in roughly a south-eastwards direction. 'I reckon it will be down *that* way,' he says, although his tone is noticeably speculative rather than confident.

'Whatever you say,' says Sally with an indulgent or possibly semi-ironic smile. 'Lead on! You're the nerd and I'll simply follow in your footsteps!'

'Thanks.'

They continue to look at house numbers as they walk away from North Rampart Street and slowly make their way back towards the old US Mint building and the distant river. They chat as they walk. Sally asks questions about the book – how long did it take, what sort of research was required and was the reaction in any way anticipated, given the nature of the book? And Martin asks questions about Stefan – what instruments does he play, does he like jazz and how many CDs/LPs does he possess? When the conversation dwindles, Martin wonders if the parents might have recently emigrated to New Zealand and prior to making his first visit the man had mailed the painting to them as a housewarming present. 'Madame X' could be bored and lonely while adjusting to her new environment, hence her online distractions. Such a scenario might possibly work but he fears he might already be growing weary of the idea.

But mainly they point out the houses they like to one another, speculate on real estate prices and read out the numbers. The house numbers are based on the block system, which Sally understands far better than her father, and each time they traverse a junction the numbers drop from 1100 and something down to 1000 then down to 900 until eventually, after walking for about ten minutes, they reach the 600 block.

Sally notices it first and instantly experiences the strongest urge to laugh. 'There you go,' she says, pointing.

'What are you – oh fuck!'

She hits him playfully on the arm. 'Way to go, nerd! Didn't see that coming now, did you?'

What Martin had not seen coming was the fact that 649 Barracks Street stands out from the buildings on either side because of a disabled access ramp that runs from the street right up to the front door. The directions had nothing to do with Rampart Street and Martin now feels a warm tingling sensation in his cheeks. Before he has a chance to compose himself or think of a suitable response, Sally is already tapping on the glass panel of the front door.

'Hello, hello,' she says in the sort of breathy, light-hearted sing-song tone that comes quite easily when you're twenty-two. Martin remains on the sidewalk a couple of yards away; he glances up and down the street as though wondering if they are being observed. A legacy of 'Recent Events'; it is not a question of the true reason or the motive behind one's actions – it is only how it may appear to others.

'Hello...'

The door is now opened by an African American lady in jeans and a loose-fitting floral shirt. Martin would place her somewhere in her mid to late sixties.

'Yes?' she says bluntly but not entirely without kindness.

'Hi there,' says Sally.

'Y'all lost or something?'

'No, ma'am, my name is Sally Bonehouse and this is my father, Martin.'

'Hi there,' says Martin.

The lady nods but doesn't say anything. She seems to be taking a step backwards into the cool, dark sanctuary of her home and Martin pictures the loaded shotgun she keeps just inside the door.

'Are you guys Australian?' she asks suddenly.

'No, I'm English actually,' says Martin, warily stepping onto the ramp for the first time.

'And I live in Montreal.'

'You don't say.'

'I love your house,' announces Sally, keen to keep the conversation going. 'It's really pretty.'

'Well, thank you, sweetie; you're very kind but what do you guys want? You got some Jesus stuff you want to tell me about? Or you got some insurance thing going on?'

'No, nothing like that,' says Martin approaching the front door. 'I was given this address by a guitar player on Royal Street and I was really hoping to speak to A.C. Monroe.'

'You mean Arthur? He's my son, yeah, he's here all right. You got an appointment or something?'

Martin toys with the hair above his right ear. 'Well, no,' he intones languidly, 'not exactly. But it's about; well ... it's to do with a book I'm writing.'

'A *book* you say?'

Martin nods. 'Yeah, that's right.'

'Oh, y'all better come in, then. I'll take you through; he's in the back. He ain't going no place anytime soon.'

She calls her son's name a couple of times, in a manner that suggests she is alerting rather than summoning him, as she leads Martin and Sally through the house. The interior of 649 Barracks Street is cool and airy with polished wooden floors and dark wood ceiling fans. Martin glances at the books on the shelves as he passes, as is his custom and Sally notices the original artworks on the walls, landscapes and abstracts of a pretty high standard and she wonders for a moment if Arthur or his mother is the artist responsible.

Mrs Monroe knocks on a door towards the rear of the house and gestures for her visitors to join her. 'Hey, Arthur, some people here to see you, son.'

There is no reply.

'You be nice to these people now, you hear me, son. Man is writing a book and they just come all the way from Australia to see you.'

'That right?' says a voice.

She pushes open the door and turns to Martin and Sally. 'Y'all go on in and make yourselves comfortable. Y'all need anything, y'all just holler now.'

'Thank you,' says Sally.

Martin now steps timidly through the doorway. 'Mr Monroe,' he says to the man in the corner of the room who has his back to him.

'Thank you so much for seeing us. I really app–'

'So what's all this about exactly?' A.C. Monroe deftly reverses his wheelchair and executing a perfect 180° manoeuvre, he turns to face Martin. He is probably the younger man by

208

a few years and although dressed casually and unshaven, possesses a commanding and authoritative demeanour quite evident at first glance. 'Who did you say you were?'

Martin takes a step forward. 'My name is Martin Bonehouse,' he says, nervously offering his hand, 'and this is my daughter, Sally.'

Mr Monroe fails to notice Martin's outstretched hand and declines to look at either of his visitors. 'How y'all doing?' he enquires vaguely.

'I'm sorry to barge in like this but I was given your address by Little Vee. You might know him; he's a guitarist –'

The man smiles. 'Yeah I know him. But he was Vernon when I knew him. I used to teach Sociology at Dillard and he was one of my students. This was a good few years ago but he'll always be Vernon to me. Not the brightest boy in the class and probably a better guitar player than he ever was student, that's for damn sure!' He chuckles to himself and now looks at Martin and Sally for the first time. 'Yeah, folks, come in and find yourselves some chairs somewhere,' he says, gesturing with his hand in a manner that is possibly more theatrical than specific. 'Y'all can just move all those papers, put 'em on the floor if you have to.' He then adds, as though to forestall any further comments, 'Housekeeping just ain't my thing.'

The room, which obviously functions as an office or workspace, is incredibly untidy but it has that sort of academic disarray which Martin always finds comforting in some way. As much as his brief inventory can ascertain on this occasion, most of the books on the shelves that line almost every inch of available wall space seem to be related to social history or political theory. But everywhere he looks there are scattered papers, open books and journals. On the desk there are three high-end, large screen laptops, each displaying a different page of text. It is, in short, precisely the kind of room that Martin has always wanted to inhabit.

Eventually, they find two chairs in opposite corners of the room and sit down.

'So why exactly did Vernon send you to me?'

'Well ... um...' says Martin, wondering where best to begin.

'Dad's writing a book,' says Sally suddenly, summarising the situation with her customary acuity.

'Is that right?'

Martin nods. 'Or maybe an article; I don't know yet.'

'That must be nice for you. You want to tell me what it's about?'

Martin's shallow inhalation betrays his apprehension. 'Well, it's basically about this obscure musician and performer from New Orleans. His name was Oscar Oliver Brightwater.'

A.C. Monroe shakes his head. 'Don't know the name, I'm afraid.'

'He worked from the late thirties up until the seventies. He never used his real name. He mainly worked in medicine shows and was known as Sweet Papa Stalebread and then Tambo Bones and then –'

'Woah, woah now! Just stop right there! I know *that* name!' Mr Monroe's eyes flash with sudden anger. 'Are you serious with that? Tambo Bones was like the last surviving minstrel, for god's sake, a blackface minstrel! Surely you know that already and you've come to my house to talk to me about a blackface performer! Is this some racist redneck hillbilly cracker bullshit you tryin' to pull on me? Where's the hidden webcam?'

'No, no, please, it's nothing like that,' says Martin in a sudden tone of mild desperation. 'Look, I understand perfectly –'

'Oh, you *understand* do you?' he asks, in an exaggerated mocking manner. 'You've shared in the pain and the degradation and humiliation, have you? You know just what that is like?'

'I'm sorry,' says Martin. 'I don't mean to give offence.'

'Offence? *Offence?* And you be dragging your sorry ass

into *my* home to talk to me about blackface. Have you the slight–?'

'Did you know,' asks Sally, interrupting suddenly and showing once again her habitual flair for decisive action.

Both men now turn instantly towards her. The accent had modified certainly but the intonation and precise cadence of the three words was unchanged with its distinct emphasis on the last two syllables – did *you know*? Thankfully, from Martin's perspective, on this occasion, she does not follow up the query with a piece of unsolicited information about dinosaurs or the Spice Girls.

'Did *you know* that in 1967, right, that's like four years after the March on Washington, three years after the Civil Rights Act and two years after the Voting Rights Act, right? Well, in 1967, the US Government, actually the United States Board on Geographic Names, to give it its proper name, replaced the, er ... N-word in a hundred and forty-three place names in the USA! Isn't that, like, just amazing? Like the word was *actually* in a hundred and forty-three place names in 1967!'

A.C. Monroe narrows his eyes and looks at Sally coldly, but his tone is curious rather than accusatory. 'Are you sure 'bout that? It wasn't 1867 you're thinking of?'

'No, it's definitely 1967. We did it in college with Mr Gotterher. I had to write an essay about it.'

'You serious, girl?'

'Yeah, I'm absolutely serious!'

Mr Monroe thinks for a moment and then shakes his head. He grabs a piece of paper and a pen from his desk. 'I'm writing that down. That's going right in my blog tonight. 1967? Shit! How many was it again?'

'A hundred and forty-three.'

Martin looks at Sally with a combination of gratitude and wonder, which might be another way of describing love he thinks, and they both watch in silence as A.C. Monroe writes.

He mutters to himself as he does so but only the words 'un-fucking-believable' are actually discernible from a distance.

Sensing that this might be his last opportunity to speak, Martin feels obliged to clarify the matter. 'It's really only one particular song he recorded that is of any interest to me,' he says, his voice teetering on the apologetic.

'Uh huh.'

'Are you familiar at all with the song called "Georgia Blues"?'

'Er ... no, I don't think that I am.' A.C. Monroe's tone of voice now seems to somehow imply both suspicion and disinterest.

Martin goes on to describe the song in some detail and what he feels is its unequivocal message. He quotes the lyrics from all three verses and concludes by saying, 'It's an amazing song and it was recorded here in New Orleans in 1941!'

Mr Monroe's face now breaks into a smile. 'You people sure have a thing with dates, don't you? Is that like a *thing* where you come from?'

But Martin is not about to be distracted. 'For 1941, it is almost unprecedented. It has all the powerful imagery and the underlying meaning of a great protest song: one that you could easily associate with a movement that was almost twenty years in the future.'

The other man shrugs in a manner that suggests the information is of little consequence to him.

Martin now leans forward in his chair and continues. 'But the thing that is often overlooked is the fact that behind the character of Tambo Bones and underneath all that black makeup, Oscar Brightwater was not a white man but actually a mixed-race Creole.'

'Now,' says A.C. Monroe raising his index finger to his lip, 'I'm listening.'

Martin glances over at Sally who smiles at him and taking this as some kind of cue, he now excitedly paraphrases the opening spoken segment of the song. He quotes, as accurately as he can, the dialogue during which Tambo makes the point that the listeners, who are quite clearly white by implication, only enjoy blues songs because it gives them a chance to revel in the black man's misery. 'This really isn't one man's reading; it's not my interpretation. If you hear the song there is absolutely no other reading.'

'That's a rather arrogant stance if you don't mind me saying.'

'But I think if you heard –'

'And furthermore, Creole or mixed race, you'll never get over that blackface thing. Not anymore.'

But Martin is not easily dissuaded. 'But that's the thing. This wasn't from a film or a show. It was a record. Blackface is a visual, shall we say, motif or device? What would be the point of an audio recording? It doesn't work? It's an absurdity, a paradox. Even if the intention was to be humorous in some way it just can't work on that level, right? Therefore, it must be the singer's intention to have the song listened to on its own merits, right? Do we know or need to know that the singer is actually in blackface? Is that part of the intended entertainment?'

'I don't think you can just ignore something like that so easily.'

'But it's just a song and does it actually matter what we can't see?' Martin's tone of voice now becomes noticeably more excited. 'Look, Billie Holiday could have been half passed-out under a piano with a needle in her arm when she sang "Strange Fruit" – it's the message that's important. The Miles Davis Quintet could have been raping kittens when they made "'Round About Midnight" but the music is all we've got, right?'

'Oh, thanks so much for that image, man! That's going to stay with me all day!'

'Sorry,' says Martin smiling.

'Thing is, regardless of your area of interest or study, without hard evidence you can only ever speculate and you'll never know for certain intention or motive. It's simply the realm of the possible and you'll always be struggling with the question of interpretation and no interpretation is definitive. Ask any so-called *historian!*' He intones the word with evident disdain. 'It's all about perception. Always has been.'

'But I really don't think it's possible to have any other interpretation.'

A.C. Monroe shakes his head vigorously. 'There are always other interpretations! Don't matter if it's social history or cultural history, without solid evidence, nothing is an absolute truth.' He alters his position in his chair and reflects for a moment. 'Look, when you first go to school and you study science and math and geography and history you are led to believe that history is like science – it's the study of simple unassailable facts. But history is equally the art of *presenting* facts as much as it is about the facts themselves.'

Martin shrugs and intones wearily, 'The nightmare from which I'm trying to awake.'

'Yeah, something like that! Look, History is how facts get *displayed*. It is not a science – it's marketing. No disrespect to you or your integrity, but look at it objectively; you're just a white male with some obviously great need to exonerate or redeem some justifiably obscure performer. You're wasting your time! You think you're going to enlighten the masses, turn public opinion? It'll never happen, not for you and certainly not for Tambo Bones. You'll be accused of racial insensitivity for one thing and probably a lot worse. Leave all that stuff to the historians.'

Sally chooses this moment to re-join the conversation. 'But you just sounded like you have little respect for historians.'

'Damn right!' says A.C. Monroe in a loud, booming voice, suggesting he was going to enjoy this shift in the conversation. 'Historians like order. They like finding patterns and seek

214

consolation in the certainties they have constructed. They're sometimes like those people who see images of Jesus in the clouds. They love finding connections that aren't there. They despise chaos, random acts or anything that doesn't fit or conform precisely. Your perception of Tambo Bones is an anomaly. Believe me, sir, it would not be tolerated.'

Martin looks at his shoes then glances at Sally and wonders if this might be a time to say their farewells. But A.C. Monroe hasn't quite finished.

'Young lady,' he says, addressing Sally, 'could you be so kind as to reach behind your left shoulder and take down that maroon folder that's lying there on its side next to that little statuette thing. Yeah that's it.' He turns once again to Martin. 'So, Martin, this isn't a trick question but if I said Jim Crow to you what sort of thing would that conjure up in your mind?'

Shit, thinks Martin, why is he asking me this? He reflects on the question for a moment and speaks slowly as though mindful that in his haste he may say something he might regret. 'Well, I know it was from a song or a show from the minstrel era and it later came to be used as a euphemism for segregation and racist policies and attitudes.'

'Yeah, that's pretty much the accepted view.'

Martin feels the tension draining from his shoulders. 'Well, that's what I thought.'

'But I can show you another interpretation, another *perception* if you will.' He turns to Sally. 'Just hand that file to your old man, would you? Thanks. And you, sir, if you just open the file and look at the picture that's in the plastic sleeve right on top there. You see it?'

Martin does as he is requested and finds that he is currently looking at a copy of an old engraving of a blackface minstrel. The lettering at the bottom of the picture is feint; the first line is more or less illegible but in the subsequent two lines he can clearly make out:

England and America
Mr T.D. RICE

'So, who is this guy?'

Mr Monroe frowns. 'That man, my friend, is Daddy Rice performing at the Bowery Theatre in 1833. The illustration is probably the best and clearest one available of him performing 'Jump Jim Crow', the song that made him famous and gave us the term we still use today.'

Martin looks at the picture again. The man is standing on one leg and his head is turned to one side strangely. By the contortions of his legs and arms, one gets the impression that the artist was attempting to depict a man in the process of dancing.

'Like I say, it's possibly the most detailed representation I've been able to source. Given its history, it's a hard image for any African American to look at, but once you go beyond the blackface and the garish clothes, the more you start to notice certain other details. You notice the odd gait of the head; the way the neck is tilted to me immediately suggests curvature of the spine or mild scoliosis.'

'I did notice that,' says Martin.

'Then I direct your attention to the man's hands. Particularly consider the posture of the left hand. What do you see?'

Martin gazes hard at the picture again. 'Uh ... looks like he might be miming playing, I don't know ... an invisible banjo?'

A.C. Monroe shakes his head. 'Well, that might be another *perception* I suppose. But look again at the very particular way in which they've been depicted. You see, I can recognise instantly that this man's wrists are displaying what is known as internal rotation. It is a symptom of people who suffer with cerebral palsy. I've spoken to a number of specialists and they agree with my observation.'

'I'm sorry,' says Martin with an awkward shrug, 'but that's not something I could really comment on.'

'So you put the internal rotation of the wrists alongside the scoliosis, which is also a symptom of cerebral palsy, and things start to take you in a new direction.'

Martin nods and for a moment he wonders if the nature of Mr Monroe's disability is also cerebral palsy.

'Right, now, here's the interesting part. What is not generally known is that Daddy Rice based his whole 'Jump Jim Crow' routine on an actual man named Jim Crow. Jim Crow was historically a real person. If you turn over to the next page in the file you'll see a copy of an article from the *New York Times* in 1881. You got it there?'

'Yes.'

'The article is called "An Old Actor's Memories" and in the right-hand column there are a couple of paragraphs about Daddy Rice, including a section on how he first met Jim Crow. The original Jim Crow was an old slave from Louisville who worked in a stable behind the theatre where Rice was working. Crow used to sing to himself while he was working and perform this little dance, which he called "Jumping Jim Crow". Rice saw this first-hand and attempted to accurately mimic his entire song together with his funny little body movements and adapt it for the stage. As we know, it was a huge success. But what concerns us is that in the same article, Jim Crow is described as "very much deformed". There are other references in other sources to him being crippled or handicapped. So, given all that information, I think it's perfectly rational to assume that old Jim Crow had some variant of cerebral palsy.'

'That's, like, so interesting,' says Sally. 'Are you planning to write about this?'

'That, young lady, is pretty much the problem. You see that whole file you're looking at was my working notes for an article I wrote for the university paper. The piece was called "Jim Crow – A New Perspective" and publishing that article was probably the most stupid decision I ever made in my whole damn life.'

'Not well received?'

'That's putting it mildly.'

'Was this article,' asks Sally in slow, fairly sombre tones, 'like, the reason why you don't work at the university anymore?' A.C. Monroe chuckles at this. 'Wow, the girl's on fire today, my man! Actually, there were a couple of other transgressions, shall we say, but the article had a totally different effect to the one I was intending. But, as I discovered, history is still all about the recording and retelling of simple choices, like those between good and evil or right and wrong, anything in fact divided by a clear unassailable boundary. Anything that challenges or straddles that boundary, or recognises multiple or alternative choices, is rarely encouraged.'

'That's really sad.'

'Yeah, but it's a lesson learned and maybe it's one that your father needs to hear too. Some things you just have to leave alone. Look at me; I'm a wheelchair-bound African American, I'm forty-six years old and not some kind of naïve white boy idiot and I wasn't disrespecting my people or the four-hundred years of oppression and brutality we have been through; I just felt it was time for handicapped people to fight back as well. I thought we could use a rallying cry, too! So, maybe when a wheelchair-user is turned down for a job or can't use the restroom in a restaurant or maybe can't even get into the damn restaurant in the first place, maybe when he's treated like a freak or mocked because he can't make himself understood, he could shout 'Jim Crow, Jim Crow!' and the message would get gradually through! And the message will bring people together. I tell you, that's all you can ever hope to do, man, just get that message through. Don't matter if it's two people or two million! OK, I was wrong, but I kind of thought of myself, stupidly, as a self-propelling Toussaint Louverture!'

'That must have been, like, really disappointing.'

'Well, it's like my mother says: if I was the kind of person who gave a shit that would be exactly the sort of thing I'd give a shit about.'

'I'll remember that,' says Martin smiling. 'If you're ever thinking of running for mayor, I would definitely use that as your campaign slogan.'

Mr Monroe smiles. 'Yeah, maybe I will. But seriously, I swear to you, it was never my remotest intention to claim the term on behalf of the handicapped – absolutely not – but I hoped that if the situation warranted it then it might be used by any oppressed segregated peoples. Jim Crow was a handicapped black man *period* not a black man who also, by the way, happened to be handicapped or a handicapped man who, coincidentally, also happened to be black. It's a question of emphasis. But, like I say, intentions can be misinterpreted and what you think you've written isn't always the same thing as what folks read.'

The day stops for a moment and these words now hang heavily in the air; they fill every inch of the space between them and quickly begin to drain the oxygen from the room. Martin watches the ceiling fan rotate then he lets the top shelf of the opposite bookcase claim his attention. This is not an issue he feels comfortable exploring in any depth and for a few moments he finds that he does not wish to make eye contact with either of the other two people in the room. Fortunately, A.C. Monroe moves onto another subject.

'Funny thing about the article is that the previous year I'd written a long piece for the paper about, what I called, "Virtual Blackface". It was about how minstrelsy survived into the era of rock 'n' roll and beyond and that even traces can be found in the music of today. I cited Mick Jagger, on account of his singing style and stage manner, as the greatest exponent of virtual blackface. But I used other examples too. Jimi Hendrix was interesting to me as he seemed to be a psychedelic reimagining of the character of Mars Napoleon Sinclair Brown or Zip Coon, the gaudily dressed dandy and ladies' man, complete with his anglicised manners and pretensions. In the same piece I even wrote that some hip-hop artists still today take on the personas of stereotypes from the minstrel era. Anyway, that particular article was highly regarded around the university and I even received a degree of praise for it. Not the slightest suggestion of controversy. So, I had this great idea of doing something about Jim Crow and you know the rest, right?'

'So did you try to get another job?' asks Sally with the kind of candour that both betrays and celebrates her youth.

'Nah, I'd had enough by then. I get by doing private tuition and grading exam papers. But my blog has over three thousand subscribers and that's my real area of interest nowadays.'

'We'll subscribe, won't we, Dad?'

'Definitely,' says Martin, slowly getting up from his chair. 'Look, thank you so much for your time, but I really don't want us to impose any further.'

'No problem. Just don't go stirring things up. You can speculate as objectively as you can over the issue of motive or intention, but it will only ever be speculation. Just don't go confusing theory with history. On the basis of a single recording, you can't know for certain what was high moral purpose or what was just basically a bad joke.'

'Well,' says Martin, 'I suppose I could go and ask him.'

A.C. Monroe offers a cold, mocking laugh. 'And just how you propose doing that, my man?'

'I can go and see him!'

'What? What are you sayin'?'

Martin grins in a manner which unfortunately teeters on the self-satisfied. 'Yeah, he's in his nineties now but Oscar Oliver Brightwater is still with us. He's in an assisted-living place somewhere over in Timberlane. Nowadays, he uses the name Washington Adams, apparently.'

'Wash – Jesus, man, are you serious with that?'

'Absolutely.'

'Then what are you waiting for? Get your ass over there!'
Martin leans over and now, on his second attempt, he manages
to shake the man's hand. 'Thank you so much for your time.'
'Y'all come back and tell me about it.'
'We totally will,' says Sally as she plants a kiss on his
cheek. 'We totally will.'
When they are back on Barracks Street, Sally is the first
to speak.
'Wow, that guy was just so totally awesome, didn't you
think?'
'Yeah, he was something all right. Thanks for helping me
out in there, by the way. It was about to get a bit – you
know. Thanks anyway.'
'No problem,' she says with a dismissive pout. 'I can't wait
to tell Stefan about him. I'm going to sign up to his blog
just as soon as I get back on my netbook.'
'Yeah,' says Martin vaguely, 'might be interesting reading.'
'Maybe he'll mention us! So, Dad,' she announces as she
takes his arm, 'are you coming to meet Stefan tonight? We
thought about six thirty; maybe find somewhere nice in the
Quarter to eat?'
Martin sighs. 'Oh Sally, I'm sorry, I can't. Er ... not tonight.
I really need to go and see Clayton and tell him what I found
out from JuJu Jones.'
'But I promised Stefan.'
'Look, I'm sorry. Maybe later in the week.'
'But we might not be here then. Stefan is, like, freaking
out about Tintin and wants us to go back home.'
'Tintin?'
'Stefan's cat. His neighbour's feeding him but Stefan is really
funny about him and doesn't like leaving him on his own.
He's had him for, like, forever.'
'Tintin as in "Hergés Adventures of"?' asks Martin, lapsing
affectionately into an approximation of the booming
introduction to the old TV show.

Sally looks at her father suspiciously. 'I don't think so. It's not his full name as Stefan is always telling everyone. It's actually Tin Tin Deo.'

'What?' says Martin sharply.

'What do you mean "what"?'

'Stefan named his cat Tin Tin Deo?'

Sally looks indignant. 'So, is there, like, a law or something?'

Martin smiles to himself. He likes Stefan. Any man that would chose to name his cat after an old Dizzy Gillespie song, particularly one that was co-written by the legendary Cuban percussionist Chano Pozo, would obviously be a good man to know.

'What time did you say we were meeting up again?'

11

Thanet Talk Radio

Tambo Bones presents a great number of problems to the historian. Historians loathe chaos, random acts and anything that challenges a sense of clear order. They tend to regard the progress of mankind as a sequence of simple choices between opposing ideas.

Martin's eyes dart left and right suspiciously. 'Yeah, yeah I know,' he whispers conspiratorially. 'He won't mind; I'll make sure he gets a credit in the notes or something.'

With Tambo, the starting point of any investigation is the blackface and it is also the point to which we invariably return. Artists as diverse as Jelly Roll Morton, Bessie Smith, Furry Lewis, Louis Jordan, Hank Williams and Rufus Thomas (born in 1917, the same year as Tambo, incidentally) all performed in blackface early in their careers. But the issues are complicated and multi-faceted and continually raise further questions. Without factual certainty, we can only speculate, interpret or surmise. It is an admittedly controversial point, but without a clear indication of motive we should hesitate in branding him a racist. Was it his intention to mock, humiliate or denigrate for our amusement? Or was his crime simply one of racial insensitivity?

Martin wonders if he needs to clarify this point, racism being a deliberate, conscious conviction contrasted with insensitivity, which could, by definition, be a consequence of simple ignorance rather than doctrine. The tendency for the older generation to use certain once-correct racial terms that are no longer acceptable is a good example of the latter. But perhaps the differences were subtler, less clear cut. Were they in fact just varying degrees of the same mind-set? It is not a debate he feels comfortable in starting and so he deletes the final two lines. He tries a different angle.

Nowadays, it might be well regarded as an ambiguous act, but having your country's national flag tattooed on your arm doesn't ipso facto *qualify you as a racist. Of course, you might possibly be a racist (in which case your tattoo might serve as visual assertion) but the tattoo* alone *does not qualify as hard irrefutable evidence of racial prejudice.*

Again, he feels he is adopting the inflammatory tone of an embittered apologist. Furthermore, on rereading the text, he wonders if the point is a little beyond the scope of the project. Once again, he seems to be returning to a version of the same problem that has been nagging away at his thinking for the past hour. Politically, Martin has always considered himself an old-school socialist; philosophically, however, he would claim to be a liberal and a libertarian. So, if a man believes, as he does, absolutely and unconditionally, in freedom of speech, and this must be regarded as an incontrovertible human right, then that freedom must be accorded to those people whose speeches will make him physically sick. To unequivocally adhere to such an ideology, he should be prepared to lie down and die defending the rights of Nazis, racists and necrophiliacs to hold any beliefs they choose. In short, Liberalism, as they say around these parts, is a total motherfucker. And you know what they say: one man's moral certainty is another man's blinkered prejudice.

New paragraph.

Was it possible that Tambo felt that the medicine shows were based on long-established entertainment traditions and the conventions they adhered to were no more bizarre than clowns or drag acts and in

224

This, thinks Martin, is roughly the same as claiming racial insensitivity as an excuse. Since when was it an excuse anyway? It isn't as though he wanted to make a case for it being downgraded to the racist equivalent of manslaughter.

It all has to go.

The real issue remains entirely the question of motive and intention. Is 'Georgia Blues' the great lost protest song of the twentieth century? Or was it simply Tambo Bones's idea of a joke? Mr Monroe was entirely correct in what he said as they were leaving and Martin knows what he must do. He needs to talk to perhaps the only person still alive who can answer this question. He hasn't yet spoken to Clayton beyond leaving a message on his voicemail but he is starting to feel now with increasing conviction that the resolution to this crucial matter is something he must seek on his own.

He glances at the clock on his laptop toolbar and performs the usual subtraction. It is 6.23 p.m. and he's going to be late.

Bernice's reply was not the one he'd been expecting. 'That's a bit disappointing, don't you think?'

'Why do you say that? I thought you'd be really pleased.'

'I *am* pleased,' she says defensively. 'Look, this is my pleased face.' She smiles manically as though attempting to illustrate her point.

It is a Friday evening in March 2010, Wes has recently retired to his room and Martin and Bernice are sitting together at the kitchen table. They are sharing a bottle of Sainsbury's Spanish rosé and until a few moments ago, Martin was under the impression they were celebrating.

'So why are you disappointed then?'

Bernice looks at her empty glass suspiciously. 'Oh, it's nothing, really.'

'Come on.'

'Well, I just thought you'd actually be going to the radio station and doing the interview in their studio. You know, like the BBC or something. Jason's mum made them sound like they had these huge premises.'

'I'm sure they do, it's just they mainly conduct phone interviews for the show I'm on.'

'OK, but it's still a tiny bit disappointing, don't you think?'

'Maybe. But actually getting on the radio is the important thing.'

Bernice sighs and refills her glass. 'Fair enough. Anyway, what else did they say? Was it Jason's mum who rang?'

'No, it was just some researcher from Thanet Talk Radio. She told me that my "segment", which is what she kept calling it, would be on Monday's show just after the one o'clock news and she told me to be by my phone from about twelve fifty-five. I should have about ten or possibly fifteen minutes. I'm on the Steve Perry Hour, whatever that is. Apparently it's their most popular show.'

'Really?'

'That was what she said. It seems he also likes "lively debates".' Martin intones the words as though such things were highly disreputable. 'Anyway, rather than all the usual blather, he actually engages in conversations with the guests on his show and prefers to discuss issues on air. That's what the researcher told me, anyway. He's not a young bloke from what I gathered; I think she said he was a journalist for many years so it should be interesting.'

Bernice stifles a yawn. 'Anything else?' she asks, suggesting that she is now growing weary of the subject.

'Not really. They said they'd received the copy of the book we sent over and they were going to take a look at it over the weekend. Then she just told me not to be nervous.'

'Are you nervous?'

'Not until she said that, I wasn't.'

'You'll be fine. Anyway, I've got some more good news for

you,' she announces breezily and with the clear emphasis of someone introducing a welcome change of subject.

'Really?'

'After I went to Sainsbury's, I just happened to pop back into the town and I just happened to pop into Waterstones and then I just happened to glance at the shelves where they have your book and guess what?'

'What?'

'You've sold a copy of your book! Seriously! There were four there on Tuesday and now there are only three! That's something, right? You have to start somewhere.'

Bernice's enthusiasm, which Martin has, on account of the difference in their ages, always categorically refused to preface with 'youthful', has so often been a source of consolation in the past. It is, however, on this occasion, sadly misplaced.

'No, actually I haven't sold any books,' say Martin blandly.

'Yes, you have! I can count!'

'No, it was me.'

'You mean,' says Bernice, her brow furrowed in confusion, 'you actually bought your own book?'

Martin shrugs defensively. 'I didn't mean to, it just sort of happened. I was in there yesterday morning and I thought I'd take a picture on my phone, just to have record of one of my books being in a book shop. I was trying to be a bit sneaky, which probably made it look suspicious. Anyway, it took a couple of attempts as it was out of focus and blurry and then I was approached by this lady who asked me if I needed any help. So, I sort of felt compelled to buy the book.'

'Oh, Martin, that's just so sad,' she says slowly, but not without affection.

'You don't want to see the pictures, then?' asks Martin, but Bernice has already started making her way upstairs.

The following Monday, Martin is waiting by the telephone when it rings shortly before one o'clock. On account of what he fondly believes to be dignity, he lets the phone ring three times before answering it.

'Hello?'

'Hi there. Is that Martin?' says a vaguely familiar woman's voice.

'Yes, it is.'

'Great, this is Shelley again from Thanet Talk Radio. Just to let you know you'll be talking to Steve in about ten minutes. So I'd like to ask you at this stage to stay on the phone and stay right where you are.'

'Sure thing.'

'Right then, sit tight and wait for Steve. We go out live as I mentioned before so don't be nervous and enjoy the ride!'

'OK, thanks, Shelley.'

The line goes dead for a few moments then suddenly crackles to life once more and he is listening to the one o'clock news, followed by the weather, followed by the local traffic news and then suddenly it is happening.

'Hi there and welcome to the Steve Perry Hour here on Thanet Talk Radio, part of the Thanet FM network. I'm your host, Steve Perry, and we've got a great show lined up for you this afternoon...'

A piece of horrible music, which Martin recognises from somewhere, begins playing as Steve Perry lists the guests appearing on that afternoon's show: a local politician, a lady canoeist, someone talking about an exhibition called Unknown Margate and an actor who Martin truly believed was dead, before concluding, 'and that's all coming up in the next hour but our first guest this afternoon is on the line right now. Martin Bonehouse. Good afternoon, Martin.'

'Good afternoon, Steve.'

'Now, Martin is a writer who lives in the charming little village of Wickham, just outside Canterbury, and he's got a book that's just come out and I'm going to be chatting to him about that. So, Martin, if I could just ask you, is this your first book?'

'Yes, it is. I've written a number of other things but this is my first actual published novel.'

'Right. Well, the book is called *An Unhealthy Interest* and that rather sums up the main theme of the story, would you agree?'

'Partly. But it's certainly not its only theme. On some level it's a love story I suppose but really it's more about ignorance and bigotry and –'

'I don't wish to cut in here, Martin, but surely you realise it's an extremely controversial book.'

'I don't agree,' says Martin, discovering there to be a sudden confidence in his voice. 'Its subject matter might be judged controversial but no, I don't think the book itself is controversial.'

'Well, that's not a view I could personally endorse,' says Steve Perry in an abrupt, dismissive manner. 'You see, I imagine many people tuning in this afternoon might well consider themselves liberal, permissive and even broad-minded but I think even they may well find aspects of your novel, shall we say, difficult.'

Here we go, thinks Martin. Is this the 'lively debate' he was warned about? 'Well, look,' he says, gathering his thoughts, 'I don't wish to give away too much but when you get to the end of the novel the whole perspective of the story shifts and –'

'But your book is basically the story of a paedophile lusting after a fourteen-year-old girl.'

'Actually,' says Martin, 'that's a fallacious statement. The girl, as you rightly point out is fourteen. Therefore, the correct term in this case would be hebephilia and not paedophilia. I know paedophilia has become a demonising word which the righteous and ignorant bandy around hysterically nowadays, but that term actually refers to generally younger, usually prepubescent children.'

And this is it.

This is the point after which things will never be the same.

This is that tragic low punch in the second round when the referee should have stopped the fight.

This is the moment he steps into the hurricane.

There was life before this moment and life after, but this will remain the precise division that separates the two.

You might just about get away with sounding smug and self-satisfied on the radio (hundreds, probably thousands, do so every single day) particularly if you're feeling a little nervous. But you never *ever* correct an experienced broadcaster like Steve Perry on air over his use of English.

Furthermore, you should never suggest that the man is ignorant.

The man in question is quick to respond. 'Thank you for clearing that up for us, although I'm not absolutely sure our listeners will be happy to be referred to as stupid! The fact remains your book is about the salacious and disgusting fantasies of some pervert and you seem to be asking us to sympathise with this character's bestial cravings for an underage girl. I mean, are you actually suggesting we should lower the age of consent?'

'What? Absolutely not. How can you even –?'

'And if you don't mind me asking, how did you, as a writer, manage to get into such a person's mind? To me, the book reads like a sort of confession. Is it a confession?'

The agitation in Martin's voice is now all too evident. 'Of course it isn't! Look, obviously you haven't read the end of the book, the whole purpose –'

'To be honest with you, I wasn't able to get past the first couple of chapters. It was like some twisted pornographic fantasy.'

'No, no, that's not it at all.' There is now almost a pleading aspect to Martin's voice. 'If you'd read the ending –'

'Frankly, I doubt that most decent-minded people would get that far!'

In his panic, Martin now begins to repeat himself. 'But the book is more about bigotry and judgement...'

'Usually, I would ask a writer about the research he undertook for his book but in your case that might not be something I'd be prepared to discuss on air.'

Uncertain if the comment is serious or intended as a joke, Martin replies slowly. 'I actually did a lot of reading, statistics, case studies and that kind of thing. If you can wade through the hysteria you get a very different viewpoint. In some studies as many as 30% of sexual acts on underage girls are committed by underage boys. But that's not the sort of thing that interests us; that doesn't satisfy our vigilante bloodlust, does it?'

'So how do you propose we treat paedophiles or, for that matter, *hebephiles*?' The broadcaster intones the word with mocking sarcastic emphasis and the point is clearly made.

'Well...' Martin takes a moment to consider the question. 'That's not something I could really comment on,' he says in a tone that edges towards the evasive. 'But I don't think treating it as an extreme sexual orientation is the right approach, surely it's some form of psychiatric dysfunction as much as anything else.'

'So it's not a crime in your eyes and we should feel some sort of sympathy with people who molest children, is that what you're saying?'

'Of course I'm not,' says Martin feebly. 'But this really has got nothing to do with my book.'

Sensing the time is approaching to conclude the interview, Steve Perry now prepares to make his final point. 'One other question, Martin. I notice your book is published by Authorland, which, as far as I can gather, is a sort of self-publishing enterprise. Presumably this was because no other reputable publisher would touch it with a barge pole. Would that be correct?'

'Look, Steve, I really think you've missed the point here. If you had actually read the ending you'd find it's not the book you think it is and that –'

But at some point during this final remark the line has gone dead and he is currently addressing his comments to the dialling tone.

AN UNHEALTHY INTEREST

Chapter Fourteen

I don't blame my mum for doing what she did. I think she could see that the situation was slowly getting out of control. I don't imagine she contacted them herself but she probably asked someone from her Bible group to make the call. Most afternoons that week they returned to our house at roughly the same time. Sometimes they just banged the door but on other days I could hear them calling my name through the letterbox. If my mum was at home she would tell me to answer the door but I'd just ignore her. She couldn't make me and she knew that and so she'd usually just quote the Bible at me some more. It was usually from Proverbs. 1:7 was often mentioned; 'fools despise wisdom and instruction.' She would use that one a lot. Or there was that one from 18-something, 'an intelligent heart acquires knowledge, and the ear of the wise seeks knowledge.' I'm not stupid, I wanted to tell her and of course I knew the point she was making but it wasn't something I could think about anymore. I'd not seen Lucy for a while and everything in my head was becoming confused once more. When I was seeing her every day there was a real clarity about things, a sort of order to my life I could understand. It was like she'd gone into my head and rearranged all the stuff there and just handed everything back to me. Everything felt safe when she was there. But when she stopped visiting every day I had problems keeping all the really bad thoughts away. The day I remember most clearly was probably the last really hot day we had that summer. It was getting on towards the end of August and the sky was so blue and clear, the sort of day when you never see a cloud. I suppose it was mid-afternoon and I was at my desk in the spare room working on a model of a Dornier Do 217 E-2. The Dornier was considered a more powerful bomber than the Junkers Ju 88 but it was the design of the plane that appealed to me; it looked really solid and sturdy. I'd made a good start but because of what happened later that day, I have never wanted to finish it. Actually, I think it's still in a cupboard somewhere. I guess my thinking at the time was that it might have brought me bad luck or something. I often think things like that; the Heinkel HE 177 was responsible for Lucy arriving and that was good luck, whereas the Dornier had the opposite effect. I'm sure you've probably guessed that while I was working I kept glancing over at the patio next door in the hope that Lucy had returned without my knowledge. If that was the case it probably seemed reasonable that she might wish to take advantage of the sun. Sometimes if I half-closed my eyes I could make myself believe that she was lying down there on that red and black check blanket. It was like I could actually make her appear! It was just for a few seconds and then she'd be gone again but that was enough for me. She was wearing the black bikini with the top half undone – like she did that first time. I doubt that I will ever be able to imagine anything as beautiful as Lucy sunbathing and I don't want to be able to. Absolute certainty in our lives is rare and so I will cling to every memory I have of Lucy. I never touched her in the way you think I did. I wanted to, I thought about it all the time and maybe I regret not acting upon it. I understand that it's wrong, I understand that touching myself is wrong too, I even understand that cutting my arms is wrong, but I've never seemed able to stop. That afternoon, I thought about Lucy a lot and it was distracting so, almost as an experiment, I forced myself to concentrate on the Dornier instead. I really made an effort. I'd started applying glue to one side of the fuselage when something really odd happened. Something that I'm sure had never happened before. I started hearing voices! Not the kind you hear in your head sometimes when you have really bad thoughts but real voices, like people talking and the sound was coming from downstairs, from the room immediately below where I was sitting. No one ever came to our house and I know for a fact we haven't got anything worth stealing! So I rushed downstairs to investigate and found my mum sitting in the lounge with two ladies. They were both quite smartly dressed and the lady who looked slightly older was holding a briefcase. As I entered the room they stopped talking and stood up. They both looked at me and then the older one spoke.

'Oh good. I'm so pleased you've decided to join us.'

I didn't say anything. I just looked at my mum.

The lady continued. 'We've been trying really hard to get in touch with you; actually, we've been coming round here and trying your door for quite a long time. I was beginning to wonder what your neighbours might think!' She looked at the other lady and they both smiled at this.

I knew this was my mum's doing, she'd done this to me. She'd let them into our house; it was like she'd decided that she couldn't punish me herself so she'd given the job to someone else.

I hated her at that moment so much.

'So, Samantha, come and join us,' the lady said, indicating the vacant armchair.

They both sat down again and I did as I was requested. 'I prefer Sam,' I said.

'Oh, but that's such a shame, isn't it?' She smiled in that way that people do when you can't trust them. 'Samantha is such a lovely name.'

'I hate it.'

'OK, as you wish. Sam it is.' She opened her briefcase and started pulling papers out. 'Right, shall we get down to

business, then?' She eventually found the document she was looking for. 'Now, according to our most recent records, you haven't attended school since the start of the year. So, conservatively we can assume you've actually missed about six months of school.'

'If you say so.' I didn't think it was right that they could come into my house and just talk to me like this. On any level you care to name, it just wasn't fair.

They were just like all the others.

'We do say so, Sam. Most definitely we do. And I just wondered if you had anything to say on the subject.'

'No,' I said, a little above a whisper.

'Really?' said the other lady.

'Well, I had to look after my mum, didn't I? She wasn't well and she needed me to help her.' I looked across at my mum but she had her face turned away.

The older lady looked at me suspiciously. 'Well, I'm sure that's very laudable in its way but you can't just stop going to school like that. I'm sorry but it's the law, Sam.'

'But I'm sixteen,' I said. 'I don't have to go to school if I don't want to. Loads of people leave school at sixteen.'

'I'm sure they do but you're fifteen, Sam! You're not sixteen until next March. We have your records here. We should know!' She laughed a bit at this and then the room fell silent for a few moments. I looked at my mum again and suddenly I understood. All that hatred I felt towards her just a moment ago vanished and left no trace whatsoever. In that second I could see all her pain and all the terrible things she'd had to endure in her life. I knew why she'd done this; I knew why she arranged this visit. She was just trying to do the right thing for once. I stood up, walked over and stood next to her.

'So, Sam, we need to go through some alternatives with you this afternoon...'

Her hair had got very grey, I noticed; maybe she'd let me dye it for her.

'...obviously you've missed a great deal of work this year and it hardly seems fair to expect you to catch up in a few months when it's your GCSE year...'

Nothing too drastic, maybe a sort of gentle brown, a bit like her original colour.

'...spoken to the headmaster and he'd be happy for you to drop back a year and re-join your education at the start of year ten. That way you can start your GCSEs all over again. This is a mixed school, Sam, which we all agree will be better for you than another all girls' school...'

I reached out my hand and started to stroke her hair.

She turned to me and silently placed her hand over mine.

Again, Sally's tone falls somewhere in between confusion, anger, sympathy and exasperation, and is thus a fairly accurate summation of her current state of mind. 'So why didn't you, like, just explain the ending when you had the chance?'

'I know, I know, and you can't possibly know how many times I've asked myself that exact question!'

'Then why didn't you?' Exasperation. Solely.

'I probably had this mad idea in my head that I was trying to sell the book or something and if people were intrigued by the ending they'd all rush out and buy themselves a copy. If I just announced what happened at the end, why would they bother? Yeah, but, on reflection, I suppose when the tone of the interview started to turn a bit nasty I should have said something.'

'And maybe, like, suggesting the guy was ignorant wasn't one of your best moves either!'

'Yeah, I know. Not exactly a recommended interview technique!'

'Interview?' asks Stefan, absently inserting his little finger into the neck of his empty Rolling Rock bottle. 'No way that was an interview, dude. It sounds more like an ambush!'

Martin smiles. 'Yeah, that's probably a pretty fair interpretation.'

Sally, Stefan and Martin are currently seated around a window table in a Pizzeria on the junction of Iberville and Decatur. It would not have been Martin's first choice of restaurant but it was located opposite the New Orleans Music Company, which Stefan had been keen to visit beforehand.

'So, Dad, like, what happened next?'

'Actually, not much happened for a day or so. First thing I heard was that our local branch of Waterstones no longer had the book on their shelves. You know, the funny thing is that I actually thought they might have been sold! Can you believe that?'

'So, what was going on?'

'Bernice called in there after work and asked the manager if they would be reordering more copies. They told her that they'd had a complaint and would no longer be stocking the book. That was the first inkling I had, I think, of the direction in which things were heading. But that's always easy to say with hindsight.'

Sally shakes her head as sympathy finally triumphs. 'Oh, Dad.'

'Then everything just started snowballing and it was like I was powerless to do anything. I had to just sit around as my whole life collapsed around me. It was like some terrible, insane circus I was being forced to watch. All day, every day, even if I ignored *it*, I was therefore acknowledging *it* and therefore participating in *it*. A few days later I was about to take Wes to school but when I opened the front door I saw that someone had sprayed *PAEDO* across it. Seriously, I didn't make the connection for a minute or two and thought it was a mistake but then I realised. Obviously, I tried to make light of it to Wes and said it was probably someone's idea of a joke, but to be honest I was frightened. I washed it off but the next morning it was back. Then someone took a key or a knife or something and scratched *KILL THE PAEDO* on the boot of Bernie's car.'

'Shit,' says Stefan, 'isn't there a law against stuff like that? I mean, couldn't you call the police or something?'

'Oh yeah, I called them, but there wasn't much they could do. They just told me to keep some sort of record of the incidents.'

'Jesus!'

'I even tried getting in touch with Steve Perry, after all he'd mentioned the name of the village where I lived on air; I thought maybe he'd have me back on the show so I could clear up a few things but he never returned my calls.' Martin glances downwards for a moment as the memory triggers another. 'We had three windows broken in two weeks. It would happen in the middle of the night when we were all asleep and by the time I rushed downstairs the perpetrators were long gone. I don't really know what I thought I could achieve by confronting them. I suppose I could have pointed out that the book was fiction and that in the end it is revealed that the main character is actually a fifteen-year-old girl.'

Glimpsed now for the first time in Martin's features there is a suggestion of sadness or possibly resignation. 'Or maybe I could have reminded them that the whole thing was an essay on bigotry and narrow-mindedness and therefore their actions had just proved my point. I don't know, but I just didn't see that working in my favour somehow. Maybe I should have read out your assignment, Sal?'

For the first time that evening Sally can think of no suitable response.

'Oh yeah and then the letters started coming, some in the mail, some hand-delivered. Basically death threats or threats to castrate me if I ever went anywhere near blah-blah street or such-and-such school. The spelling was usually terrible.'

'I had no idea about any of this,' says Sally, with the suggestion of panic now in her voice.

Martin drinks the last of his beer. 'Some gentleman – well, I presume it was a gentleman although I have no real way of knowing – went to all the effort and trouble of sending me a human turd in a sealed padded envelope.'

'Oh, that's just so disgusting.'

'Come on, you're seriously telling me the police can do nothing in cases like this? Just what kind of country you living in, dude?'

Martin shrugs. 'I kept trying but they probably had better things to do. They just kept telling me to keep a record.'

'That's, like, so *lame*.'

'But I tell you, it's really difficult to go about your day, feeling that despised and loathed by people. All because of a book which obviously no one had bothered to actually read! The only crumb of consolation was that it remained a local story the whole time and never made it as far as the national press. Although I did get an email from the publishers reminding me that according to the terms of my contract, the actual content of the published work remains at all times the sole responsibility of the author. The subtext was clear; I was basically on my own! To be honest, I'm not sure if the book is even available anymore. It was taken off their website fairly quickly but as it was a print-on-demand arrangement it's not like they have any unsold copies kicking around. I think they just discreetly backed away from the whole mess, although they still manage to send me an email every few days with news of some fabulous new promotion or another.' Martin attempts to smile at the irony. 'Did you know there were even a few death threats posted as reviews on their website? I think that might actually be some sort of first!'

'I think you need another beer, Martin,' says Stefan, attempting to attract the attention of their waitress. There is a bold, brash confidence to the gesture which seems to come entirely naturally to him. Assertive but in no way arrogant, precisely the kind of thing that Martin usually fears the British aren't terribly good at.

When the beers arrive Martin returns to 'Recent Events'. 'You see,' he says, jabbing the air with his finger for emphasis, as though summoning an invisible lift. 'You see, right there at that point, if it had all stopped completely and hadn't gone any further there was a chance Bernie and I might have coped with it. Maybe if everything had just calmed down or someone else in the area became the unwitting focus of moral outrage and panic, it might have turned out differently. She was so supportive for the first week or so and then everything changed when Wes got dragged into it.'

'That's such a cool name. Is he named –?'

'Not now, Stefan,' hisses Sally. 'Just ignore him, Dad, please carry on.'

'There was a series of incidents at school, boys picking on him and bullying and generally doing what boys usually do. He'd been a fairly popular boy up until then with lots of friends, but suddenly that all changed after the interview went out. It started with all the predictable name calling but then it quickly got a lot nastier. They kept on and on at him all the time asking him if I'd ever touched him or done anything sexual to him and the kid is only twelve and it's his first year in secondary school and he really doesn't know what's happening to him or why he's being singled out like that. Time after time, I tried to sit down with him and explain the situation to him, but he just kept on yelling at me, tears streaming down his face. "Why did you do that? Why did you do that?" I didn't really have an answer for him. We talked to the school but very little changed. He got in trouble for fighting back a few times but he's not like that; he was just confused I suppose.'

'Poor little thing,' says Sally. 'I expect he was.'

'Then one day he just stopped speaking to me and wouldn't even be in the same room as me if Bernie wasn't there as

well. Like he needed a chaperone! It was as though he suddenly couldn't stand to be anywhere near me. I never discussed it with him or rather he would never discuss it with me but I imagine he was frightened that there was some grain of truth in all the taunts and insults. Then, about the same time as this, Bernie's attitude towards me and towards the whole situation in general began to change. It started quite subtly at first; I noticed that she no longer defended me to Wes with quite the same authority and then there were a few remarks that I felt were a little unfair, but I could see she was under a lot of stress too, so I didn't respond. But these built and built over the weeks and eventually turned into blame and then finally flat-out accusations. She kept telling me she was only thinking of Wes and that I should grow up, do the same thing and try and behave like a father for once. But it was a miserable couple of months I can tell you.'
Martin's voice trails off into a quiet reflective murmur. At the outset, he'd imagined that if he restricted himself exclusively to a catalogue of the simple facts he would be able to speak of 'Recent Events'. Sadly, this might have been a slightly optimistic forecast.

Sally and Stefan glance at each other but neither feels that this is the time to speak.

'So I did the only practical sensible thing I could do under the circumstances. I packed a bag and went to stay for a couple of days at Mr Price's old flat in Canterbury. I told you, didn't I, that he left it to me in his will? I'd thought about renting it out or selling it but I just wasn't ready to deal with it all, so I'd just left it. I'd sorted out all his personal stuff but hadn't got around to things like selling the furniture by that point. I used to pay the bills and I'd call in now and again to collect the mail but it was basically just sitting there unoccupied. I tell you it felt so weird being there on my own at first, but then gradually I started to find it oddly comforting – I came to regard it, quite literally, as a

241

sort of sanctuary. Initially, I thought if I gave Wes and Bernie a bit of a space for a couple of days, it would all blow over and things would return to normal. But then it was the weekend and then a couple more bags and then another week and suddenly I discover I've accidentally moved out. But it wasn't "maybe for the best" or "these things happen" or "we just grew apart"; it was nothing like that. It really was the only available option. I'm still on reasonable terms with Bernie but we usually stick to practical issues like money; we never discuss the future but I don't think either of us is under any illusions whatsoever. This is the way it has to be and that's it. Wes still won't speak to me. He's still fighting and skipping school and his grades are going from bad to worse. He's got expulsion hanging over him and I suppose with some justification he blames me for everything. Just before I came out here I sent him a long letter trying to explain things again but he absolutely refuses to read it.' Again the voice trails off.

'What happened to all the vigilante shit?' asks Stefan, 'after you moved?'

Martin seems relieved to return to the earlier subject. 'I think when I moved they saw it as some sort of victory. Bernie said they never returned to the cottage after I left. I'm pretty anonymous where I am in Canterbury although I hardly left the flat for about a month and only went shopping at the twenty-four-hour Asda at ridiculous times of the day, like two thirty in the morning.' Martin smiles bravely at the memory. 'Now that's where you can really meet some *interesting* people. I tell you, my friends, we are definitely the new underground! Just give us a couple of years!'

Welcoming the introduction of a note of levity, Stefan chuckles nervously. 'So, dude, how come you fetched up in New Orleans of all places?'

Martin feels that maybe this isn't the right time to introduce Mr Price into the conversation and so he answers simply,

'Well, after all that had gone on, I just needed a change of scene, I suppose. Although I think I probably liked the idea of being in exile for a while. I just wanted to turn my back on everything. Nobody seemed interested in my side of the story. In a sort of final desperation, I even tried writing a few letters to our local paper. I was actually drafting one a few days ago, but it's useless. I even offered them an exclusive interview if they'd give me the chance to get my version of things into print. But they never replied and they never printed a single letter. So I chose exile and I chose New Orleans.'

There is a pause now in the conversation until Sally asks, 'So, when are you going back to England then?'

Martin grips the bridge of his nose between his thumb and forefinger. 'Now you're asking,' he says, gathering his thoughts. 'I've got a flight booked in a week or so but I may reschedule and stay a bit longer.'

Sally's eyes suddenly widen. 'But you should totally come up to Montreal and stay with us for a few weeks before you go back, shouldn't he, Stefan?'

'Absolutely,' says Stefan. 'That's actually a great idea, Sally.'

'Stefan can take you to all the jazz clubs and I can take you round to see mum to totally freak her out! Come on, Dad, it'll be mega!'

Martin smiles. 'Jazz clubs?'

'You bet,' says Stefan with evident enthusiasm. 'We got some brilliant clubs up there; we got The House of Jazz, the Griffontown; there's loads of places and there's always some great music going down every day of the week.'

Sally then explains that mainly on account of Stefan's cat, she and Stefan will be returning to Montreal on a flight leaving New Orleans the following evening. But that Martin would be welcome to visit whenever he liked for as long as he liked.

'You could maybe do some work on your Tambo-thingy project while you're there,' she says by way of conclusion.

'Yeah, I could,' says Martin, clearly warming to idea.
'That's the blackface guy, right?' asks Stefan.
'That's right.'
'Yeah, Sally told me about him earlier on. Sounds like such
an amazing story. You know, sometime, if it's OK with you,
I'd love to read what you've got written so far. Sally says
the dude is actually still alive!'
'Yeah, that's right. He's over in the Maison de Belle Vie,
in Timberlane on the opposite side of the river. I was planning
on heading over there sometime tomorrow.'
'Wow!' says Stefan, clasping his hands to his forehead.
'That is just the coolest thing ever!' Suddenly a thought flashes
through his mind. 'Hey, how you planning on getting over
there?'
'Er, a taxi, probably,' says Martin.
'No, no, you don't want to get a taxi. Why don't we drive
you over there? What do you think, Sally? We could do that,
couldn't we?'
Sally nods emphatically. 'Totally.'
Stefan continues. 'What do you say, Martin? The last
seminar of the day finishes about three and we're not flying
until ten and I'm dropping off the rental car at the airport.
So we could easily take you over there and get you back in
plenty of time. I think it would just be so great to be a part
of this – it's such an amazing story.'
'Well, if you're sure,' says Martin, 'if it's not going to make
you late.'
'No, it's totally cool, really it is. We'll swing by your hotel
about three thirty. I've got GPS on the rental so we won't
have a problem finding the place.'
'Thank you,' say Martin, genuinely moved by the offer.
When something restores one's faith in human nature it
often serves as a timely reminder that it has been rather
desperately requiring restoration.
'No problem. Hey, I got something to show you here. Wait

until you see this!' Stefan reaches under the table and produces a New Orleans Music Company carrier bag from which he produces a 12" vinyl LP. 'Here, Martin, take a look at this. Couldn't resist it. Great little shop, I've got to say. They had all those racks of old vinyl at the back of the shop and there it was. BLP1573. A genuine first pressing. Bit pricey but definitely worth every cent.'

Martin looks at the cover and reads the title: *John Jenkins with Kenny Burrell*. Martin is unfamiliar with either this particular record or the name John Jenkins. The record dates from 1957 and was released on the legendary Blue Note label. The cover, however, was not a classic and with its brightly coloured blocks of orange and yellow, it fell some way below the usual high standard of Blue Note's artwork of the period.

'Obviously I know Kenny Burrell,' says Martin, having just decided that honesty would probably be the best approach, 'but I must admit I don't know John Jenkins' work and I'm amazed you've found a Blue Note record that I've never even heard of!' He hands the LP back to Stefan.

'Well, you're missing a treat. Great alto player, there's a bit of Bird in there, bit of Sonny Stitt, maybe a bit of Jackie Maclean too. He made one record as leader for Blue Note and it's a real gem. Totally underrated. I've got an MP3 version on my hard drive back at the hotel. I'll burn you a CD later.'

'That would be really kind of you, thanks.'

'I always say about Jenkins that there is some parallel universe somewhere where everything has shifted up a gear or so and where Hank Mobley has the same status of, say, Coltrane or Rollins. In that universe John Jenkins will have moved up into Hank's old position.'

Martin swallows and attempts a smile. It was during a conversation about jazz, not dissimilar to the current one, that he first befriended Mr Price. Everything goes in cycles, he thinks, you can't avoid it, as simple and natural as the opening and closing of a circle. Of course, there is absolutely no doubt that Mr Price would have loved John Jenkins. He wouldn't even have to listen to him. He would have simply loved him for precisely the same reason he loved Bill Evans, Elvin Jones and Tony Williams – because he sounded Welsh.

Stefan excuses himself to visit the rest room and Sally immediately seizes the opportunity. 'So, anyway, Dad, what do you think?'

'What do I think about what?'

'Stefan, of course!'

'Well,' says Martin, relishing the moment, 'I think if you decide not to marry him then I might give it a shot myself!'

'Dad!' says Sally slapping his hand playfully. 'Behave yourself! Anyway, I saw him first.'

'Can't blame a girl for trying.'

'But he just *totally* gets me.' Then she adds shyly, 'A bit like you.'

Martin now glances left and right and without speaking he reaches into the Wallgreen's carrier bag that is currently at his feet. He places on the table in front of Sally a bulky A4 cardboard envelope.

Sally regards the item with suspicion. 'What's this, Dad? You haven't kept that man's poo, have you?' she asks, breaking into a laugh. 'Top secret government plans to destroy Canada? Wow, are you, like, a whistle-blower too? That would be so cool.'

'Nothing like that,' replies Martin in flat, neutral tones. 'Sorry.'

'Do I open it?'

'If you want. But I can save you the trouble. These are a few of the last remaining copies of *An Unhealthy Interest*.' Martin speaks slowly in a manner that suggests caution as much as sentiment. 'Well, for one thing, I thought you'd like a less tatty copy and, I don't know, as you seem to live in the only place in the world where people have actually read it, it seems right, somehow, that you should have them.'

'Oh my God! Thanks,' she says, opening the envelope fractionally to view its contents. 'Wow! That's just so brilliant. Can I give one to Mr Gotterher?'

'Do whatever you like with them.'

'Maybe I'll sell it to him; that would be cool, wouldn't it? But does this mean you don't, like, have a copy of your own book anymore?'

'I've got a couple of copies left in England.' Martin then goes on to explain his original plan to distribute copies amongst the book shops in the Quarter and the reasoning behind it – a plan he realises he abandoned shortly after his first encounter with Tambo Bones.

'That's always been my problem with you, Dad. Sometimes you do stuff and I can never, like, figure out if it's really cool or really sad.'

Martin takes an unhurried sip of his beer and smiles.

'Dad!' says Sally suddenly in a tone of mild admonishment.

'What?'

'You're doing that *thing* with your hands again.'

12

Flapdoodle Empires

History is a reflection of attitudes and perceptions as much as factual reportage.

The free people of colour in New Orleans actually owned slaves.

Less than 6% of the slaves that left Africa actually ended up in the USA.

The greatest anti-segregationist anthem of the war years was performed by a man in blackface.

Of course, our initial reaction is that none of those statements can be true. They are inaccurate, surely. They offend our sense of the past; they confuse and confound our need to divide issues into simple right and wrong. The story of Tambo Bones, which touches on so many aspects of American history, illustrates how complex and unfathomable these issues can be.

Not sure about that, thinks Martin. He fears that, with some justification, the tone might give the reader the idea that they've stumbled upon some fundamentalist, right-wing revisionist essay on the subject of slavery. A.C. Monroe would not be pleased. Select. Delete.

In a matter of a few hours, he keeps reminding himself, he will be raising these precise issues with Tambo Bones himself. As a consequence, this morning he will admit to feeling excited, nervous and fully prepared to be disappointed and he is being truthful about the first two. He has already gathered together various photos and clippings from Clayton's original file in the hope that they might jog the old man's memory if his powers are failing. The main purpose of the visit he tells himself is to establish a sound factual basis for the project and thus, he will no longer have to rely on conjecture and perception. It might be that the tone of the work will shift and some of his ideas might well be rendered obsolete by this evening. He tells himself he is ready for this, as whatever transpires his story will have its ending. The pursuit of truth is always a noble cause, but like many men who seek the truth he suspects what he is actually seeking is only confirmation of his own theories.

It is not my intention to address the historical stigma of blackface performers or the numerous issues surrounding minstrelsy. It is, however, impossible to separate the story of Tambo Bones from the ugly side of

No, too apologetic. I'm sorry if what you're about to read is racist, offensive garbage but hey, it's not my fault, right? Besides, as he intends to send Stefan a PDF of the first 11,000 words or so, he is keen not to give the impression that he's learned nothing from 'Recent Events'. Or else has some strange urge to recreate a very similar situation for himself. He deletes the previous paragraph and saves the document. Mr Price used to say in reference to himself that a man's life is measured out by the sell-by dates on supermarket ready meals. Martin is beginning to wonder if his own markers might be some great long sequence of deleted files.

Ever since meeting Stefan the previous evening, he's been thinking a lot about Mr Price. It is probably the jazz thing, he's been telling himself all morning, and has no desire to delve any deeper than that.

He opens his email browser and now writes

Dear Stefan,

Please find attached

Then, as though succumbing to some inadvertent urge to prove his earlier point, he closes the file and deletes it.

The day is overcast and humid and Martin occupies himself as best he can. At one point during the afternoon, sensing that perhaps his quest is nearing its conclusion, he finds himself being drawn towards the place where it had all begun and he makes his way to the New Orleans Music Company. Sadly, there is no sign of Hugo today and so he idles away the better part of an hour browsing through the second-hand vinyl section at the rear of the shop, where Stefan had found his John Jenkins record. Despite not owning a turntable, Martin likes looking at the covers and losing himself in the world they still evoke. He picks up a Japanese pressing of 'Soul Station' by Hank Mobley, and he stares at the cover for a good five minutes. Now this one, he would confidently assert, is a classic Blue Note sleeve. The lettering, the uncharacteristic serif font, the layout, the vivid blue tint and the way Mobley smiles and the cavalier, almost disrespectful way he holds his saxophone – everything about it is perfect. It is gratifying to be somewhere, he thinks, where one might still believe, if only for a moment, that such things are still relevant and important. He reads the song titles and in his head he can hear the music so clearly, that great first track and how the whole thing just swings from the very first beat. There is no introduction, no teasing piano refrain or snare drum fill; the whole band just comes right in with
Buh der-der... Buh-der...
No, that's wrong, he thinks; surely a more accurate phonetic approximation would be
Per-dido... Per-di...
He smiles. And this is how New Orleans just takes over your life. Perdido Street was a couple of blocks away from Gravier. Almost as legendary as Basin Street, it ran the length of what was once Black Storyville, or, as the area was also once known, Back O' Town.
Everything now aligns perfectly.
Only in New Orleans can you recite the street names and make them sound like jazz.

Per-dido... Per-di...

He wanders out of the shop feeling oddly uplifted by the discovery – a man reacquainted with his own small certainties. Recalling this moment at regular intervals, he remains in a good mood for the rest of the afternoon and a couple of hours later, just after five o'clock, he is sitting in the rear of a Chevy Impala being driven by Stefan as he negotiates the late afternoon traffic on Route 90. As they cross the Mississippi, Martin glances down at the great, mighty iconic river – brown, murky and unremarkable this afternoon and like so much of New Orleans, blatantly disinterested in its own mythology. Sally, who is sitting in the passenger seat, glances at the GPS screen and turns around to reply to her father's earlier question.

'Crescent City Connection.'

'What?' utters Martin in disbelief. 'Are you sure?'

'That's, like, what, it says on the GPS here.'

'You mean, this mighty structure,' he exclaims dramatically, 'this fabulous feat of design and engineering; you're telling me this magnificent bridge is actually called Crescent City Connection?' He intones the words with mock disdain.

'I do.'

'But it's such a terrible name. Who thought of it? I mean if it's an episode of *Starsky and Hutch* or a covers band that you hire for your wedding then it's a perfectly fine name...'

Stefan chuckles. 'I hear where you're coming from, dude.'

'They named the airport after Louis Armstrong; why couldn't they name a bridge after Sidney Bechet? Or Morton or Buddy Bolden?'

'Or Lester Young?' offers Stefan.

'Er...?' says Martin awkwardly.

'Hey, I got you there, didn't I? Didn't know that, did you? OK, as we get over the other side of the river, look out to your left and you'll see a neighbourhood called Algiers and that, dude, was where Lester Young grew up. Seriously, he was born somewhere in Mississippi but he grew up right here!'

'Really?' exclaims Martin in a tone of genuine surprise. 'I had no idea.'

'Hey, you should have worked this out by now; whatever you think you know about New Orleans there's always shit loads more you don't know. I've been down here a few times but this place is always full of surprises. Am I right?'

'Yeah, you are,' says Martin quietly as the mention of Lester Young has just triggered another half-forgotten memory of Mr Price, who once claimed the legendary saxophonist was the first love of his life. This is approximately the moment that Sally decides to re-join the conversation.

'So, Dad, have you, like, worked out all the questions you need to ask this guy?'

'Well ... um, more or less.'

'Is that, like, a no?'

'You know,' says Martin, in an increasingly evasive tone, 'it's probably best just to play it by ear, see if he feels like talking.'

'Yeah, totally,' says Stefan.

They fall into silence as Martin gazes out of the window. On the opposite bank, away from the Quarter, The Marigny and the Garden District, New Orleans has a further surprise in store for the visitor. For it suddenly becomes quite ordinary. Staid, conservative and with very few features that will ever trouble the memory, it doesn't feel to Martin like a sudden shift in urban development as much as it feels like waking from a dream.

About twenty minutes later, Martin is wrenched from his deliberations when Stefan, slowing down the Impala to make a right turn off Lapalco Boulevard, suddenly announces, 'Here we are, dude!'

Martin looks out of the window and feels something hard like a man's fist pressing into his right temple. He sees the large sign at the roadside with the simple legend *Maison de Belle Vie*, which will transpire to be the centre's only memorable feature. In truth, the Maison de Belle Vie presents itself as a large, rather depressing, single-storey structure which becomes more depressing the closer one approaches. There are no details to the building that catch the eye or suddenly reveal themselves as one negotiates the short slip road towards the car park. It remains grey, drab and municipal, and if you wanted to design a place to keep secrets then it would look like this.

The fist pushes harder into his temple.

He closes his eyes as Stefan reverses the car into a parking space.

'Come on, Dad,' says Sally, breezily, as she opens the passenger door. 'Let's find someone we can talk to and let's, like, shake up this devious old so-called Washington Adams. See what the old buzzard has to say for himself.'

Martin gets out of the car and finds that he is now rather unsteady on his feet. He turns his back on Sally and Stefan and starts walking away from the car in the opposite direction to the entrance of the Maison de Belle Vie.

'Dad,' Sally calls after him, 'are you all right?'

His legs shake and his head is now pounding.

'Hey, Martin, what's up, dude?'

Martin stops walking and turns around. He looks at his daughter and her good, decent, honest boyfriend and struggling for the right words, tries his best to smile. 'I'm so sorry, I really am; I'm sorry to have dragged you all the way out here like this. It's really not fair to do this to you.'

Sally now walks towards him. 'Dad?' she asks in a tone of concern rather than admonishment. 'Do what to us exactly? What do you mean?'

'I can't do this. I'm sorry, I just can't.'

'You're kidding, right?'

'No, Sally, I'm serious.' He puts his arm around his daughter and together they walk back towards the car. 'You know, I've just realised something that's been quietly nagging away ever since I spoke to JuJu Jones. I don't know what it is exactly but I'm terrified and I can't do this now.' He shrugs apologetically. 'Maybe it's because I'm just not brave enough to confront a man who may very well shatter all my illusions about him and I suppose, by extension, about all music in general. Seriously, no man could ever be equal to the stories I've distilled from that man's life in the past few days or so! But that's just it right there! It's the stories, you see. Clayton was right! The stories are everything! They may actually be the only things that ever really matter; they are very precious and ... very fragile and...' Martin hesitates. 'You see, whatever happens...' He waves his forefinger in the approximate direction of the entrance. 'Whatever happens in *there*...' He gives the word a peculiar emphasis, 'will completely change the whole story.'

'You can't know that for sure,' says Stefan.

'But I can't take that chance. I just feel this great need to protect my – yeah, OK, guilty as charged – my *perception*, my version of the truth, if you like.' Martin pauses for moment to gather his thoughts. 'It's stupid, I know, but I honestly thought that I could actually shift public opinion! Can you believe that? God bless A.C. Monroe! He was absolutely right. This stuff should be left alone.'

'But what about the book?' asks Sally.

'Well, maybe it needs to be a different book now. You know, thinking about it, I suppose this is my story now and if you think about it it's *our* story too. Face it; it's all just become another one of those stories that attaches itself to New Orleans. That's all it's ever going to be and nothing more. But I'm happy about that, really I am. The stories survive. They can demolish and plough Storyville into the ground; the ending doesn't matter; we don't want to know about the bulldozers, right, because the legends of Storyville will last forever. It doesn't matter about the actual conclusion. Not anymore. Look, I'll show you.' Martin takes a step backwards. He mimes the gesture of opening an imaginary book and reads out loud to Stefan and Sally and the cars speeding by on Lapalco Boulevard.

Oscar Brightwater is an incredibly quick-witted and lucid nonagenarian with an enthusiasm for anecdote and conversation that would be impressive in a man two decades his junior. I took his arm (or pushed his wheelchair or helped him with his walking aid) as we took a tour of his home's impressive grounds one afternoon in October. That he'd been given the opportunity to finally clear his name was evidently a source of great comfort to him.

'OK, that's definitely the one we're all hoping for, right? But what if it plays out differently?'

Oscar Brightwater a.k.a. Tambo Bones remains an uncompromising individual. Age has not withered or mellowed him in the slightest and within a minute of our meeting the first sneering racial insult has passed his lips. It is followed by a whole sequence of others. I am then subjected to a series of racist jokes and stories and even spoken lyrics to songs that 'nobody had the goddamn fucking balls to release.' One would be tempted to attribute his views to a form of dementia if it wasn't for the fact that his memory and the consistency of his doctrine seemed incredibly clear that afternoon.

'So is that any better? How do you think I turn that into a great study of twentieth century American music? Some great classic ending that would be, right? Maybe that stupid song was some bad sick joke just like Clayton said it was. What do you think the moral would be exactly and how would all that sound to A.C. Monroe? Maybe I should be hoping for something completely different?'

In his nineties, Oscar Brightwater presents a sad spectacle to the visitor. Virtually bed-ridden since Katrina and unable to understand much beyond the most simple commands, he no longer recognises the staff or the doctors at thegfh home and his rare utterances nowadays are simply requests for refreshment.

'You think that's what I'm going to be writing tomorrow morning? Is that how the story of Tambo Bones, The Back O' Town Boys and "Georgia Blues" must end? That's the ultimate fucking tragedy of reality; it so often lacks the big finale. There's no vast significant moment waiting for us, just things carrying on as before. Normal is a bitch and normal always wins out in the end! So try this one.'

Following my enquiries at the main entrance I am shown into the doctor's office. A genial white-haired man in his sixties is sitting behind a desk and he invites me to sit down. He asks me how well I know Washington Adams, the name by which Oscar is known at the centre – is he family? Are we old acquaintances? I explain my story as briefly as I can and then even before he replies I sense what he is about to say. He removes his glasses and says in a tone of voice that suggests a lifetime of similar rooms, similar conversations and similar conclusions, 'I'm so sorry to inform you but Mr Adams passed in the night.'

'So now do you see? There doesn't actually need to be an ending, really there doesn't. This is the ending; we're standing in it! It's the three of us here in this car park, just like this. That's what happens in this place! We all just get swallowed up and become part of another story: the one about the middle-aged failed writer from England! Yeah, he escapes to New Orleans to hide from some idiotic self-inflicted controversy, but accidentally stumbles upon this song. Perhaps he is just sublimating, but he becomes absolutely obsessed with the artist responsible and makes all these wild, unsubstantiated claims on his behalf. Along the way he meets all these people, maybe acquires a little self-awareness and then reconnects with his own daughter, blah, blah, blah. That's us; that's what we are now – a story passed on by whoever… Clayton Palmer or Monroe or even Hugo from the shop.'

'I think,' says Stefan slowly, 'I actually feel where you're coming from.'

'Thanks, Stefan,' says Martin, touching the younger man on the shoulder, 'and I'm really sorry for wasting your time.'

'No problem, dude.'

'You know, it was a song this time, maybe next time it will be a pirate treasure map. It doesn't matter; it's all the same.' Martin's face now contorts into the approximation of a smile. 'Besides, I guess it's just another Flapdoodle Empire.'

Sally looks suddenly alarmed. 'Another *what*?'

'It's what Mr Price used to call it. According to him, all men have their Flapdoodle Empires. It is that which we invent or construct solely to conceal the irrefutable daily evidence of mortality, decay, failure and our own terrible mediocrity.'

Stefan smiles but wisely says nothing and lets Sally ask the question instead.

'So what are you, like, going to do now, Dad?'

'You know,' says Martin, letting his head loll reflectively and speaking in a voice a fraction above a whisper, 'if I was the kind of person who gave a shit that would be exactly the sort of thing I'd give a shit about.'

Sally now knows everything she needs to know; she looks at her father and smiles. 'Come on, guys...' She opens her passenger side door and the sudden dull mechanical sound bisects the afternoon and serves as a suitable indicator that the day's business is now concluded.

In New Orleans, the evening falls quickly in late October and as they return over the Crescent City Connection, the street lights are already lit all across the Quarter.

For the second time that afternoon, Martin glances out of the car window at the Mississippi and wonders what stories will be washed up with the tide tomorrow. He may get to hear them, he may not, but someone would pass them on; of that much he is certain. Maybe they'll embellish a little, personalise some aspects, re-work a few details here and there but the whole thing just keeps rolling.

Now, just about audible over the sound of the traffic, and gradually becoming more distinct, he begins to hear it again. It is everywhere, inside him and outside him; it is the most beautiful thing in the world and the most inevitable.

But now it is more than that. It is comforting.

But this is not a sound from childhood, rather from that faraway, dying bed of all his days.

'Roll 'em, Mr Bones, Mr Bones, Mr Bones,
Roll 'em, Mr Bones...'

New Orleans, Louisiana. Thanksgiving Day, 2012